DURHAM RED
THE UNQUIET GRAVE

Red bounced to her feet, snarling. The bald man was lying still, but his companions had dropped their chains and were racing towards her. Plasma fire ripped out across the deck.

She dived aside, behind the axle, letting off two shots as she went. Each shot hit a man in grey; superheated blood and bone fragments exploded back into the walls. Red peered back around the stone column, just in time to see Ketta blur out of the corridor and into the surviving attackers.

There was a sudden cacophony of screams, blows, and breaking limbs. It ended mercifully quickly – in five seconds, maybe less – until all the grey-clad men were dead. Red didn't even see it happen. She was already looking up at Godolkin, trying to see how the cuffs would come off.

A heartbeat later, she was flying back into the axle, her face a mask of pain.

DURHAM RED

THE UNQUIET GRAVE

PETER J EVANS

To Nicola
Who makes everything work
Especially me.

And to Kent
Who came up with the goods.

A Black Flame Publication
www.blackflame.com

First published in 2004 by BL Publishing, Games Workshop Ltd., Willow Road, Nottingham NG7 2WS, UK.

Distributed in the US by Simon & Schuster, 1230 Avenue of the Americas, New York, NY 10020, USA.

10 9 8 7 6 5 4 3 2 1

Cover illustration by Mark Harrison.

ISBN 1 84416 159 5

A CIP record for this book is available from the British Library.

Printed in the UK by Bookmarque, Surrey, UK.

The Legend of Durham Red

It is written that in that year of 2150, the skies rained down nuclear death, and every family and clan lost father and brothers and sons. The Strontium choked our beloved homeworld and brought forth mutants, squealing and twisted things.

Yet such mutants were not weak things to be crushed underfoot, for the same radiation that had created them warped their bodies, making them stronger than any normal human. They became hated and feared by all, and were herded into ghettos and imprisoned in vast camps. There they plotted rebellion and dreamed of freedom amongst their own kind.

Some, it is told, were able to escape from the shadows of ruined Earth, to join the feared Search/Destroy Agency. They tracked wanted criminals on worlds too dangerous for regular enforcement officers. They became known as the Strontium Dogs.

The one they call Durham Red became an S/D Agent to escape the teeming ghettos of her devastated homeland. Shunned even by her own kind because of a foul mutant blood-thirst, she soon found that her unsurpassed combat skills served her well as a Strontium Dog. The years of continuous slaughter took their toll, however, and the tales relate that in the end Red willingly entered the deep sleep of cryogenic suspension, determined to let a few years go by without her.

All know of the unexpected twist that the legend took. Her cryo-tube malfunctioned. Durham Red woke up twelve hundred years late.

While she slept, the enmity between humans and mutants had exploded into centuries of total war, leaving the galaxy a shattered shell, home only to superstition and barbarism. Billions of oppressed mutants now worship Saint Scarlet of Durham – the mythologised image of Red herself! The bounty hunter from Milton Keynes has now become almost a messiah figure for mutantkind – and a terrifying blasphemy in the eyes of humans.

Half the galaxy is looking to her for bloody salvation. The other half is determined to destroy her at any cost. The future is a nightmare, and Durham Red is trapped right in the middle of it...

1. GLOW

Judas Harrow was late arriving at the Chamber of Sensation. By the time he got there, the orgy was already in full swing.

The gallery was overflowing, lesser acolytes of the Osculum Cruentus jammed against the handrail in their dozens; a solid wall of crimson cowls. Harrow had to force his way to the front, sliding through the ranks of the faithful with an equal mixture of stealth, apology and brute force. No one complained, even though Harrow was certain he'd felt someone's rib crack after a particularly vicious shove. The owner of the rib might have gasped but the chamber was already ringing with gasps, and worse. Nobody paid any heed to one more.

Harrow reached the rail, inwardly cursing himself for not getting to the chamber sooner. Part of his problem was the cowl. Its previous owner had been taller and the garment was too big, voluminous and long. He had to be on constant guard not to trip over the cursed thing. Falling flat on his face would do his attempts at subterfuge no good at all.

Neither would the look of shock on his face when he peered over the edge of the gallery, but there was nothing he could do about that. Luckily the cowl's hood covered his expression and no one seemed to be looking at him anyway.

They were too busy watching those participating in the orgy.

It was the first time Harrow had managed to gain access into the chamber, and from what he saw with his own eyes, it was far worse than he could have imagined.

The chamber itself was a broad, circular cavern, maybe a hundred metres across and a similar distance from floor to ceiling. The walls were hung with huge tapestries; scenes of gruesome debauchery so extreme that even Judas Harrow, who had seen some sights in his time, took one quick look at them and decided that he would see no more.

Above the awful hangings, diamond-analogue windows formed a wide, domed ceiling. Distant starlight speckled in from outside, through coloured panes that formed images almost as foul as those on the walls. Halfway up the chamber was a ring of metal walkway, bolted precariously into the dark stone – the viewing gallery on which Judas Harrow, and almost a hundred sweating acolytes, now stood. The floor below was lost in darkness, but from the centre rose a blunt cylinder of black iron, its flanks stained and pitted with rust. The upper surface of this, the dais, was where the attention of the ranked acolytes was fixed. Harrow forced himself to turn his gaze the same way.

What he saw sickened him.

Down on the dais, lovers writhed in mindless abandon. Harrow tried to count them, but gave up after a few seconds. Ten, twelve, maybe more, he couldn't tell. There seemed to be no division between one bacchanalian and the next: the dais was a tangle of limbs, a squirming mass of pale, sweat-slicked skin and glittering metal.

Despite the rapt, lust-soaked stares of the acolytes, Harrow could find nothing arousing in the multiple coupling below him. The lovers moved spastically, like failing machines. A physically active associate of the orgy on Harrow's side of the dais fell slightly away from her fellows shuddering uncontrollably, and he saw that the curve of her spine was studded with interface jacks, black metal sockets stapled brutally through her white skin and into the vertebrae beneath. Rumour had it that those who engaged in the orgies spent the long hours between rituals in a storm of neural transfer; plugged directly into the temple's data-engines and force-fed imagery both erotic and terrifying, priming them for the rigors of ceremony. Harrow saw that the woman's mind had already been driven apart by days of torturous hypnotic input. All that was left to her now was pain and raw, animalistic desire.

The woman turned her head. She had no eyes, just another two interface sockets, riveted into the bone of her skull.

Harrow gripped the rail hard and tried to keep his stomach from reeling. The stench of those who partook in the orgy – musk, vanilla and bitter machine oil – was assaulting his nostrils and the harsh glare of the spotlights illuminating them hurt his brain. He found a spot on the dais that appeared to be empty, and fixed his attention on it, trying to breathe through his mouth.

Abruptly, the section of dais he was staring at moved.

A jagged section of metal dropped and then slid away. With a soft whine of concealed hydraulics, almost lost amidst the cries and groans of the sexual debauchery, a long, gleaming blade rose up, slowed and locked into place.

More blades were emerging from the dais – long, curved knives on hinged poles, little serrated scalpels peeking from the iron floor, spikes, needles. In seconds, the grinding and pumping bodies were surrounded by a lethal glitter of edged steel.

Despite himself, something in Judas Harrow soared. He had been wondering if he was in the right place, or if he had stumbled on another deranged pleasure-cult. This, however, told him that he was indeed on the right track, even though the sight of it stopped the breath in his throat.

The eyeless woman cried out, her back arching, her head thrown back. In doing so she met a blade and the razored edge parted her bald scalp down to the bone.

Blood flowed from the exposed wound like crimson lava and began to slick down the woman's neck and shoulders. If she noticed the horrific injury, she made no sign of it. Nor did the other writhing participants, as they too found sharpened metal with pale skin.

In moments, the surface of the dais was bright red with blood. Its sickly sweet odour rose to meet Harrow, strong enough to block out the musk and oil, and for that he was grateful. He had smelled enough blood in his time to make the reek of it almost comforting.

The dais was carved with dozens of intricate channels. He hadn't noticed them before, but now they stood out against the black iron as they filled with warm blood, taking it from the lacerated bodies and down into a system of open drains. Harrow squinted, trying to see where the blood was forming up, and as he did so he noticed movement below the dais. He strained to see into the darkness.

There was a platform below the dais, a mesh ring set further down the cylinder. Harrow saw two men there; mutants. One had arms that moved with a boneless fluidity under the sleeves of his robe, the other bore a random, unfocussed mutation that turned his face into a maze of rifts and scars.

Judas Harrow was a mutant too, although his genetic changes were far subtler.

The snake-armed man was lifting a wide bowl and the other operating a valve set into the cylinder's iron flank. Liquid, dark and thick, gurgled faintly as it flowed into the bowl and filled it.

As Harrow watched, the man at the valve turned a control, stemming the flow, and then reached into his robes. He brought out a vial and held it with a reverent pride. As his companion held the bowl close, the man uncorked the vial.

From the mouth of it poured a sickly, greenish radiance.

Harrow held his breath. There was little doubt, now – he was where he needed to be. And, of course, in mortal danger just by his very presence. One false step and he'd be down on the dais by tomorrow night, eyeless and brains pulped to a sexual mush, bleeding into a bowl. A shiver inched down his spine, and at that moment he was quite glad of the cowl's heavy fabric.

His life had been simpler once. He was sure of it.

Concentrate, Harrow! There was no time for reverie now; the man with the bottle was already dipping into it with a long spoon, taking out a tiny measure of fine powder. The spoonful gave off a ghostly light as he lowered it to the bowl and carefully, lovingly stirred it in.

The powder's strange radiance faded into the liquid, but it never quite went out. Harrow watched the luminous disc bob in the gloom as the scarred man lifted the bowl above his head.

"Blood!" he roared.

His voice was harsh and powerful, as deep as a funeral drum. It cut effortlessly across the weakening cries of the grinding bodies. Harrow felt the acolytes around him tense.

Was this the moment?

"Blood," the man called again. "Blood born of pleasure, born of pain. Blood born of sensation, true sensation. True enlightenment!"

The acolytes cheered, howled and beat at the rail with their fists. They had been waiting for this moment as well, but for different reasons to Harrow. For appearances, he slapped the rail a couple of times too. "Hooray," he croaked weakly.

The snake-armed man joined his fellow. "This blood is the libation we give to our high-priestess, so that she may bless its creation for us." As he spoke, there was a grinding hiss: a door was grumbling open, down near the floor of the chamber. Light flooded in, blue-white and fluttering. In the staccato glare Harrow saw that the men were standing at the top of a shallow ramp, which led from the platform down to the doorway.

The door itself was massive, armoured and saw-edged.

The robed mutants turned without another word, and strode down the ramp, holding the bowl of gleaming blood between them. Harrow was too far around the gallery to see what lay beyond the opening, and he couldn't risk moving and losing his place. He needed to see what would happen next.

What happened for several minutes was nothing, save the continued gyrations of those partaking in the blood-spattered orgy. Harrow noticed that a couple of them had lost too much blood and had fallen still and silent. If their fellows had any sanity left at all, he thought to himself, they would have envied their fallen companions. Instead, horribly, they continued to couple with them. They couldn't have enough wits left to know the difference between the living and the dead.

Thankfully, the robed priests returned. The snake-armed man raised the bowl sinuously above his head and as one the acolytes gasped.

It was empty.

"Rejoice!" the scarred mutant roared. "The priestess has tasted our libation and pronounced it good. Now you shall taste enlightenment as she has done."

With that, panels concealed around the wall of the gallery slid aside with a rusty groan. Inside were filthy metal beakers, brimming with dark, faintly glowing blood.

The acolytes rushed at the open panels, grasping for the stained beakers, gulping the contents down. Judas Harrow, however, was already making his way off the gallery. There was nothing for him here, and he had no desire to sample the blood taken from the cut and wounded bodies. He had been dosing himself with an antidote to Glow, the luminous narcotic powder, for three days now, ever since he had arrived at the temple, but there was no sense pushing his luck. The vile stuff was everywhere, even in the air, and he would not risk drinking it as well.

Once outside, in the corridor that led to the accommodation cells, he allowed himself a single curse. "Sneck!" he swore.

He had been hoping that the priestess would show herself, that somehow the priests would bring her forth and present her to the faithful. Just a glimpse would have been enough.

Enough to prove that he was right, that after all his months of searching he hadn't come here in vain. Enough to show him that she was alive.

Because if he was right, the high priestess of the Osculum Cruentus was the woman he would love and worship until he died. Saint Scarlet herself.

Durham Red.

Harrow had come to the temple of the Osculum Cruentus well prepared. Hidden beneath the folds of his cowl was a variety of equipment more suited to the professional burglar than the religious adept: the crimson fabric concealed a light-drill, a data-pick, a reel of mono-bond climbing line, a plasma-derringer and a long, wickedly curved knife. The last item hadn't been part of his original kit, but almost as soon as he had entered the temple an acolyte had tried to stab him with it. Which had been something of a mistake – Harrow was no warrior, but he knew how to take care of himself.

The acolyte had lost his knife, his life and his cowl – roughly in that order – and had provided Judas Harrow with both a disguise and a useful weapon. A problem too, since the man's body had been folded into a cupboard for nearly three days. Glow-addled most of the Osculum might be, but it wouldn't be long before the smell of the carcass alerted someone.

All the better if Harrow was gone from this place, and soon.

He hurried along a passageway that, by his reckoning, must have run roughly alongside the Chamber of Sensation. The walls of the passage were rough-cut from the same dark stone as the rest of the temple, lit by meagre panels ranged along the ceiling. The inside of the temple, as Harrow had discovered during his time here, was a maze: an insane network of ramps, corridors, halls, chambers, vaulted rooms and terrifying, vertiginous stairways. Before the orgy he would have had no idea of even which direction to head in, and the place had been full of wandering acolytes. Now, with the faithful still gulping down mouthfuls of blood in the chamber, Harrow had almost free run of the temple.

That situation wouldn't last long. Those involved in the frenzied orgy could only have so much fluid left in their bodies, blood or otherwise. He had to move fast.

The passageway branched left and right. Harrow paused at the junction, trying to picture the layout in his head. In a normal building left should have been the way to go, but that corridor led to a flight of stairs heading down: wasn't he still on the right level? The other passage disappeared around a corner that plainly went back in the direction he had come from. Harrow nibbled his lower lip nervously and chose right on a whim. Maybe it would turn again.

He was halfway down the corridor when he heard heavy, measured footsteps approaching him. He froze, wondering where to hide. The odd acoustics of the passageway were making it hard to tell where the footsteps were coming from.

Harrow had just about convinced himself that he was being approached from around the next bend when a door slid open directly behind him. He span, and came face to face with two servitors.

Like those in the orgy, they had been human once. They had a similar look to them: hairless, their skin the same dead-looking white, devices of glossy black metal riveted brutally into their bodies. But these modifications were designed for hard labour, not lust. Both had their arms replaced with piston-operated grabs and braces mounted through their shoulders and backs to support loads that would break a normal man's spine. As they drew close, Harrow saw that in place of eyes the servitors had crude sensory feeds, clusters of lenses that chattered and whirred like ancient, rusty cameras as they focussed on him.

Their mouths had been sewn shut.

The creatures were right on top of him; there was nowhere for Harrow to go. Running away would have certainly aroused their suspicions and although the idea of hauling out the derringer and blasting the pair of them crossed his mind, common sense quickly overrode the notion. Gunfights, he knew from bitter experience, were loud.

He could do nothing but stand where he was as the servitors' deliberate, mechanical pace slowed and stopped. He heard servomotors in their joints winding down.

"Acolyte," one of them said. Its voice, a reedy grating, emerged from a grill mounted in the side of its neck.

There couldn't be too much detail in their sight, Harrow realised. They could tell his rank by the broad shape of his clothing, but little more than that. He decided to try bluffing his way out. "Servitors. I've come to tell you that your presence is requested in the flight hangar."

There was a faint chattering sound; crude relays working in the servitors' brains as they tried to process the new information. Harrow suppressed a shudder of disgust.

"Negative," quavered the one that had spoken before. "New order cannot be processed. Existing orders are not open to revision."

"It is time for the milking," said the other. "Step aside, acolyte."

Milking? Harrow shrugged and moved out of the way, watching as the servitors stalked past. At least they hadn't raised an alarm. Presumably, it wasn't unknown for acolytes to try ordering the creatures about. It must have been something they were programmed to ignore.

He waited, breathing hard, as the sound of their piston-engine footfalls faded off around the corner, then shook himself and carried on along the corridor. He had known that the Osculum Cruentus had a reputation for harbouring horrors, but things here were worse than he could have imagined.

Were the servitors also suffering? Were the people they had once been still in there somewhere?

The corridor angled to the right, which Harrow felt certain was entirely the wrong way, and before long he found himself at the foot of a narrow, winding stairway. He cursed and was about to turn back when he noticed light filtering down the stairs from above. There was a quality to it that was oddly familiar, although he couldn't put his finger on why.

It was enough to intrigue him though, and he began to climb.

The stairs climbed for quite a way – two levels, maybe three – in a twisting, looping spiral, before terminating at one end of a short hallway. Harrow paused near the top, peeking over the last few steps to make sure that no one was in sight.

Compared to the treacherous stairs and the cramped, gloomy corridors, the hallway seemed bright and sumptuously decorated. Tapestries lined the walls and the ceiling was a high, vaulted series of stone arches. The far end opened out into what looked like a smaller version of the viewing gallery from the chamber, with a platform extending out into a larger space, ringed with ornate handrails.

Light, blue-white and flickering, was spilling in through the far end of the hallway. Harrow had seen a similar stuttering glare past the armoured door in the Chamber of Sensation, when the priests had taken the bowl of blood to their priestess.

Hardly daring to hope, he crept towards the rail, keeping his back against the wall. The room beyond the platform was large, maybe half as big as the Chamber of Sensation, and gave the impression of being perfectly spherical. As Harrow edged closer he could see arc lights set into niches in the curving inner surface, pouring out an incessant, painful glare. At least one of the arc lights was malfunctioning, and sputtering fitfully. The air stank of ozone and burnt insulation.

The handrail was just like that on the gallery, black iron, worn smooth along the top by a century of use. Harrow peered over it and into the chamber below.

For a second, his heart froze in his chest, solid as a bone.
She was here.

There was no furniture in the chamber, no throne or altar.
Instead, the concave floor was covered with a deranged pro-
fusion of fabrics: old rugs, redundant wall hangings, filthy
tapestries, even a discarded cowl or two. The litter must
have been a metre deep, maybe more. It looked as though
it had built up over decades, more layers dropped over the
top as the ones below rotted away.

And on this grimy, reeking mass lay Durham Red, the
Scarlet Saint herself.

She was clad in shapeless robes, and her once-crimson
hair had been hacked into a messy, dull-looking halo around
her wasted face. She sprawled over tattered, bloodstained
cushions, her eyes closed, her breathing shallow. Her skin
was a sickly white, almost transparent under the arc lights,
and gleaming with sweat. There was dried blood on her chin
and neck. It looked like it had been there for some time.

As Harrow watched, shivers wracked her. This was no
priestess. This was an animal, tied up and left to howl.

He sagged back, feeling a queasy rage filling his gut. To
have come so far, searched so long and found her like this...
It was too much to bear.

One way or another, he would have vengeance on the
Osculum Cruentus.

The time for disguise was over. Harrow shrugged his way
out of the cowl and dropped it behind him. The floor
around Red's unconscious form might have been softer
than it looked, but Harrow didn't want to risk a broken leg
jumping down to find out. He unclipped the mono-bond
line from his belt, fastened one end around the rail, and
opened the casing's integral handgrips.

He was just about to climb over when a door slid open
below him.

He ducked back and down, behind the rail. The armoured
door to the Chamber of Sensation was still closed, he could

see that from where he crouched. No, a smaller entrance had opened, showing dark against the smooth stone interior of the sphere.

After a few seconds, figures stepped through the opening and down onto the crumbling rugs: servitors, two of them, and the snake-armed priest from the orgy. The servitors looked exactly like the pair Harrow had tried to bluff earlier.

The altered slaves strode towards Red. As Harrow watched, one of them grabbed her left arm in its massive claw, and hauled her roughly up into a sitting position. She sagged like a rag doll in the machine-man's grip, until the other servitor took her by the shoulder, holding her steady.

Her head, unsupported, dropped forwards. The robes she wore appeared to be open at the back, falling apart to reveal a white expanse of neck. There was something between her shoulder blades that should not have been.

Harrow clamped a hand over his mouth. A black metal socket had been driven into Red's spine, fixed as brutally and solidly as the devices sported by those who suffered terribly in the orgy. The skin around it was puckered and grey-pink. It looked horribly infected.

If Red had been awake, she would have been in agony.

The snake-armed priest crouched behind her. He took a device from within his robes, something that was part bright steel, part glass. Making sure that Red was held securely by the two servitors, he pushed it into the socket at her back, and twisted it.

There was the sound of metal locking against metal. And of Durham Red, whimpering almost imperceptibly in protest.

Liquid, water-thin and slightly cloudy, began to fill a glass tube in the device. And suddenly, Judas Harrow understood.

The milking!

They were drawing off her spinal fluid. Kept drugged with huge quantities of Glow, she was fed with tainted blood from the orgy, and then the priests milked her spinal fluid for some unholy purpose. By the state of her, they must have been doing this for weeks, if not months. They had even inserted a valve into her spine to make extraction easier.

Harrow slipped the plasma-derringer from its holster and thumbed the priming key. As soon as those bastards stepped away from her...

Alarm gongs ripped out across the chamber, a deafening metallic chime. The sheer volume of it made Harrow wince and curse under his breath.

Somebody must have found the dead acolyte he'd shoved into a cupboard.

Behind him, a door slammed open. He whirled, still crouching, and saw a servitor guard barrelling into the hallway, raising the guns bolted into the severed stumps of its wrists.

Harrow snapped the derringer up and put a shot through the creature's sternum. The plasma charge cracked like a whip as it superheated the air around the barrel, and the servitor's torso exploded in a crimson shower. The arms span away, wrist-guns firing on reflex. Frag-shells screamed around the hallway.

Ducking shrapnel and debris, Harrow grabbed the monobond reel in his free hand and dived over the rail.

The line paid out fast, squealing, dropping him onto the stinking rugs before the priest below could even shout. He dived under the swinging grab of one servitor, but the second lashed out and caught him a stunning blow across the back of the head, sending him sprawling. The derringer flew from his grasp.

He rolled over. The servitors had left Red to drop, and were hammering towards him. He scrambled away, dragging the light-drill from his belt and slapping it to full charge with the heel of his hand. A violet thread sprang from the nozzle, searing and bright, and when he played it over the nearest servitor the creature tripped over its own feet and collapsed instantly, severed cables spraying oil, sparks and blood.

The second servitor paused as its colleague fell and Harrow drilled it clear through the forehead. It sagged to its knees and toppled, its suffering well and truly over.

The priest was trying to get away, the tube of Red's spinal fluid grasped in his hand.

Harrow ran at him, scooping the mono-bond reel off the floor as his did so. He flipped it, sending a loop around the priest's neck. The man took one more step and then his head came off.

That was a surprise: Harrow had meant to strangle the man, to leave him hanging from the handrail, but the mono-bond line was thin and very strong. As the priest ran, his own momentum was enough to draw the line clear through his neck. His head dropped away in a hissing shower of blood and his jerking body fell in the opposite direction, tentacle arms wind-milling and thrashing the air.

Harrow stared, resolving not to go climbing with mono-bond any more.

Alarm gongs were still pounding. Durham Red had collapsed into a heap nearby, slumped pitifully against some rancid cushions. Harrow stepped over the body of a servitor and lifted her tenderly; she was frighteningly light in his arms. "Holy one? Can you hear me?"

She made no answer, other than a slight flutter of the eyelids. To Harrow, that was enough. It was time to be away.

Judas Harrow had searched long and hard for the Osculum Cruentus. It had taken him months to track them down, partly because they simply didn't want to be found, but mainly because he was looking in the wrong place. He was expecting to find their cult-temple on some backwater planet, or hidden beneath the surface of a forgotten moon. All the sites where one usually put such things.

He certainly never thought to look for them in the heart of an asteroid.

But there they were, and had been for the last hundred years, tunnelling away in the dark and conducting their loathsome experiments in pain and pleasure. Deep within the iron-black stone of a planetisimal as big as a mountain, hiding since their excommunication, only venturing out to harvest local planets for fresh orgy victims and servitors. Over the decades they had expanded natural caverns in the rock into a nightmare maze: the Chamber of Sensation, the spherical room of the priestess, and all the corridors, cells and halls surrounding them had been nibbled out metre by metre.

Which left Judas Harrow with a unique problem. Even in the most crowded of asteroid belts, the distances between planetisimals are great, and starships are large, bright, hot objects in the icy darkness of space. An asteroid isn't something one can easily creep up on.

Harrow had a ship of his own, a tiny super-light yacht he had named *Crimson Hunter*. Once in the Kantallis Belt he had managed to get it safely to within a hundred kilometres of the Osculum's rock, judging that the cultists would have set their sense-engines to detect larger prey. He had left the ship on the shadow-side of a planetisimal not much larger than a tower block, powering it down but instructing a small, unsleeping part of its systems to await his call. He then sealed himself into a stealth-coated vacuum-shroud, strapped another to his belt for Durham Red, and stepped out of the airlock.

It had taken a long, lonely hour to reach the temple.

Once he was there, he had located a small service airlock and opened it with the data-pick, making his way inside and closing it behind him before the temple's surveillance engines knew anything was amiss. He had stripped off the vacuum-shroud, hidden it and its twin carefully and then an acolyte had tried to stab him in the face.

The yammering of the alarm gongs was giving Harrow a headache. It looked as though the dead acolyte was finally getting his revenge.

He was scrambling back through the temple towards the service lock, the derringer in one hand, the other arm wrapped tightly around Durham Red's waist. He was leaning her sideways slightly so she would slump against him and keep more or less upright, but her bare feet were still dragging along the stone floor. Even though she was thin and light, Harrow found himself wishing that the asteroid's artificial gravity had been set a little lower.

At least he remembered this route well enough. He had made sure that he knew it off by heart – could walk it in the dark if necessary – over the past couple of days. If life among the stars had taught him anything, it was to always have a good escape route handy.

He rounded the corner into the service lock and stopped dead. There were servitors there, looking right at him: priests behind them, acolytes. They had found the vacuum-shrouds.

The body of the acolyte he had killed must still have been in the cupboard, a nasty surprise waiting for the next man to put his cowl away.

Harrow swung Red around so that his body was between her and the enemy, and loosed off three shots with the derringer. One struck the head of the closest servitor and detonated its skull, sending fragments of grisly shrapnel spattering wildly around the lock. The priests ducked back, but the servitors weren't so easily cowed. Harrow just managed to fling himself back around the corner before the air filled with exploding frag-shells.

He fired another shot around the corner, hitting nothing, looking madly left and right for another escape route. Why had they discovered the body now? Didn't these people have a sense of smell?

There was a doorway opposite him, although getting to it would mean crossing what was rapidly becoming a solid wall of frag-fire. He took a deep breath, counted to three and then dived into the maelstrom, keeping low and slapping out shots with the derringer as fast as he could pull the trigger. Its supply of ammunition wasn't inexhaustible, but if he didn't use it now he'd never get another chance.

One of the shots hit a priest, blowing away everything from the centre of his chest upwards, and a second ripped a servitor in half. The survivors were packed in around the service lock, and that was Harrow's advantage – every time one of them fell prey to a plasma discharge, the others would be sprayed with his ruins. By this fact alone, Harrow managed to get himself and Red across to the doorway without being blown apart.

He dived through, hauling her with him. Past the entrance were long racks of what looked like tiny accommodation cells, their circular doors identical and stacked three high. For a moment Harrow didn't recognise them, their design was so old.

They were life-shells, programmed to open in an emergency and allow escape from a stricken starship or space station. In normal times, however, their doors were kept firmly locked, to stop people stealing their supplies.

Which meant Harrow needed an emergency.

He set Red down gently against the nearest shell, then took the acolyte's knife from his belt. He had to work fast; the fire from the corridor was beginning to lessen, as the servitors began to realise they weren't hitting anything. They could come stalking through the doorway any second, and what Harrow had in mind would leave him somewhat short of weaponry.

The point of the knife was slim but strong enough to flip open the derringer's access panels. He stabbed feverishly at the gleaming components inside, snapping the safeties away from the ignition chamber, jamming the knife blade down into the charging cell. Red had showed him how to do this once, but it had been a while ago, and he'd had more time.

From around the corner, he heard the piston-engine tread of a servitor.

The life-shells were racked near an airlock. If they were programmed in the usual way, he wouldn't even need to fracture the lock, just cause superficial damage; that should

be enough to get the shells open. Harrow pulled the derringer's trigger hard back, feeling it stick. Instantly the
weapon was scalding hot against his hand, and a thin
whine rose from its insides. He ducked around the corner
and threw the gun past the approaching servitors.

He heard a priest shout in warning, and the derringer
exploded.

It wasn't difficult to rig a plasma-discharge weapon to
explode – the things were notoriously prone to do so. Easy
or not, the effects were spectacular. Harrow had to dive
back into the doorway again as a searing column of white-
hot flame spat back along the corridor towards him.

The noise was amazing.

He risked a glance back outside. The service lock was a
roiling, smoke-shot inferno. Things moved fitfully amid the
flames, but not for long. It must have simply been the
effects of heat on flesh, scorched tissues twisting away from
blackening bone. Nothing could have survived the blast.

Well, he thought. That's it for the vacuum-shrouds. He
darted back to the shells, expecting to see ranks of opened
hatches.

All of them were closed.

The lock must have withstood the effects of the exploding derringer far better than the cultists inside. The plan
hadn't worked, and in the distance, Harrow heard the
shouts and sounds of weapons being prepared. Despite
himself, he used a word he had heard Red say once or
twice.

"Bugger!" he snarled.

At that precise moment, the airlock exploded again.

The noise was worse this time, enough to drive Harrow
to his knees, even around the corner and out of the direct
blast. Hot wind whipped at him. Something in the fire must
have grown hot enough to detonate – the servitors' ammunition, probably.

After the blast, there was another sound; a thin scream of
escaping air.

The life-shells were beginning to open. Harrow chose the one that looked the least decrepit and dragged Red through the hatch and into the cramped interior, ignoring her murmured protests. As the hatch slammed and locked behind him, he found something to hang onto and braced himself.

Here was a long, terrifying pause. The shell had a window, a domed diamond-analogue viewport. He could see flames lapping towards him, dragged into twisting points of vapour by the airflow.

The face of a servitor, half burned away, slammed against the port.

Harrow screamed in horror and as if on cue, the shell's explosive latches fired. The little vessel shuddered violently, almost shaking Harrow free of his handhold. He felt acceleration yank him as the shell engaged a reaction drive, blasting it free of the asteroid.

They were away.

Harrow gave a whoop of triumph. Against all odds, they had made it.

There was one last piece of equipment he hadn't used; a comm-linker, keyed to *Crimson Hunter*'s code-frequencies. The yacht wasn't sentient by any means; the art of building intelligent machines had long since been lost to the universe. But it had enough sense to come when it was called.

Harrow glanced across at Red. She was beginning to shiver violently and her eyes roved ceaselessly under her lids. He knew that her mutations gave her quite startling regenerative powers, and had witnessed her recover from near-crippling injuries in a matter of days. But this was the worst he had ever seen her. Even though he had finally located and carried her to freedom, he began to wonder if she would survive.

Past her, in the shell's domed viewport, he caught a glimpse of the temple asteroid. Flickers of light were showing around its edge.

For a moment he wasn't sure what he was seeing, whether there actually were tiny flares around the giant rock's periphery, or if it was just a trick of the eye. But as he watched, he saw that the floating mountain was moving, very slightly, against the backdrop of stars.

Manoeuvring thrusters. The asteroid was rotating around its axis towards him.

Harrow didn't like the look of this at all. He didn't know why the Osculum might be re-orientating their temple, and he wasn't quite sure he wanted to. He was very glad indeed when he felt *Hunter*'s parasite grabs latch onto the life-shell and draw it close.

As the two vessels embraced, *Crimson Hunter* opened its airlock. Harrow opened up the life-shell and carried Red over the threshold and into the yacht, easing her gently down onto the deck. She mumbled something and curled into a ball.

The airlock was still open. Harrow turned to close it, and saw through the life-shell's viewport why the Osculum had been turning their asteroid around. They were bringing their guns to bear.

The sky was yellow with antimat fire.

Great gouts of raw energy were ripping out of the asteroid towards him. Antimat guns were the kind of ordnance used by capital ships against each other. If one of those ragged bolts even clipped *Hunter*, the little yacht would be annihilated in an instant.

Harrow slammed his hand flat against the lock control, and even before the doors had cycled shut he was in the command throne.

Suddenly, *Hunter* fizzed. Harrow felt a thrill of latent electricity race through the vessel's structure, making the console lights flicker, sending tiny blue-white sparks up from the controls and into his fingertips. One of the antimat bolts must have come close, within a kilometre.

The next salvo could be right on target. Harrow brought the fusion core up to full power, gripped the throttle bar and poured energy into the drives. The ship leapt forwards, maximum thrust forcing Harrow back into the seat cushions. Distantly he heard Red sliding backwards along the deck as the acceleration grew, but his attention was fixed on the superlight indicators. Bars of light were growing there, reaching towards maximum...

He hit the jump key and, with a thunder of phased-transfer engines, *Hunter* left the universe of men for a better, cleaner place.

Durham Red was safe aboard his vessel. The ship was in jumpspace, heading off on the first of a series of programmed spatial leaps guaranteed to throw the Osculum off his trail. He hadn't been caught and turned into a drooling bacchanal.

All things considered, Judas Harrow was quite pleased with the way things had turned out.

He sat back in the command throne for a moment or two, allowing himself to relax for the first time in eight months. He felt he deserved it. Not for too long, though: Durham Red needed medical attention, and quickly. Luckily, Harrow had kitted *Hunter* out with an advanced medicom unit and a trauma spider, just in case.

There was a sound behind him, a scraping. He turned, and was stunned to see Red hauling herself upright. "Holy one," he whispered. "What–"

At the sound of his voice, she snapped around. There was nothing in her eyes but scarlet madness, nothing in her voice save an awful, steam-kettle hiss of pure animal rage. Fangs bared, she leaped.

She was on him before he could move, before he could speak, backhanding him with impossible strength into the wall of the cabin. His skull slammed into the metal, detonating novas of pain behind his eyes. He felt the deck whirl up and smash into the side of his face.

He tried to say something, anything, but words were beyond him. It was all he could do to keep breathing.

A shadow fell across him. The last thing he felt, before darkness became the world, was Durham Red's fangs at his throat.

2. RELICS

There was a wind coming up off the Great Scour, fast and brutally cold. Matteus Godolkin could feel it buffet him as he stood on the tower roof, could feel the frost it carried stinging the exposed skin of his face around the breath-mask.

He was alone on the roof, which was his preference. It was the place where he felt most able to meditate properly. The meditorium, at the back of the chapel, was too cluttered for him to feel completely at peace, and he didn't really like the Vision Hall much either. There was no point being able to see the harsh landscape of Lavannos, he had decided, if you couldn't feel it.

Lavannos was a deadly little place, a bitter, frozen enemy of a world. Matteus Godolkin had no time for an enemy he could not face.

The tower had a surrounding wall, waist high, turning its flat, square top into a terrace of sorts. Godolkin gripped the wall tightly, his big hands almost as white as the smooth stone under them, daring the wind to strike him. It was a habit he had grown into over the past few months; every day he would climb up through the tower, barely noticing the exertion of the multiple flights of steps, and make his way onto the roof. There he would stand, for hours at a time, feeling the frosty wind cut into his scarred, bleached-out skin, chilling his augmented bones. The daytime temperature on the bright face of Lavannos rarely rose above thirty degrees below zero. Without fail, Godolkin went up to the roof stripped to the waist.

His only admission of weakness was the breath-mask. Matteus Godolkin could do many things, but not even he could breathe the rarefied atmosphere of Lavannos for very long.

"Quite beautiful, isn't it? In a lethal kind of way…"

Godolkin didn't turn away from the wall. He had heard the abbot climbing the stairs behind him – the last three flights, in fact. "I had not noticed."

"Come now, Matteus. Are you trying to tell me that an Iconoclast has no appreciation of beauty?"

The abbot walked briskly across the roof and joined Godolkin at the wall. He was tall, although nowhere near as tall as the Iconoclast, and slender. A heavy thermocowl was draped over his narrow, stoop-shouldered frame, and his long hands were covered with electrically warmed gloves. His breath-mask was a full-face design. Godolkin looked across at him and saw himself reflected in twin lenses as bulbous and facetted as the eyes of an insect.

He pondered for a moment. He and the abbot had spoken of many things over the months, but beauty wasn't one of them. "Perhaps our training requires us to be more… focussed. To see beauty would be an inefficiency and dangerous. We might be required to destroy that beauty without hesitation."

"And recognising it might give you pause?"

"Anything that slows the reactions is potentially fatal."

The abbot nodded. "Yes, I can see that. Still…" He gestured at the frozen vista before them. "Appreciate it now, Godolkin. Have a good look at that and tell me you see no beauty."

An exercise, then. Godolkin was always ready to test himself. He looked.

And saw…

The sky of Lavannos was split in two across a shallow diagonal. Above the horizon, wider to the west, was a narrow, curving strip of deep, rich blue, turning almost black at its highest point. Above that, and covering three-quarters of the sky, was the vast, yellow-orange ball of the gas giant Mandus. Wide, stormy belts of darker cloud roiled and swarmed across the face of the giant, constantly changing in a slow, ceaselessly chaotic crawl.

As for Lavannos itself, Godolkin had never seen a world like it.

At some time in its distant past, the little planet had been exposed to a source of heat that beggared comprehension: the entire surface, to a depth of dozens of kilometres, had been rendered liquid. And then, while that liquid had still been leaping and frothing with huge bubbles of super-heated gas, Lavannos had abruptly refrozen. Whatever geological variations the planet had once possessed were boiled away in that searing heat, leaving a landscape of gleaming black glass. The surface was peppered with great blisters and cysts, rough as plague-wracked flesh.

Gravity, and the stresses of close orbit around Mandus, had caused most of the bubbles to collapse under their own weight. The crust had been left pockmarked with craters, deep and smooth-sided, their bases littered with shards of obsidian which were sharp enough to scythe a man in two.

The largest crater was also the closest: Eye of God was ninety kilometres across, and almost thirty deep. Its base was forever lost to darkness and its near-vertical sides rimed with metres of frost. The gaze of the Lord, however, was slightly lopsided; God's Pupil, an unbroken bubble of glistening black glass the size of a small town, rose off-centre and misshapen from its depths.

The Church of the Arch, and the tower on which Godolkin and the abbot now stood, nestled close to the rim of Eye of God. The drop in front of the building was sheer, and kilometres deep.

To the east, Godolkin's right, the congress of two cysts formed the lethal Bridge of Splinters. To his left lay the Great Scour, shallow and ragged and wide enough to swallow fleets. North of that was the part-collapsed blister of

Fracture Peak, and in the distance, half hidden beneath drifting slopes of ice, rose the gaping maw of Mount Solace.

Cysts and craters, black glass and white frost: Lavannos was a lifeless, oily foam. Godolkin had seen lovelier cesspools.

The abbot was waiting. "It is," Godolkin admitted finally, "impressive."

Beside him, the older man gave a wry chuckle. "And is that your tactical appraisal?"

"No. That would take longer."

The abbot nodded. "I would be intrigued to hear it, my friend." He glanced about, his movements reduced to mime by mask and cowl. "But not here. My bones, unlike yours, are just made of bone. And they get cold."

The abbot had quarters two levels down, under the Vision Hall. It was warmer there. Godolkin removed his breath-mask and shrugged into a heavy, armoured jacket, then fastened his grey attendant's cloak around his throat. The abbot had stripped away his mask and thermocowl on the way down.

The rooms were not especially large, although they were considerably bigger than those occupied by Godolkin and the rest of the attendants. Simple rugs lay on the floors, while plain luminescent panels provided light. The walls were unadorned and slightly narrower at the ceiling than they were at the floor, following the slope-sided profile of the tower.

The abbot liked to keep things simple, Godolkin had learned. He had only one indulgence the Iconoclast was aware of. "I'm making tea. Would you care to join me?"

Godolkin nodded and found a chair that would take his weight, while the abbot fussed with hot water and tiny cups and a tall, long-stemmed teapot. He had taken tea with the old man several times since arriving at the Church; the abbot seemed to enjoy engaging the Iconoclast in conversation, although Godolkin did the lesser share of talking by far. He had once asked the abbot why he was singled out for these discussions; there were other attendants at the retreat, after all. The abbot had told him, other than for his interesting past, it was because most of the others had taken a vow of silence.

Godolkin had to admit that would make things difficult. He had made no such pledge himself; he had taken vows in the past and had seen them come to ruin. He would not do so lightly again.

The abbot was coming over to join him, carrying a small tray. Two cups, perched on exquisite saucers, steamed on it. "Sugar?"

Godolkin shook his head, then sniffed. "The composition is different today."

"Well spotted, Het." The abbot lifted a cup to his lips and sipped delicately. "Mmm. This is, I am reliably informed, a tea called Earl Grey. It dates back to pre-Accord times; an archeotech who stayed here recently taught me the trick of it, and gave me a living tea-plant. I keep it in the Vision Hall, where it can find at least a little sun."

Godolkin reached for a cup. His fingers were too large to go through the tiny, looped handle, so he wrapped his whole hand around the container, feeling its warmth against his massive palm.

He brought the steaming liquid closer and sniffed it again. And as its fragrance reached his nostrils he had a sudden vision: a massive warrior, his grey-white skin a network of scars and intricate charm-tattoos, sitting in a comfortable chair with a hot cup of tea in his hand. He blinked, suddenly amazed at himself. "Insane," he muttered.

"Excuse me?"

Godolkin looked at the old man. "Het Abbot, I am – I *was* – an Iconoclast First-Class, a warrior in unswerving service of the Accord. I have led planet-wide purges, overseen the execution of thousands. I have watched oceans boil and continents burn. And yet here I am, sipping leaf-infusions from ceramic containers, discussing the finer points of tea-making…" He shook his head. "An insane situation."

The abbot shrugged. "The universe is brimming with insane situations, Het. Wars fought over the most trivial genetic differences have killed billions. Worlds starve in order to meet planetary tithes that no longer have any meaning. Battlefleets powerful enough to snuff out suns are sent to punish the misdemeanours of a single man."

"And vampires live among us," Godolkin whispered, staring into his teacup.

"One, at least." The abbot lifted his own cup in ironic salute. "And there, Iconoclast First-Class, is the whole root of your problem."

Of all the mad horrors in the universe, it was the vampire that had occupied Matteus Godolkin the most.

In the aftermath of the Bloodshed – as historians had come to call the great war between human and mutant – the Iconoclasts had become the most potent military force in the Pan-Species Accord. Their evolution had begun during the Bloodshed itself, but had accelerated massively during its final stages. Their duties had now grown far beyond the simple protection of the human species: they were charged with suppression of mutant activity on a thousand fronts, collection of planetary tithes, patrol of Accord territorial borders and most important of all, the complete annihilation of the underground mutant cadre known as the Tenebrae.

For their part, the Tenebrae represented the dripping knife-edge of anti-humanism. The days when they had been a simple sect of blood-worshippers were long gone. United behind the image of Saint Scarlet of Durham, they had become a potent military organisation; secret yet overt, hidden yet able and willing to strike with genocidal force. Only the vastness of the inhabited galaxy allowed them to remain little more than myth in most quarters, and yet command battlefleets.

Iconoclast and Tenebrae: never before or since had two more bitterly opposed forces come to be.

The Tenebrae drew strength from their worship of the arch-vampire, Durham Red. The Iconoclasts believed with unshakeable conviction that the vampire was the most deadly threat to the human race that existed. Thus, they became vampire-killers.

Iconoclast soldiers were not simply indoctrinated to hate and fear the vampire or trained to kill it; they were physically altered for the task. Counter-vampire charms were burned into their skins, a network of sacred tattoos protecting their arteries and surface blood vessels. Their bones were reinforced, their nervous systems rewired. Eyes were altered to receive input from vision amplifiers, their senses of smell, taste and hearing jacked-up to insane levels. An Iconoclast at the height of their powers could hear a man's heartbeat at ten metres, a breath at a hundred. He could see thermal differences of a tenth of a degree.

He could detect a mutant by smell alone.

All this, Matteus Godolkin could do. And when he finally met a vampire, a real one, none of it was the slightest use.

In response to a wild tale of the mythical Saint Scarlet's revival, Godolkin and his team had been sent to purge the university world of Wodan. Unfortunately for him, the tale had been true. Durham Red herself had attacked him.

That had been something of a surprise. But up to the last moment, just before her great leap had brought her teeth to his throat, he had still believed he would prevail. His charms, his training, his belief would save him.

He'd been wrong, of course.

She had knocked him flat, torn the anti-vampire weapons from his grasp, ripped away his vision amplifier, and sunk her fangs into his neck. Which would have been the end of Matteus Godolkin and all his works, had the Blasphemy's mutant companion, Judas Harrow, not hauled her away.

Every day, without fail, Matteus Godolkin climbed to the top of the tower at the Church of the Arch and stood staring out over the Eye of God, willing the Almighty to somehow transport him back to that day and let Durham Red take those last, fatal drops.

He was trapped by her now. Her poison was in his blood, her fangs at his throat no matter how far apart the two of them were. From that moment on, Godolkin had ceased to be a warrior of the Accord and had become a slave to the fiend herself. The Blasphemy's word had become his law.

It was intolerable and horrible. He was sworn to destroy her, and yet, with a single utterance from her, he was bound to protect her. For weeks after that day he had been her unwilling companion, until finally, blessedly, she had grown tired of him and Harrow. Told them they were cramping her style, whatever that might have meant. She had ordered Godolkin to leave her side; a command he followed willingly.

His wanderings after that had taken him to world after world, before he had at last found the Church of the Arch, and a kind of peace.

If only he could stop dreaming about Durham Red.

She came to him again that night, after the Earl Grey, striding through mists and darkness, a sly smile playing about her lips. She was as he had last seen her, on the pleasure-moon; dressed in black synthetic leather, the cut of the garment showing every curve, every plane and angle of her perfect, hellish body. Her hair was long, scarlet and black, and her eyes glowed a deep crimson. "Hey, Godolkin," she purred. "I've missed you."

"Blasphemy," he hissed. "Come no closer, or I swear you will fall."

"Aw, honey, don't be like that." She whirled girlishly, spinning on one impossibly high heel. "I know you want me."

He shook his head, violently. "No. Your body is a poison, a house of death. You sicken me."

"Really? Not the impression I got." She leaned close. "Still, if you don't want my body, I know you want my mind…"

She reached up with both hands, crooking her long fingers down to meet in the centre of her scalp. Godolkin saw her wrists tense, heard the cracking of bone as she forced her fingertips downwards through hair and skin and skull. Blood spilled from the wound, ran down over her smiling face.

Slowly, horribly, she wrenched her hands apart.

Her head split, scalp to jaw, her face coming apart in two equal sections as she levered her skull open to expose the steaming mass within. "Come on, Godolkin," she grinned, fangs awash with blood and fluid. "I know you're hungry. Dig in!"

And he rose to her, mouth watering, opening his jaw impossibly wide to take that first succulent bite...

There was no real night and day on Lavannos. The monastery ran on an artificial diurnal cycle, based on the Galactic Standard Hour. It was a well-known system, the same used on starships, and easy enough to adapt to. Matteus Godolkin had no problems adjusting to the most wildly different day-night lengths, due to a mixture of training and biochemical implants. None of the other attendants, however, had this advantage. As far as records showed, no other Iconoclast had ever been to the Church of the Arch.

Lavannos and its gigantic partner, Mandus, orbited very far indeed from their sun. The star, Godolkin knew, was called Shantima, and occasionally he was able to spot it during his meditations on the tower. From this distance, though, it was nothing more than a bright point in the sky, barely able to cast a shadow. No heat reached Lavannos from Shantima either – thermal emissions from Mandus provided the only warmth on offer.

Almost as if Lavannos acknowledged the debt it owed Mandus, it kept one face turned continually towards it; tidally-locked to its giant companion by the vast gravitational well.

Thus the foamed landscape of Lavannos remained unchanging, save the occasional drift of frost off the Great Scour. Perhaps, Godolkin thought, gripping the tower wall hard, that was why people came here. In a frantic, baleful universe, maybe even this deathly peace was enough to ease the soul.

He wished it would do something for his own.

Godolkin had not seen the abbot for some days – the old man was spending most of his time elsewhere. Hardly surprising, given that the old man had seventy monks, thirty attendants, the church, the monastery and everything within its walls to keep track of. There were times, it was said, when he would disappear for weeks.

As an Iconoclast warrior, Godolkin would be the first to tell anyone that he needed no company but his own. Self-reliance was of paramount importance in the field of battle. While it was important to know how to fight as part of a team – and recognise one's place in the vaster armies of the Accord – it was also essential to be able to operate completely alone, without succour or supply, for indefinite periods of time. Matteus Godolkin, Iconoclast First-Class, knew this better than most.

But he still wished the abbot were around. He had, against all his training, grown rather fond of the old man. Plus, of course, the abbot was the only person who he would confess to and reveal the torment that was ripping his mind apart.

The dreams had been getting worse.

Contrary to popular belief, Iconoclasts dreamed just like anyone else. They just didn't talk about it. But Godolkin's dreams were becoming so intense, so disturbing, that they were threatening his sanity. Night after night, for weeks, he had been visited by the Blasphemy, and drawn with her into the foulest acts imaginable. He had seen terrible things in his time and done terrible things, but the images that haunted his nights on Lavannos were far, far worse. And he didn't know what to do.

He could leave Lavannos, ship out on the next supply tender, only a few days away. But would the dreams stop if he did? They might get worse, once he was returned to the harshness of the galaxy. Not forgetting, of course, that he was still a wanted man.

The vampire's taint was in him, now. Any Iconoclasts he met would immolate him on sight.

Abruptly, his reverie was broken by the sound of someone climbing the tower steps. The atmosphere of Lavannos was unbreathably thin – if it hadn't been for Mandus, it wouldn't have had one at all – and the lack of air impaired his hearing. He still heard the footsteps well before anyone emerged onto the roof.

He could also tell that it wasn't the abbot. "Prior Rinaud."

"Het Godolkin." Rinaud was the abbot's second-in-command, a severe woman with the lean, angular frame of someone who had spent a long time on Lavannos. The light gravity did that to people. "I was told I could find you here."

Godolkin blinked. He hadn't been aware it was a secret. "By whom?"

"The abbot. He sent me to find you, to give you a message." Rinaud hadn't crossed the roof. She was keeping near the steps, with the trapdoor open. Godolkin could hear her shivering, even with a thermocowl covering her from head to foot and heat washing up the steps from the levels below. "Sneck, it's cold up here. Lord, pardon my foul tongue."

"Was that the message?"

Rinaud snorted through her breath-mask. "No, Het, the message is this: 'Look to the *Rule of Lavann,* chapter seven, verse four.'"

Godolkin raised an eyebrow. "'Idleness is the enemy of the soul'," he quoted. "I am intrigued."

"He said you would be." Rinaud turned away, and began to bob back down the steps. "He's in the reliquary."

. . .

Unusually, the reliquary was on the other side of the monastery from the chapel. Godolkin could have reached it through the pressurised, heated areas of the building, but the quickest way was across the courtyard. Once down the tower steps and back at ground level he took a small side-corridor past the chapel and the west cloister, and out onto the plain black tiles of the open court.

A small attendant, masked and hooded against the chill, peered at him as he strode past. Godolkin caught a glimpse of a woman's face under the hood, and felt a strange jolt of recognition. "Good day, Het," he muttered, using the universal honorific. Past the breath-mask he couldn't be sure if she smelled of human or mutant.

The woman said nothing, and turned away. Godolkin was puzzled for a moment, but then put her out of his mind. She had probably arrived on the same supply tender he had.

The reliquary was a small building, as blocky and unadorned as the rest of the monastery and coated in the same radiation-reflecting white stone. Godolkin found the heat-lock and keyed the chime set into the frame. A few moments later the lock hissed out a small cloud of condensation and swung aside.

Godolkin stepped in and heard the outer door seal behind him a fraction of a second before the inner one opened. The monastery's heat-locks were efficiently built and scrupulously maintained. To go through one was little more effort than walking through an ordinary door.

They were, however, built a little low for someone of Godolkin's height.

The reliquary felt warm after the icy cold of outside, but not as stifling as other areas of the monastery. Godolkin tugged his breath-mask free and sniffed the air, picking up the dead tang of atmosphere control instantly. Whatever relics the building contained must have been of some delicacy to require such precise monitoring of their air and climate.

The interior of the reliquary was not what Godolkin was expecting. Most churches kept their sacred relics in grim, forbidding places, bedecked with symbols and the gilded skulls of the honoured dead. This, however, was more like an operating theatre.

Flat, silvery panels of insulation lined the walls, reflecting soft white light from the low-level ceiling. The floor beneath Godolkin's boots was black antistatic carpet, silent as he paced inside, and shelves, stacked neatly with artefacts, rose in symmetrical banks on either side of him. At the far end of the reliquary was what looked like a small but well-equipped laboratory with multiple data-engines and holo displays centred around a coffin-sized scanning deck. Godolkin drew closer, noting several items that had no normal place within a place of prayer: an electron microscope, a phase-breacher, a quantum probe.

This was not worship. This was intense study.

He was alone in the reliquary, the only sound a faint chattering from the lab's engines. "Het Abbot?" he called.

There was a soft noise of concealed panels sliding away.

Godolkin turned. A doorway had appeared between two sets of shelves and the abbot's face was peering out of the shadows behind; it was oddly close to the floor. "Ah, Matteus!" he smiled, beckoning. "Come down. I've got a job for you."

Godolkin padded back to the doorway. The abbot was already descending a steep set of stairs, leading down into the gloom. "I'm glad Rinaud found you," he was saying, his voice echoing harshly. "She was rather loath to venture onto the tower, I'm afraid."

"The view is not to everyone's taste." Godolkin lowered himself down onto the first step, and then began to descend.

"Nor the climb." The abbot looked back, making sure that Godolkin was following. He carried a bright hand-lume, casting bluish light up the tunnel. "Take care, by the way. These steps are carved out of the crust of Lavannos, and they can be slippery, to say the least..."

Godolkin's old black boots were Iconoclast standard issue, with grips that would keep him upright on wet ice in a gale. Still, he took his care. The steps, and the tunnel that surrounded them, were indeed that same black, glassy stuff as the rest of Lavannos, like a kind of bubble-flecked obsidian. It was not only slippery, but razor-sharp.

"Het Abbot? I am puzzled."

"About what?"

"The reliquary. Are the items there holy things?"

The abbot chuckled. "Only in as much as Lavannos itself is holy to us. Its appearance to Saint Lavann is still an accepted miracle among his followers."

And a heresy to the orthodox faith of the Accord, thought Godolkin, although he kept his silence. Lavannos was, thankfully, well outside Accord space, almost on the fringes of the Vermin Stars. "I had expected to come face to face with the bones of Lavann himself."

"Oh no, our blessed father left nothing so crass." The abbot turned back up the steps to Godolkin. "A few more metres, Het, and then all will be revealed."

The abbot's words, Godolkin discovered moments later, were perfectly true. If something of an understatement.

It was perfectly logical, when he thought about it. The titan bubbles of gas that gave Lavannos its foamed structure couldn't all have reached the surface before the crust refroze. Millions of them must still have been buried.

Like the one he stood in now.

It was vast, a flattened ovoid space as big as a freighter hold. The inside surface of it, where the light from the abbot's lume reached it, was as glossy as black silk. Barring a few imperfections – smaller bubbles, minor pits and cracks – it was almost completely featureless.

"Large, isn't it?" grinned the abbot, his voice reverberating insanely around the cavern. "Lavann be praised, it's the biggest void under the monastery by far. I've had nightmares about something the size of Eye of God opening up under my feet."

Godolkin, who had enough nightmares of his own to worry about, just nodded.

The abbot was walking away, towards the furthest wall of the bubble. "And over here, my friend, is why I called you down here. I need your strength. And your silence."

Godolkin followed him, boots crunching on glassy dust. "I will take no vow, Het Abbot. I've told you that."

"I know, Het. This is trust on my part, believe me." He raised the hand-lume. "But it would give rise to more questions than answers if we made this too well-known."

Matteus Godolkin, for all his iron will, only barely stopped himself from uttering one of Durham Red's infamous curses.

The wall of the cavern was studded with objects, frozen into the rock.

This was where the reliquary's artefacts had come from – he could see the places where they had been chipped and wrenched out of the glass. There were strange objects he could hardly recognise, some burned and melted by the intense heat that had ruined Lavannos, some almost intact. Pieces of metal, plastic, other materials he could not name. Items of technology, pieces of reinforced structure, furniture. Human bones.

"Look at this," The abbot directed the lume's light onto a gleaming artefact, what looked like part of a metal hand. The finger joints were intricate, subtle workings of metal and ceramic that was nothing like the brute technologies of the Accord. "Have you, in all you travels, seen anything like this?"

Godolkin shook his head. "I have not."

"But you do see why this mustn't, for the moment, be revealed. To the other attendants or anyone else."

"I believe so." Godolkin straightened. "I am no archeotech. But I see these technologies have no current analogue. Abbot, do your relics date back to before the Bloodshed?"

The old man rubbed his chin. "We think so. This cavern was only discovered ten years ago – ten years standard, of course. We've been studying the finds ever since, with the help of any attendant we felt we could trust, and whose knowledge might have been useful." He too stood straight, putting a hand to his lower back. "It may turn out to be nothing, curios from some vessel that crashed hard enough into Lavannos to melt part of the crust. A jumpspace accident, maybe. But if we call in a university or Accord archeotechs the administratum will be all over Lavannos like a nasty rash, if you'll pardon the analogy."

"And your holy retreat would end up as nothing more than a farworld dig, laid open and swarming with historians." Godolkin put a finger to his black lips. "A sad end to the church."

"I'm glad you agree, my friend." The abbot winced. "God! Curse these old bones of mine. The indignities of seniority. Which is the other reason I brought you down here, Matteus. You translated my message?"

"I did." Godolkin had read the rule of Lavann upon entering the retreat, just like every attendant. Once he had read something, he didn't forget it. "And far be it from me to let my soul fall prey to an enemy again. Where would you like my strength applied?"

"Here." The abbot moved a few metres further along the wall, where a large, flattened cylinder jutted from the rock. Around its ridged surface the cavern had been chipped and scored into a deep crater, exposing more of the artefact. Godolkin could see that most of it had been freed, almost three metres of gleaming metal.

Something about it jolted inside him. He shook the feeling away. "Do you wish me to simply pull it free?"

"More or less." The abbot gestured at the rough surroundings of the cylinder. "I don't want to use the light-drill any more – it's at too awkward an angle, and I don't want to score the metal. I think that with the right leverage…"

Godolkin put his arms around the cylinder, feeling a slight warmth from it, a subtle vibration. The aftermath of the light-drill, no doubt. He pulled.

There was a sharp cracking sound. Bits of glass splintered away and scattered across the bubble floor.

Boots firmly planted, Godolkin bettered his grip on the cylinder and heaved. For a second there was no movement, but then the glassy wall of the cavern groaned. There was a squeaking, snapping report.

The cylinder came free.

Part of the wall shivered to fragments behind it, collapsing in a dusty heap around Godolkin's feet. Still holding the cylinder, he moved back, careful to avoid the larger shards of glass, and set the artefact down before the abbot. "You were correct," he said. "It was almost free."

And then, in the light of the abbot's lume, he got a good look at the thing.

And realised where he had seen it before.

For the first time, the tower roof seemed cold to Godolkin.

He'd been able to hide his recognition of the cylinder from the abbot, and the horrified shock of seeing what he had freed from the cavern wall. At that moment, more than at any other time, he'd wished he had never set foot on Lavannos.

And yet, that awful thing in the cavern, and whatever nightmare it may contain, could lead him to salvation. It could bring him to a final confrontation with Durham Red.

To do so was madness, he knew. What he had found might have lethal consequences: for himself, for Lavannos, for the Accord. It could raise Durham Red to true supremacy or destroy her utterly. Or it might do neither. But one thing it would do, of that he was certain.

It would bring her to Lavannos.

He couldn't contact her. Even if he knew where the arch-bitch was, she had ordered him not to. But he had no other choice. The dreams were shredding him. From whatever hellish lair she had secreted herself in, she was driving him insane with these nightmares.

He would stand before Durham Red again, and one of them would fall. Either way, the torment would end. Godolkin felt as though he were teetering on the Bridge of Splinters. Razor-edged shards of black glass in every direction and a sheer drop of five kilometres on either side.

Communications from the monastery were normally forbidden, and the Shantima system was so out of the way and so far from a relay station that messages from Lavannos back to the Accord might take days. Godolkin, however, had access to technology very few others had even seen. One of these, kept concealed in his room ever since he had arrived, was a military comm-linker, with full encryption.

Godolkin checked around him, making sure one final time that he was alone on the tower roof. Then he activated the linker and set the channel to the crypt-key used by the mutant, Judas Harrow.

"Hear me and take heed, Harrow," he began. "I am at the Church of the Arch, on Lavannos, Shantima system. You must do what I cannot – find your sainted bitch, Durham Red, and bring her here. There is something on Lavannos that she must see."

He paused, gazing out over Eye of God. The thin winds of Lavannos were whipping the frost into glittering dust devils along its eastern edge. "I am enclosing a sense-scan of an artefact, found buried under the monastery of Saint Lavann. She will recognise its significance, as will you. Get this message to her, Harrow. At all costs."

He closed the transmission, and let out a long breath, watching it steam away through the mask. It was done. Suddenly, he was immensely tired.

Nightmares or not, he needed sleep. It had been days since he had last rested. He turned away from the Eye of God and started walking back to the tower.

When he was halfway across the roof, the trapdoor opened up from the inside. Godolkin halted, something inside him ringing a warning.

He hadn't heard any footsteps.

The trapdoor was a heat-lock, set level with the tower floor, the inner door at the bottom of the top flight of stairs. It could be motorised, opened from elsewhere.

He whirled, lightening quick, and dived for cover. He was almost quick enough, but the gravity on Lavannos was light. He was still in the air when he should have been on the ground, and the shot – fired from the chapel roof – took him in the left shoulder.

It spun him around, slamming him into the tower wall. He fell away and rolled onto his back, hands scraping at the stone. He couldn't get up.

For a moment, all he could see was the huge, roiling ball of Mandus above him, filling the whole sky. Then it was blocked out. Godolkin squinted up through a haze of pain, into the insect eyes of a breath mask.

Before the other three shots slapped into his chest.

3. INTO THE FIRE

There was a digital display on part of *Crimson Hunter*'s control board, a clock showing Galactic Standard time and date. Durham Red couldn't stop looking at it.

Eight months. She'd been out of the loop for almost eight months.

She was hunched in the navigation throne, wrapped up in as many environment blankets as Harrow had been able to find in the ship's supply locker. There was no way she could sit upright. Even trying to do so sent barbs of pain slicing up between her shoulder blades. The spinal socket was gone, removed the day before by Harrow's trauma spider: the wound it left, however, was still in the process of healing.

Red didn't feel as though *anything* were healing. Everything hurt. She'd been through enough bad times in the past, but she honestly couldn't remember feeling anywhere near as rotten as this. To say she was weak didn't even come close to describing the situation – there were times when she couldn't lift an arm. Her spine was a column of raw ache at her core, and waves of searing inner heat and shuddering cold were washing up her body, from her feet to the top of her pounding, heavy head; alternating roughly, by the display on the clock, once every four minutes.

Hot or cold, she couldn't stop shivering. And every time she saw the clock display again, the date on it jolted her like a kick in the ribs.

Eight months…

She felt as though she could no longer hold onto time. It kept slipping away from her, dancing out of her grip just as she thought she had a handle on things. Time, she decided, was getting its revenge, making her suffer for trying to throw it away, all those centuries ago.

All she'd wanted to do was drop a couple of years, let the world go by without her for a while. And look where she'd ended up.

The rear hatch, at the back of *Hunter*'s egg-shaped command cabin, slid open. Red turned, wincing as the motion set her head swimming. Judas Harrow was clambering in from the yacht's spinal corridor.

He still looked fairly wobbly on his feet, and there was a large bio-dressing on the left side of his neck. Red hadn't been gentle when she'd fed from him. From what he'd been able to tell her, it was even betting which of them had needed the medicom more after that little encounter.

Lucky for him, she'd come to her senses before she'd drained him dry. Lucky for them both, in fact.

Harrow sat down next to her, in the command throne. "How are you feeling, holy one?" he asked softly. "Any better?"

"Well, I haven't thrown up for at least twenty minutes, so that's a bonus." As she spoke, a tide of rubbery heat washed up from her toes and she groaned. "Sneck, Jude. What did those bastards do to me?"

Harrow looked at her warily. "I'll tell you when you're feeling stronger."

"Oh yeah." He'd tried to tell her before, the first time she'd asked. He was less than a minute into his explanation before Red had been sick over him.

He gave her a wan smile. "What do you remember?"

Nothing. She remembered nothing. The last eight months were gone in a haze of distant agony and constant, suffocating need. Before that...

"Gomorrah," she said finally, her voice little more than a whisper. "We went to Gomorrah."

• • •

Gomorrah was a pleasure-moon. Red had found a reference to it in the ship's data banks, under "Proscribed Territories". It was the first, and indeed the only part of the planetary database she'd looked at. "To you Jude, this is 'Here Be Dragons.' To me, it's a holiday brochure."

They had a different ship, back then. It was a larger vessel, the one they had stolen from Pyre, just before the planet had been sterilised by Iconoclast kill-fleets. Even though it was a small ship compared to most, for a crew of three it was cavernous. Wandering around it for days on end, while Godolkin made random superlight jumps, had been starting to drive her insane.

There had been excursions; planetfalls on the way to pick up supplies, and for Red to try and find a little fresh blood, willing or otherwise. None had ended well. After a while, they had just stopped trying.

Stars raced past, seemingly without end. Days, too. Durham Red felt the metal walls of the ship closing in on her, nearer with every hour. Suddenly, it wasn't big enough. She took to wandering through its holds and cabins, skulking about the darkest corridors, even putting on a vacuum-shroud and prowling the outside of the hull. Anything to avoid Harrow's doe-eyed devotion and Godolkin's baleful obedience.

And then she'd discovered Gomorrah.

Most of the worlds classed as proscribed were listed because they were dangerous; home to vicious beasts, lethal diseases and terrible natural phenomena. Gomorrah, on the other hand, was a danger to the soul. The debauches practised on the world, it was said, would drive even the most pious traveller mad with desire.

To Red, that was the best sales pitch she'd heard in a long time.

Harrow, of course, had tried to persuade her not to go. "It's a lawless place, holy one. All they care about is pleasure, at any price."

"Cool." Red had already set a course by this point. "Can we go any faster?"

The two of them had been alone on the bridge. Godolkin was at devotions in his cabin, poring over his books of scripture. Red was lounging in the command throne, shades on, high-heeled boots resting on the navigation cascade. She was picking her teeth with a combat knife, largely to freak Harrow out. By the look on his face, it was working.

"Red, please listen. Gomorrah might sound like fun, but it's far more dangerous than that. You still have a price on your head, you know."

Red found something with the knife, a tiny fragment of tissue or dried blood. She held the blade up to the light to inspect it. "You worry about your head, boy, and I'll worry about mine."

"That's the point. I do worry."

The knife whickered out of her hand and embedded itself in the headrest of Harrow's chair. "Dammit Judas, you are such a snecking drag!" She glared at him from behind the shades. "Just lighten up, willya? You're beginning to sound like Godolkin."

"But we shouldn't–"

"Ah!" she snapped warningly, aiming a finger at him.

"But–"

"Ah!"

He dropped it. If only Godolkin had been so easy to sway.

Gomorrah was a revelation. It lay on the fringes of the Pan-Species Accord, and seemed totally untouched by the baleful puritanism that pervaded Accord life. In fact, the place was the complete opposite of anything Red had seen so far.

It was a small world, about the size of Vadis, tumbling around a giant planet that seemed to consist entirely of ocean. But where that little backwater had been almost life-less, Gomorrah seethed and pulsed.

The pleasure-moon was belted by a single, titanic city, a thousand kilometres wide and so long that it stretched clear around Gomorrah and met itself again on the far side. Great towers thrust up from the centre of every city-block, livid with brilliant neon, holograms and whirling, sweeping searchlights. Around the towers, streets spread out in concentric rings, the buildings that crowded them offering every kind of pleasure imaginable. The sky was constantly dark, laden with sweet-smelling mist, and there was music everywhere – not the ever-present monastic chiming of the Accord worlds, but a grinding, driving sound that made Red's bones leap and thrill with the life of it. The entire planet had a beat.

Once she was off the ship, she had wanted to race away, fling herself into the nearest party and never leave. Godolkin, however, had other ideas. Unlike Harrow, he never tried to persuade her to leave. He simply insisted on accompanying her everywhere, vetoing any tavern or sense-palace she tried to head for.

They were in disguise, the three of them, with false papers and simulated brand-scars. But even with his Iconoclast tattoos hidden and his amplifier-eye covered by a data monocle, Godolkin still had an air to him that discouraged casual conversation, to say the least. More than one playful soul had started to approach Durham Red, met Godolkin's implacable gaze and suddenly found other pleasures to attend.

After a couple of hours of this, Red had lost the small amount of patience she possessed; it had never been one of her greatest virtues. "Sneck off and leave me alone, you one-eyed lunatic!"

They had reached a major intersection, a vast pedestrian walkway between a multi-level twenty-six hour dance-orgy and a vaulted, heaving structure that advertised itself as the Seraglio of Sybarism. SeraSym, to the more inebriated visitor. The walkway was crowded, jammed wall to wall with thousands of pleasure-seekers. At Red's outburst, however, the three travellers suddenly found themselves with quite a lot of personal space.

Godolkin folded his arms. "Blasphemy, you told me to protect you with my life. That I shall do, even if the protection you require is from your own baser desires."

Red threw her hands up. "Jesus, Godolkin! Right now my baser desires are the only things keeping me upright! Six weeks I've had you cramping my style, whining in my ear: 'Can't go there, it's not safe. Can't drink that, wouldn't be good for you. Can't touch him, dunno where he's been!'" She stalked a few metres up the street, then whirled back to face him. "Sneck!" she snarled. "I want to have fun! I want to forget all this, don't you get it? Why the hell can't you just let me go?"

The warrior shook his great head. "You know nothing of this universe."

"I know enough!"

"Blasphemy-"

Suddenly, Red was nose to nose with Godolkin, her face a mask of murderous rage. "You call me that one more time, you snecker, and I'll-"

"What?" Godolkin met her gaze. Contrary to Red's earlier insult both his eyes were perfectly good, but the one that had been modified showed a weird, milky white. "What will you do? Kill me, and finally give me the peace I seek? You would be releasing me from a torment, Blasphemy."

Everything was abruptly still, the moment crystallising around them. Red could still hear the music, the moans – could feel the beat coming up through the soles of her boots – but inside her was a strange, thrumming stillness, like a tuning fork set too high to hear.

She was hugely, terribly angry, but there was something else in her too, creeping up cold around her heart. For that one single moment, everything was in balance, a perfect emotional fulcrum.

Her next words were very quiet. "Don't think I couldn't take you down, Godolkin."

He nodded. "Maybe you could. The question is, do you want to?"

That was it. The choice was made, the balance broken. In an instant the anger was gone, swamped and replaced by that still, empty silence.

"No," she whispered. "No, I don't want that. What I want is for you to leave."

She could see, out of the corner of her eye, Harrow gawping at her. Godolkin frowned slightly.

Red had to speak, before he did. She couldn't let him change her mind, not now. "Matteus Godolkin, I'm giving you an order, and you know you've got to obey me without question. Leave Gomorrah and don't come back. Don't try to find me. Don't try to protect me any more."

She took a step back and closed her eyes. The scent-laden air of Gomorrah must have been irritating them, for they were suddenly itchy and wet. "Go on, Godolkin. I don't ever want to see you again."

When she opened her eyes, he was already away, striding off into the crowds. In a few seconds he was gone from sight.

Red let out a long, shivering breath. She felt as though something massive that had been leaning over her for weeks, teetering on the brink of crushing her flat, was finally being reeled back. Just one more thing to do, and she would be free.

To do what? She wasn't sure yet, but it would be fun finding out.

One more thing to do.

Judas Harrow was just getting his wits back. "Holy one, you can't mean that!" he cried, pointing to the place where Godolkin had disappeared. "We need him!"

She shook her head. "No, he has to go. And so do you."

The words hit him like a bullet. She saw him jerk back, as if they had a physical effect. "What?!"

"You have to go too." She spread her hands. "I'm sorry, Jude."

"I don't understand—"

"I know." She drew close, and put a hand lightly on his shoulder. "But he was wrong. I've learned enough now. I have to go my own way. Just like you."

With that she was off, her back to him, walking away into the night. After a few steps, something made her pause. She looked back over her shoulder, saw him standing there, and gave him a sad, tender smile.

"Hey, Jude? It was fun, okay? Maybe I'll call you sometime."

And that was that.

There were four staterooms on the *Crimson Hunter*, two on either side of the spinal corridor. Red staggered into the nearest, collapsed onto the circular gel-bed and slept for two days.

When she awoke she was hungry. Harrow must have known she would be. He was there for her, within easy reach. She took just a little of his blood this time from the wrist; his neck still wasn't completely healed.

She lay for a long time, once he had gone, with the room's lights set very low and the gel-bed soft and warmly pulsing against her back. She had tried so hard to remember what had happened next on Gomorrah, but there was simply no memory left. There were a few, random images – heat, riding some kind of vehicle, the sweet-salt taste of blood under her tongue – but nothing coherent. Nothing strong enough to build up a picture of what had happened to her.

Harrow might have known more, but she didn't feel strong enough to ask him yet.

The sleep had done her good, that much was certain. The horrid shivering had abated, leaving her mildly feverish, and her back didn't hurt quite as much. The point between her shoulder blades was still tender, though. Red wondered if Harrow's trauma spider was as gentle as it could have been while wrenching the socket out of her spine.

Her stomach flipped at the thought. She closed her eyes and thought about soft sand and warm beaches until the feeling went away.

That, she told herself after a while, is a talent you've been using far too much of late. When the pain comes along, think about something else...

And suddenly it struck her, a rolling wave of loss, loneliness and despair, tearing out from that cold, still place in her heart where the warmth used to be. It swept though her, making her cry out, struggling to get upright. "Lights," she gasped. "Lights! Get the snecking lights on!"

The room brightened, just as Harrow burst in. "What? What's wrong?"

"Nothing..." Red slumped forwards, sitting on the edge of the bed, scraping her hands back through her hair. "No, sneck, not nothing. I'm sorry, Judas. I don't know."

He sighed and knelt down next to her. "You're still so weak. I know you're used to healing quickly, holy one, but this is different. You need time."

"No," she snapped, shaking her head. "Time is the last thing I need." She giggled, suddenly, the sound was strange and eerie. "Like booze, y'know? 'I'm sorry, madam, I think you've had enough!' Oh, sneck, what have I done?" Her hands were still shaking. They fluttered around her face like moths. She couldn't keep them still.

Harrow stood up and took her hands in his own, stopping their motion. "I'll get you to the medicom."

"The bridge" she muttered, letting him heave her upright. "Just get me to the bridge. I need to be in the light."

Jumpspace, Durham Red had decided, looked like Hades torn open.

There were viewports on the bridge, curved, triple-walled slabs of synthetic diamond fused into the hull plating, thicker than Red was tall. The diamond had been tweaked somehow, the molecules altered to make the slabs' refractive index pretty much that of air. Red rested her elbows on a frame and stared out through a window that looked no more substantial than a candy wrapper.

She gazed out at an infinite tunnel made of fire and lightning, and barely saw it at all.

She had thought she'd known what it was to be tired, to be burnt out. That, after all, was the reason she'd put herself into cryosleep.

God. She'd had no snecking clue.

The command cabin door slid open behind her, and in the faint reflection from the viewport she saw Judas Harrow climbing in through the low, narrow door. He was holding a cup of something. "I went to the medicom," he explained, joining her at the port. "It said your electrolytes were so out of balance they were technically off the scale, and prescribed this."

He held out a plastic goblet, brimming with sickly-looking fluid. Red took it from him and sniffed it. "Yeuch. Cheers, Jude. What did I ever do to you?"

He grinned. "It will help, holy one. Trust me."

The stuff didn't taste as bad as it looked. Red finished half of it, then rested her forehead against the port. Harrow was still looking at her, his young, blandly handsome face creased in concern.

"What happened?" he asked finally.

Red shrugged. "It all just came up and hit me, I guess." She saw his eyebrows go up. "All that time... I've lost everything, Jude. Everything I'd ever known. People, places, all the stuff I was going to do once I'd earned enough bounty. I threw it all away."

She turned herself around, leaning her shoulders back against the viewport. She didn't want to look at jumpspace anymore. "You can't think about things like that, you know? It's just too big, too scary. I've spent the last six weeks doing everything I could *not* to think about it."

"Six?"

"Oh, right." She made a vague gesture. "Eight months dosed up to the eyeballs don't count. But now it's all beginning to catch up with me. It's been trying to for ages, you know. At the back of my mind, ever since Wodan. But I've always been pretty good at shutting that kind of thing away."

"I thought you recovered quickly, at the time." He folded his arms. "But I paid it no heed. You are a saint, after all."

"I'm no saint, Jude. Sneck, I'm not even strong enough to hold it all off any more." She handed the goblet back to him. "And a cup of green sludge just isn't what I need right now."

"What do you need?"

"I need to go back to Pyre."

Harrow's expression didn't change, but a nervous tic quirked at the corner of his mouth. "You know, for a moment there I could have sworn you said–"

"I've got to get back to Pyre, Jude. I don't know why I do, I just do. You'll help me?"

Harrow rubbed a hand back through his sandy hair. "Holy one, I'm not even sure Pyre can still support life. The Tenebrae had turned it into a charnel pit well before the Iconoclasts razed it, and when the forces of the Accord burn a world, it stays burned!" He backed off and dropped heavily into the command throne. "Not to mention the patrols that might still be there. I wouldn't be surprised if the patriarch had ordered a killship or two to stay around, just in case of stragglers. It pains me to say it, Red, but of all the ideas you've had this rates among the most deranged."

"I never said it would be easy, did I?" She made her way over to the navigation throne, the seat next to Harrow. "Jude, if I don't go back, if I don't get this thing sorted out, it's going to pull me apart. You understand? I can't run away from this any more."

"But–"

"It's a done deal, Jude." She looked back at the control board. The clock was still there, little gothic characters still rolling down the display. Eight months. Twelve hundred years and eight months. "Either you'll take me or I'll get there myself."

Harrow sighed. "Holy one, you can't even get to the fresher by yourself." She gave him a look and he put his hands up. "All right! I yield... But on conditions."

"You're giving *me* conditions?" For all her exhaustion, she couldn't help but smile. "You grow a pair in the last eight months?"

"When all's said and done, holy one, it is my ship."

Red put her head back and closed her eyes. "True."

"So we'll take the long way around. It will attract less attention, and give you longer to heal. Once we make orbit, we run at the first sign of trouble – from orbital weapons platforms to a chance of rain. Do we have a deal?"

The cabin was very warm and the navigation throne oddly comfortable. Red felt herself getting heavy. Was something happening to the gravity? She wanted to answer Judas Harrow, to tell him that yes, they did have a deal, but it was all too much effort. She decided to rest for a little while, and continue the conversation when she was stronger.

When she rose from her slumber, there was a blanket draped over her, and *Crimson Hunter* was speeding back towards Pyre.

4. SHALEM

There was a fire in the Angel Vault.

Antonia was already on her way there when she heard the alert chimes. The mag-car she was riding up from the Cloister Ring had relay sounders, feeding the chimes in through hidden audio panels. The car's usual background chants were suddenly drowned out by the gonging cacophony of the fire alarm.

Antonia snarled a curse. *Othniel* was in the Angel Vault.

The car eased to a stop, braking clamps hissing as they locked the vehicle down to its rail. Antonia barrelled out of it as soon as the doors started to open, clattering down the steps and into the access hall. Rows of Iconoclast warriors snapped to attention as she darted past, towards the outer lock doors, but she ignored them. This wasn't the time for drill.

Inside the airlock was the only place Antonia couldn't hear the fire alarm.

While the lock cycled through its procedures, she snapped a comm-linker free from her belt and keyed a channel. "Omri!"

"Het Admiral." Omri was Shalem's tech-prime, the temple-station's most senior engineer. Antonia had never heard him raise his voice, or speak in any manner other than one of perfect calm, not in seven years of service. He had a serenity that she envied. "Where are you?"

"Southern lock," she replied, trying to keep her voice as level as his. "Omri, the fire: is it *Othniel*?"

"Negative, Het. It's the *Novabane*."

Antonia put her thumb over the linker's pickup while she sighed in relief. As admiral of the temple-station she should have shown no preference to any one ship over another, but she couldn't help it. *Othniel* was important to her.

Novabane was tethered near the Vault's northern lock; she would need her gravity-scow to get close. "Do what you can, Omri. I'll be there in four minutes."

"Agreed, Het. Omri out."

Abruptly, the inner lock began to slide open. Antonia felt a breeze of equalising pressure, felt the thin coolness of Angel Vault air filling the lock chamber. She clipped the linker back onto her belt and stepped out onto the platform beyond.

The hazy vastness of the vault filled her view.

The Angel Vault acted as the dry dock and refit facility for the temple-station. Kept pressurised, but free from gravity, it took up the entire centre section of Shalem, a vast, buttressed sphere fully thirty kilometres across. The inner surface of it was a riot of detail, misting away into shadow and outline on either side – smoke from arc welders, fusion cutters and a hundred mighty incense furnaces tainted the vault's air, making it impossible to see right across from one lock to another, even when there were no ships inside. Antonia could smell the sweetness of it, the faint tang of ozone.

And fire-smoke, even from the opposite end of the vault. This was no minor deck blaze, she realised; *Novabane* must be in serious trouble.

She couldn't see *Novabane* from where she was standing. *Othniel* was tethered close to the southern lock, hanging in the air like a great knife-blade, blocking her view. Antonia, not for the first time, found herself looking up at it in awe; this mighty dreadnought, poised in the mist like a steel fish five kilometres high, finned, fanged and studded with the gaping, pitted maws of its hunger-guns.

For a moment, the sheer size of it stopped her where she stood. She scanned its grey, panelled hull, looking for secondary fires, seeing only the piercing sparks of welding guns, the glow of beacons and the darting flares of hundreds of gravity-scows. The open wounds along the dreadnought's starboard side had been almost entirely patched. Antonia could see helot-workers, little more than motes at this distance, scrambling about the last exposed decks.

She cursed herself and turned away. Standing around gawping wasn't going to help anyone. She began trotting down the steps that led off the platform, down to where her personal gravity-scow was tethered.

Most of the scows were simply open sleds, fitted with grav-drives and the most rudimentary of controls. Thousands of them would be drifting around the Angel Vault at any one time, ferrying helots or supplies, acting as mobile work-platforms, cranes and observation decks. In a space as vast as the vault, they were the only sensible way of getting around.

As admiral of the temple-station and master of the flagship *Othniel*, Antonia had several scows devoted to her own personal use and kept on permanent standby – one was stationed at each of the four entrance locks, and several in reserve. Antonia jumped the last few steps, landing neatly on the deck of the scow. "Pilot," she yelled, scrambling past the guard-warriors ranked against the sides. "Get us to the *Novabane*!"

The scow unlatched from the platform and accelerated smoothly away. Antonia stopped behind the pilot, steadying herself against the back of his throne with one hand. She would normally have settled into a comfortable, yet subtly armoured seat of her own for a scow-journey, but she didn't feel like sitting.

The scow angled slightly, swooping past the gaping forward section of *Othniel*. Antonia saw the cavernous mouths of spinal-mount weapons scanning past her, then they were beyond the dreadnought and out into the vault itself.

There were six ships tethered within Shalem. Antonia saw *Fearwing* close to *Othniel*'s port flank, still missing her primary drives, and the frigate *Telemachus* out in the vault's centre. Antonia strained forward, leaning over the scow's rail, trying to catch a glimpse of *Novabane*.

There, behind *Telemachus*. Antonia gasped. The support cruiser *Novabane* was ablaze from prow to stern.

Antonia was still so far from the ship, that she could cover it with the palm of her hand, but she already knew the ship was lost. The forward end of the vessel was nothing more than a billowing cloud of yellow fire, spitting great chunks of debris out into the vault as its internal munitions blew. As she watched, one of *Novabane*'s belly hangars burst, vomiting smoke and corpses, the heat of it catching several nearby scows and sending them whirling away in flames.

The blaze was moving back along *Novabane*, towards the drives.

They were closer now. Antonia could hear the fire, the muted thunder of it, the snapping hiss of molten armour. Half the ship was skeleton.

Another scow was curving in to meet them. The guard-warriors behind Antonia brought their weapons up but she waved them away. "Omri," she called. "What in hell happened?"

The other scow matched course, drawing close alongside. Omri was at the rail, his tech's robes blackened with soot. His face as well, or what was left of it. "Damper feedback," he told her calmly. "Must have been building up in the charge capacitors for weeks, some kind of power-spill. By the time we caught it the ducts were already–"

A thumping roar from *Novabane* cut him off in mid-sentence. Antonia ducked reflexively and saw pieces of burning metal whirling through the air, laying tracks of smoke across the vault. One of them whined close to the scow, passing a hundred metres under Antonia's boots before embedding itself in the wall of the vault.

Omri hadn't moved. "Het Admiral, I believe the *Novabane* to be a lost cause. Permission to withdraw fire crews and tow her outside."

Antonia paused, looking back towards the stricken cruiser. The battle around Broteus had already torn her fleet to practically nothing, eight ships out of a complement of forty. And to lose another…

But if *Novabane*'s reactor went critical in the Angel Vault, she'd have no ships and no station either. "Granted. Full authorisation to use the main lock and whatever scows are needed, tech-prime. Get that hulk off my station!"

Novabane never blew. Towed by dozens of gravity-scows into the Angel Vault's great cylindrical airlock and ejected into space, the ship burned only for thirty minutes or so before lack of oxygen killed the flames. The scorched hulk, reduced to nothing but a thousand tonnes of worthless scrap, was towed out to a safe distance by one of the temple-station's two undamaged killships.

It was still there. Antonia could see it from the viewports of her chambers, a blackened speck, tumbling slowly against the starfield. She was probably going to have to blow it up as a hazard to shipping.

As if she didn't have enough on her plate. First the Broteus fiasco, then Gaius, now this.

She turned away from the port and went back to her desk. Her chambers, in respect of her rank, were fairly spacious even by Iconoclast standards. In addition to her bedchamber, reception area, null-gravity pool, chapel and refectory, she also kept a fully-featured administration office. Previous admirals had passed such duties to lesser officials, but Antonia liked to keep the running of the station under her own, direct control.

There were times, like today, when she regretted that preference.

High Command had already sent her two requests for situation updates: one ten weeks previously, the other two days ago. She hadn't answered either of them, and the longer she left it the harder it got. What could she tell them now? That a ship had caught fire in the bowels of her own temple-station, killed almost three hundred of her people, and wrecked seventy scows before she'd finally managed to get it free? They'd have her head on a spike.

Besides, she still hadn't filed her official report on Broteus.

Antonia dropped into her seat and slumped forwards, resting her forehead against the cool, polished surface of the desk. The chambers felt warm; too warm, even though she had stripped out of her uniform armour. She'd changed into more casual attire for the night's administrative duties, a plain fabric leotard and trousers. She'd have preferred less, but Gordia, her most trusted bodyguard, was stationed just outside her door with a squad of shocktroopers. They could burst in at any moment and Antonia liked to keep some dignity, even in these troubled times.

The armour was off being cleaned. It smelled of smoke.

Eventually she sagged back in the chair and picked up the dataslate she was using for the Broteus report. She had been working on it for the past week, trying to word it so that she wouldn't be relieved of command as soon as the transmission reached Curia.

From a certain point of view, that incident could be passed off as simple bad luck. Ten months ago, when the monstrous Durham Red had managed to get her foul body dragged upright out of the grave, the Tenebrae had billowed out of their hiding places and laid waste to entire systems in her name. Had Antonia been on Shalem at the time, she would no doubt have been ordered on a punitive mission, combining forces with some of the other stations to deliver the Tenebrae fleets a crushing blow.

Bad luck indeed, then, that she was on freighter escort at the time.

The Shalem fleet was on its way back from collecting a planetary tithe. The mutant world of Broteus had given up its entire output of foodstuffs and materials for that solar year, loading it into bulk-freighters under the weapons of the Iconoclast vessels. The cost of the tithe was great – a tenth of the Brotean population would most likely starve during the coming year, but that was no concern of Antonia's. Besides, regular tithes were part of the laws of Accord dominion, and the mutant scum on Broteus bred like flies.

All had gone well until the return journey. Antonia was anxious to be back at Shalem, ready to pick up any news of Gaius as soon as it arrived. In addition, she'd left the temple-station with only two killships and a handful of support craft as protection; standard procedure on an important tithe-extraction, but one that always made her nervous.

The Shalem fleet, surrounding the freighters in defensive formation, had been preparing to leave orbit and go to superlight when they had been ambushed. One moment, the sky was clear. The next it was full of jump-flares and huge, slab-sided Tenebrae battleships.

In seconds, half of Antonia's vessels were shattered, riddled with antimat fire and flayer missiles. Most of the weapons had been launched in the last seconds *before* emerging from jumpspace: the Broteans had known that the Tenebrae fleet was nearby, and given them Antonia's exact position.

The battle was horribly one-sided. Antonia herself almost died with her flagship. The Tenebrae battlecuiser *Eviscerator* got close enough to *Othniel* to punch an antimat broadside clear through the killship's shields, ripping a track of blazing holes along her side. Half of *Othniel*'s energy dampers, essential to the ship's protection, vanished in the blast. The rest failed seconds later as the overload reduced them to slag. Without the dampers there was no way for *Othniel* to absorb shield hits, weapons recoil and reactor heat. Even the stresses of manoeuvre could rip the ship in two.

Accepted doctrine in such a situation was to accelerate *Othniel* to ramming speed and take as many of the Tenebrae with her as possible – the classic "blaze of glory" scenario. Antonia, however, held her own skin in rather higher regard than that, and instead initiated a phased shutdown of *Othniel*'s systems. In a few, frantic seconds she managed to simulate a cascade power-failure throughout the ship, with such skill that *Eviscerator*, hungry for victims, had drawn close and opened her boarding hatches.

At the last moment, Antonia had opened up *Othniel*'s fusion drives to maximum thrust, sending five sun-hot tongues of raw plasma right down *Eviscerator*'s throat.

The effect had been as instant and brutal as turning a blowtorch on a human brain. Its bridge and command functions vaporised, drives flaring, the lobotomised battlecruiser went whirling out of control. Two frigates took it without trying.

That had given Antonia just enough of a gap to take *Othniel*, and the remnants of her fleet, into superlight and away. She'd had to leave at least three ships behind, their phased-transfer engines crippled. She could only hope they'd been able to blow their own reactors before the Tenebrae boarded them.

Othniel's crew had cheered on her return to Shalem, but Antonia couldn't see the result as anything less than absolute disaster. In one battle she had effectively lost the temple-station's protective fleet, leaving it with only two active killships and its own integral weapons to rely on. Had the Tenebrae followed them through jumpspace, they could have taken the base with ease. Luckily, they had stayed to plunder the freighters, and soon after that the uprising had faltered.

The Blasphemy had vanished, never to be seen again.

Antonia took one more look at the slate, and then tossed it with considerable force against the nearest wall. It bounced off and clattered to the floor, as if it was unbreakable. She was glaring at it, resolving to stomp on it later, when the door slammed open and Gordia skated to a halt on the marble floor. "Het Admiral!"

Gordia was in full battle-gear, her outline almost totally submerged beneath multiple layers of powered armour, and her bolter was raised and primed. Antonia raised an eyebrow.

"I dropped a dataslate, Gordia. Tell me, in what way does that sound like an assassination?"

Only Gordia's eyes were visible above her gas-mask. They blinked ingenuously. "I am not sure, Het Admiral. Exactly what does an assassination sound like?"

Antonia eyed the report. "Stick around, Gordia. You may find out." She stood up, and stretched. "I'm going to bed. Rouse me at 05.00."

Gordia nodded, the armour's bulk turning the gesture into a bob of her entire upper body. "By your command, Het."

"Oh, and Gordia? Next time you hear me being slaughtered, please make sure I've not just dropped a pen."

Hours passed. She lay awake in the darkness, watching digits roll down the face of her clock-display.

Antonia slept little at the best of times, and these days she could go for a week without sleeping at all. It was quite possible for Iconoclasts to do that on a regular basis – they were built for it – but it wasn't a habit Antonia liked or encouraged. For her own part, she craved a good night's sleep.

But Gaius was still missing. While there was no word of him, she could not rest.

If asked how long it had been since the Broteus incident Antonia would have had to check a diary to get an exact figure. However, she knew that Special Agent Gaius had been officially missing for twenty-nine days, seven hours and sixteen minutes. The first transmission he had ever failed to make was that long ago.

Antonia also knew that it was thirty-two days, three hours and eleven minutes since Gaius had last shared her bed.

It was an insane thing, for them to fall in love. They had once sat together in this very bed and worked out exactly how many Iconoclast protocols such a relationship contravened. Their desires had overtaken them before they had finished counting, but it was a lot. If anyone had ever found out, they would both have been at best reduced in rank, and at worst executed. Lucky for them both that Gordia could be trusted not to hear *everything* that went on in the admiral's chambers, if she was so ordered.

Maybe, Antonia had once thought, execution would not have been the worst punishment: to be separated from Gaius would have been fouler. Immediately she had dismissed the thought as soppy, girlish nonsense, emotionally weak. Now, she realised, she had been right.

His absence was torture.

Antonia sat up in the bed and hunched, hugging her knees. She had done everything in her power to find Gaius, save abandoning her commission and hunting him down herself. She had managed to persuade Curia to send her another agent, and Major Nira Ketta was at present on the same backwater world that Gaius had last transmitted from. So far, though, Ketta had found no trace of her fellow agent, even though Antonia had authorised the activation of his tracer-implant.

Not knowing – that was the worst thing. Imagination was not a quality actively sought after in Iconoclast officers, but right now Antonia had more than she could handle. A thousand fates for Gaius roared through her mind every second of the day.

A thought struck her out of nowhere and Antonia's breath caught. Could *Novabane* have been saved if she had not been thinking about Gaius?

She tried to shake the thought away. It was too horrible. If her own failings had cost the ship and so many lives, that was bad enough, but for her feelings for Gaius to have done the same…

Antonia put her head in her hands. What was happening to her? She didn't feel like an admiral any more. She didn't even feel like an Iconoclast.

Was she really so lost?

A soft, almost inaudible chiming broke through her

thoughts. The comm-linker was picking up a signal.

Antonia leapt from the bed and darted through to the office. The linker was built into the desk, set under the polished surface. A tiny square of light blinked there, faint green in the darkness. Antonia put her fingertip to it, and the linker's screen and controls lit up across the desktop.

There was no picture. Major Ketta was too far from Accord space to be able to transmit over the usual cipher channels, and was instead reduced to punching a massively compressed datastream through jumpspace. Scratchy audio was the best she could hope for.

The desk hissed static. Antonia lowered the volume and leaned in close. "Ketta?"

There was nothing for several seconds, just the white noise of jumpspace interference. It rose and fell rhythmically, like waves on a distant shore. As Antonia listened, the noise seemed to resolve itself, become more defined. It was almost like voices, many voices, impossibly far away. They were saying something to her. If she could just hear a little better…

"Het Admiral…"

Antonia closed her eyes. She could tell, just from Ketta's voice, that something was horribly wrong.

The Iconoclast special agents were a breed apart. In terms of resources they were more expensive than a platoon of shocktroopers; in terms of effectiveness they were unparalleled. Rebuilt and modified in ways that made the best Iconoclast soldiers look like crude toys, they were trained in the most lethal forms of combat available. They were specialists in subversion, covert operations, espionage and assassination. They were experts in poisons and bioweapons of every kind. They were the ultimate warriors.

And Major Nira Ketta, highest-ranking agent this side of the Balrog Cusp, sounded as though she was going to be sick.

"Ketta, in the name of God–"

"He's dead," Ketta gasped thickly. "They're all dead. Forgive me, Het Admiral. Oh God, the sight! If you could only see–"

"Major! Control yourself!" Fine words, Antonia thought angrily. Her own tears were already hitting the desktop. "Are you sure? Tell me that you're sure!"

"I'm sure."

"You followed the implant?"

"I saw the implant!" Ketta's voice was almost a scream. "I saw it! Holy God, you have to get me out of here!"

"Ketta–"

"I need extraction, immediately. Please, Het Admiral, get me off this world!"

Antonia cut the transmission. She wiped her eyes, straightened, and padded to the door of her chamber. It slid open at her approach.

Gordia was standing outside, as always. "Admiral? Is there something you need?"

She nodded. "Gordia, you may hear some... sounds, in the next little while. Be so good as to not hear them."

The bodyguard nodded. "Understood, Het."

"I'll see you at 05.00." With that, Antonia walked away from the door, letting it close behind her.

She let out a scream that would have flung the angels themselves down from heaven.

She summoned Tech-Prime Omri to meet her at the south lock of the Vault at 06.00. He was as prompt as always, his robes and armour wiped mostly clean of *Novabane*'s soot, the eye-lenses of his sensory prosthesis polished and oiled.

Antonia, for her part, was in full battledress. "I need *Othniel*," she told him simply.

Omri turned his great head towards the dreadnought; Antonia heard the faint whine of servos in his neck. "We are on schedule, Het," he told her. "The upgraded sense-engines are en-route from Fernal, decks three-twenty through three-sixty-five are almost re-armoured, and the weapons loads are being fed in as we speak. *Othniel* will be ready for a shakedown cruise within three weeks."

"I need her operational inside forty hours."

There was a long silence, broken only by the soft whirring of Omri's eye-lenses refocussing. "That," he said eventually, "will be difficult."

From experience, Antonia knew what that word meant, coming from him. "Abandon the sense-engine upgrade for now. Pull all available helots from work on the other ships, and set them to re-armouring the exposed decks. We'll seal them and run with areas unpressurised if we have to."

"Admiral–"

"Wake and feed the operational hunger-guns and charge the antimat generators. Concentrate your efforts on drives, weapons and daggership facilities. Defence is of secondary importance." She lowered her gaze. "I'm sorry, Omri. But new orders have come in. We have a punitive mission to undertake."

Omri bowed slightly. "Thy will be done, Het Admiral. Forty hours."

"Thank you, Omri." She began walking away, back into the lock chamber. A few seconds later she heard his voice again.

"Admiral? Where are you taking her?" She looked back over her shoulder and he bowed again. "For the fuel load."

Despite herself, Antonia couldn't help but give him a wry smile. Fuel load, indeed.

"Lavannos, tech-prime. We're going to Lavannos, and we're going to melt its crust all over again."

5. SORROW

Eloise

Main sequence star, Class M5, Subclass 32664-A

0.3 Standard Masses

Eleven worlds, Tentrinn-Configuration Oort cloud

Pyre – Eloise IV

Distance from star: 2.8 Standard Astronomical Units

Diameter: 19,270 km. Density: 3.8. Gravity: 0.95 SGs

Axial Tilt: 18 degrees. Length of Day: 20 hours (GST). Length of Year: 8.55 SY

(3,749.28 local days)

Atmosphere Pressure: 1.08. Composition: Oxygen-Nitrogen-Trace

Climate: Warm, avg 288 K. Primary Terrain Type: Plains, Hills

Surface Water: 67%. Humidity: 80%

Resources: Metals, Radioactives, Organics

Some local industry

Tourism, Arable Farming

Population 3.2 Billion (Purestrain Human)

Note: This entry under revision as of 809 YA

Crimson Hunter's bridge was in near darkness. The ship was on its eight hour simulated nightcycle, with many of the internal systems powered down as the vessel sped through jumpspace. Its pilot was in much the same state: Judas Harrow slumped in the command throne, his hair flopping down over his face, snoring lightly. To Durham Red, sitting in the navigation throne beside him, he looked far younger than he actually was.

Red had given up on sleep for another night. She was very close to Pyre now, and images of its destruction were too near the surface to allow her to rest. Instead she had come back up to the command deck and, taking care not to wake Harrow, had begun trawling the planetary database again.

The entry for Pyre came up quickly. There were several pages of technical data, half of it translatable, the rest in a weird kind of church-Latin. Red hadn't been to mass in a very long time, so much of the information went over her head.

The rest was unremarkable, although she felt herself smiling wryly at the "under revision" note. The population figure was wrong for a start, she thought, scanning down the page. As far as she'd been able to tell on her last visit, it was now zero.

She sat back, stretching the kinks out of her shoulders.

The ship was largely flying itself; sentry guns unfolded, sense-engines sniffing the ether for signs of trouble. The precautions were fairly pointless in a superlight jump, as every ship carried its own little piece of jumpspace along with it. The chances of two phased-transfer bubbles ever coming into contact were remote. Still, it didn't hurt to err on the side of caution.

It wasn't a concept Durham Red had ever given much thought, but it looked like something she was going to have to get used to. Back in her own time, if people didn't like your face they'd try to shoot it off. In the Year of the Accord 809, you were more likely to get your planet blown up.

She went back to the database and typed WODAN.

There was a pause, longer than the one that had preceded the Pyre entry, and then the screen blanked. Three words scrolled up.

No Longer Extant.

Wodan had been a university world, a moon-sized space station constructed almost entirely from timber. It was where she had woken up, after Judas Harrow had lasered her cryo-tube open, and it was where she'd first discovered just how badly she'd overslept.

And Godolkin's people had taken it apart trying to get at her. They'd blasted the wooden world to scorched shavings. No one had been left alive: untold thousands had burned there, humans and mutants alike.

"No longer extant" was a rather bald way of putting things, but Red couldn't argue with the truth of it. Wodan, quite simply, no longer existed.

She glanced over at the clock and saw that the ship would begin its deceleration in a few minutes. It was time to go back to her cabin and lie to Harrow that she'd been there all night.

She got up and was about to close the database when a sudden thought struck her. She reached down to the keyboard and typed in TERRA.

There was another pause. Data systems in the Accord were not fast, not compared to the old days. A lot of technology had been lost in the dark years that followed the Bloodshed.

Red waited, making a bet with herself. "Razed by Tenebrae Assault, five to four," she breathed. "Turned into a giant training camp for Iconoclast soldiers, two to one. Left to rot as a galactic garbage dump, odds-on favourite."

The screen changed. Red stared at the words left remaining, and realised she'd lost her bet.

There was no colour left on Pyre. Everything had been burned up, washed out, rendered down until nothing but black and grey remained. Even the sun, filtering weakly through a drifting smog of ash and burned fat, was the colour of an old bruise.

Crimson Hunter had set down near a coastline, unfolding a single landing spine from its belly and perching on its splayed foot. Ten metres up, wings spread for atmospheric flight, the yacht looked oddly priggish, intent on making as little contact with the ground as possible, as though in disgust at the state of it.

Durham Red, standing on the beach, could hardly blame it.

The sand beneath her boots was dark and sticky with rotted grease. Waves still lapped, but the sea was black, a thin sludge of toxic, poisoned water and carbonised human fat. Corpses rolled in it, bloated and disintegrating after eight months in the rancid stew. There was nothing left alive in the sea to eat them.

Red had been here for a long time. Harrow had found a coat for her on the *Crimson Hunter* and she had it wrapped tightly around her shoulders. Breath steamed in front of her face. Pyre, against all her expectations, was cold.

Titanic fires had once raged across the surface of this world, hurling millions of tonnes of smoke and dust into the atmosphere. The fires were long extinguished now, but the clouds remained, blocking out almost all Pyre's sunlight. That, even more than the gigatonnes of ordnance fired by the Iconoclast fleet, had spelled doom for the planet's ecosystem – there were life-forms on Pyre hardy enough to endure the bombardment, but nothing could survive prolonged lack of sunlight.

It was a well-known scenario. First the plants die off, then the animals. Before long, even the oxygen in the air begins to bind to rock, filtering down from the air until nothing but rust and nitrogen remain. A living, breathing world is reduced to a dead wasteland.

Red stared out over the oily sea towards the invisible horizon. "Nuclear winter, they used to call this," she said. "Back then, nukes were the worst thing anyone had to offer."

She could hear Harrow trudging through the sand towards her, his boots crunching through the grease-layer. "Nukes?"

"Thermonuclear weapons."

"Oh," he said quietly. "Those."

Firecrackers now, thought Red. The weapons wielded against Pyre had made nukes look like kids' toys. No wonder Harrow remained unimpressed.

She stuffed her hands into her pockets. The silence was oppressive; it beat at the ears. It was like a pressure, squeezing her down, making her head ache. The air hung flat and heavy around her, reeking with smoke. There was no wind at all.

Harrow had stopped a few metres behind her. "Holy one," he said, his voice sounding strange and empty in the still air. "Why are we here?"

"I told you," she snapped. "I don't know."

"Then tell me how you *feel*."

She looked across at him. There was an open, quizzical look on his face. She couldn't help but smile. "You know how I feel."

"I'm sure I don't. Tell me, holy one."

Red gave a sour chuckle. "I feel like I've been hit by a bulk hauler. Like the universe took a sledgehammer, said 'Okay girlie, now it's your turn,' and smashed me into the ground like a tack."

There was a long silence, after which Harrow said: "That's not entirely what I meant."

"I know." Red scuffed a line in the sand with the toe of her boot. The grease-layer cracked away queasily, leaving soggy, dull-looking mush beneath. "Jude, I do my best communicating with my fists and my teeth." She bared her fangs at him for a second. "This isn't easy for me. All I know is, this is the closest I can get to the beginning."

"The beginning? Oh, I see," Harrow nodded. "So if Wodan still existed…"

"Jude?" She stuffed her hands deep into her pockets. "What happened to Earth?"

"Earth?" he frowned. "What do you mean?"

"I looked it up in the database, but there wasn't an entry. *Crimson Hunter* didn't know what I was talking about."

Harrow spread his hands helplessly. "Earth is… gone, holy one. It hasn't existed for, oh, a thousand years or more. Long before the database was written. Why do you ask?"

Red shook her head, bewildered. "I don't understand. How does a whole planet just go?"

"I don't know. Red, it's ancient history at best. Other than that, fairy tales. People have other things to concern them now."

She gave him a sour look. "You realise I'm quite upset about this. I was born there, Judas!"

His eyebrows went up into his hairline. "You were?"

"What, that's not what they taught you about me in Sunday school?"

"Our scriptures are hazy on your origins, holy one."

"Oh, forget it." She turned her back on him, angrily. "Whole snecking universe had gone insane. Vanishing planets just about fits right in."

She began to walk slowly back up the beach. Ahead of her, shapes were poking from the blackened ground, tipped at random angles, their outlines broken and peeling, their detail washed out by the fog into a succession of flat grey layers.

Sticks and stones, Red thought dully, picking her way across the dead beach towards them. A few sad little scraps of broken masonry and melted plastic that had once been a town.

Debris crunched and snapped beneath her boots as she walked among the broken buildings. "I wonder what it was called," she whispered.

"Hmm?" Harrow was moving parallel to her, not too close. There were few standing walls to get in the way, though. "What was what called?"

"Here. The town."

"Ah. I couldn't say."

She stopped, in front of a truncated curve that had been part of a doorway. "I'm sorry, Jude. I know I'm putting you through a lot. But I had to see this, you know? Really see it." She moved on, though the doorway. "They did this in my name. I tried to run away from that, and look what happened."

"I'm still not sure what you hope to achieve."

"Neither am I. But I'll let you know when it happens."

Three billion human beings had lived on Pyre. Then the Tenebrae came, and three billion had died.

Historians were already calling it the Second Bloodshed, that brief but vicious mutant uprising. Compared to the first great human-mutant war it lasted almost no time at all, but the devastation it wrought, the damage it did to the stability of the Accord, was almost unimaginable.

Pyre had been turned into a shrine-world; a hymn to blood and fire. The human population had been systematically butchered, their bodies fed into vast, sky-blackening furnaces, their bones fused into towering citadels. Over a period of weeks three thousand million men, women and children had been reduced to fuel.

Burned, to prove a point. And all in the name of Saint Scarlet of Durham.

That was what haunted Red, now that she was too weak to hold the thoughts back. This atrocity, and dozens of others like it, had been committed by mutants who held her as their messiah. They had slaughtered entire populations because they thought she'd want them to.

That was what she had become, while she slept the centuries away. A figurehead for a mutant cause so extreme it regarded genocide as a tool of argument.

Her footsteps slowed, and eventually she stopped and stood where she was.

She felt tired, and bitterly cold. The days spent travelling back through Accord space to Pyre had given her some time to recuperate, but she was still weak. Fairly soon, she'd have to start back to the *Crimson Hunter*, or she'd not make it.

She glanced around. Her aimless wandering had taken her deep into the ruined town. She was standing in the remnants of some kind of building; a roughly circular space in what might have been a courtyard. Objects surrounded her, burned and melted beyond recognition, arranged in concentric rings.

There were other things, too, half-buried in the ash. Little domes and rods of blackened bone.

She crouched, brushing ash away from a tiny skull with her fingertips. These ones hadn't made it to the furnaces, she realised. They must have died in the first assault.

Distantly, she heard Harrow calling her name, skating to a halt at the edge of the circle. "Holy one! I thought I'd lost you." He looked about, breathlessly. "What is this?"

The skull came up in her hands. She cradled it, blowing carbon from its eye-sockets. "It was a school."

"Oh," he said simply. There wasn't really anything else to say.

How old had this child been, she wondered, when the Tenebrae firebombs had rained down? Five? Six? When Red was six she was still in the Milton Keynes ghetto, an outcast even among her own people. Dracula, they called her. Bloodsucker.

A six year-old child, called Bloodsucker in the street.

"Nothing changes, Jude. Being different is still enough to get you killed." She stood up, and let the skull roll out of her hand. It thumped back into the ash. "There's nothing here, is there? Just soot and bones." She sighed. "Sorry."

"For what?"

"Dragging you back to this nightmare." She sniffed. Something was itching her nose, tickling the back of her throat. "Damn, this smoke gets everywhere."

He nodded. "We should get back to the ship. It'll be dark soon. Well, darker than it is already."

"Aye, cap'n." She began to walk towards an opening in the wall, then paused. She sniffed again. "That's weird."

"What?"

"I smell blood."

Harrow looked shocked. "Are you sure?"

She glared at him incredulously, and pointed at her fangs. "Er, vampire?" Her mouth was beginning to water. "I'm not kidding, Jude. Something's alive here, beside us. And it's bleeding."

The source of the smell was further than she'd thought, a few minutes' walk through the rubble. But the air was still, and Red's capacity for sniffing out blood was very good indeed.

They were at the edge of the ruins, moving up what had been a wide avenue of trees and low walls, before the bombs had shredded it. The main road into town, perhaps, or a ceremonial route. Piles of bricks and twisted lattices of metal spoke of a tall, elegant gateway.

Harrow put a hand up. "Red? Can you hear something?"

She listened hard. After a time, she nodded. "Singing. Someone's singing."

There was a song in the dead air, a slow, murmuring lament. She couldn't make out the words, or even if the song had words at all, but she could hear that it was being sung by many, many people. It was soft and low and impossibly sad.

It was beautiful. It made her throat catch to hear it.

Past the song were other sounds, she could hear them now. The steady beat of drums and the shuffling of many feet. A rhythmic noise, too; an odd, repetitive slapping that she couldn't identify. "Harrow, what is this? Have you ever heard this before?"

He shook his head, and then his eyes widened. "There," he said.

A procession was making its way through the shattered gates.

There must have been a hundred of them. A mix of humans and mutants, it looked like, although it was harder to tell now than in her own time. After all, Harrow was a mutant, a member of the Tenebrae itself, and he looked more human than she did.

The newcomers were clad in strange, angular robes of white leather and silk, their faces draped in cloth, their wrists and ankles trailing long chains of black iron. Their bare feet scuffed up great clouds of ash and filth, until it surrounded them like a captive storm.

Red moved to the side of the road as the hooded figures reached her. If they noticed her, they showed no sign of it, just kept trudging along, beating little drums with the heels of their hands, singing their tragic, wonderful song.

Durham Red shivered. The sight of so many hooded men brought back edges of memory she didn't like at all, although she couldn't remember why.

More robed figures came through the gates. Some were naked from neck to waist, and were whipping their own backs with long, bladed chains. The chains were fixed to heavy wooden handles, gleaming with years of hard use. With the handles gripped tightly in their bloodied fists, the flagellants swung the chains up and over their left shoulders, completely in unison, then down, and back up over the right shoulder. Over and over again, keeping perfect rhythm, blood sprayed into the air with every blow.

Here was the source of the blood scent and the strange sound. "Sneck," Red hissed to herself. "What a waste."

"These are heirophants of the Thanatos sect, holy one," Harrow whispered. "They must be here to say prayers for the dead of Pyre."

Red gnawed her lower lip. "Good call, I guess. But what's with the guys cutting themselves up?"

"Those are transgressors of the Thanatos code, atoning for their sins." His brow creased in thought. "Or they might be newcomers to the sect. I believe they go through a period of taking on the suffering of the dead."

Another lash, another multiple spray of blood. Red winced. "That's gotta hurt."

"There must be some who don't make it. I seem to remember..." He broke off, looking hard at the flagellants. "Sacred rubies," he gasped. "One of them's an Iconoclast!"

"You're kidding!" Red followed Harrow's startled gaze.

He was right. One of the flagellants was covered in charm tattoos. Red hadn't seen them under the blood, but there they were, a criss-cross pattern of lines burned and inked into corpse-white skin; supernatural protection against the bite of a vampire.

The man's face was hooded.

"Jude, it couldn't be him, could it?" Suddenly, Red felt her heart slamming in her chest. After all this time, all this distance.

She ran forward and ripped of the man's hood. "Godolkin, you old..."

A stranger looked back at her and gradually lowered his great head.

"Oops." Red stepped away, letting the hood drop from her hand. "Sorry, honey. Thought you were someone else."

The entire procession had stopped. So had the singing. And the drums and the bladed chains.

Red noticed that, barring the Iconoclast, everyone in the procession was looking right at her.

A man was walking towards her, leaning heavily on a black cane. His robes were the same smoke-stained white as his companions, but he wore no chains and carried no drum. He stopped in front of her, reached up and stripped the hood from his head.

Red inhaled sharply.

Something had been done to the man's face. Hundreds of carefully wrought scars around his eyes and mouth had turned his face into a paradigm of sorrow.

Red found herself taking a step backwards. "Forgive me," she muttered. "Didn't mean to stop the party."

"You are Durham Red," the man said quietly.

Red glanced quickly back to Harrow, but the mutant was looking just as baffled as her. "Um..."

"So the rumours were true," the man breathed. "I didn't believe them myself, but here you are, returned to survey your work."

Emptiness, cold and still, reached up to clutch Durham Red's heart. "Mine?"

"Whose else?" He spread his hands, encompassing everything around them. The cane remained stuck in the ash, and Red could see that the top of it was a chrome skull the size of a golf ball. "Pyre died in the name of the Scarlet Saint. The dead we sing for burned with your name on their lips."

Red looked around her, imploringly. "No, that's not fair. I didn't do this..."

"Then why are you here, Durham Red?"

The question, from the scarred lips of this terrible man, hit her like a brick. Harrow had asked her, more than once after she'd made him land here. She'd asked herself dozens of times. And every time, the same answer.

"I don't know."

The heirophant prodded the ash with the end of his cane, and flipped a blackened skull out into the light. "*They* know," he said. "But they no longer have breath with which to curse you. That privilege belongs with us now."

He fixed her with a steely glare. "Go back to where you came from, Durham Red. Go home. Your mark has been on this world long enough."

There were four systems thrones on the bridge of the *Crimson Hunter*: command and navigation faced towards the prow, engineering and tactical to the stern. Red, still bundled in her coat, was strapped into the tactical station when the yacht powered out of orbit. For a few moments she felt acceleration dragging her back towards Pyre, as if the planet was reluctant to let her go. Then the dampers kicked in and *Crimson Hunter* darted away, leaving the burned world far behind.

Red hadn't said anything for a long time, and Harrow, ever mindful of her needs, hadn't asked her to. Only when Pyre was gone from the scanners did she feel able to speak.

"Was he right?"

"The heirophant?" Harrow shook his head. "Holy one, if I've learned anything these past few months, it's that you and the Saint Scarlet of legend are two very different people indeed. Pyre was caught in a conflict that has lasted for centuries and no one sane could hold you responsible for that."

She gave him a soft smile. "You think?"

"If it hadn't been you, it would have been someone else."

"I'll keep telling myself that." She swung the throne back around to the tactical board and hit the safety release. The straps unlocked and slid away into recesses. "Sneck, I need a vacation."

Harrow appeared to consider this. "It might be no bad thing. If you don't mind me saying, you are still only just starting to recover from the Glow. A few weeks of rest would do you a power of good."

"Yep. Plus, if those happy-clappers were hearing rumours about me, it's only a matter of time before somebody else does. How much of a price do I have on my head now?"

"At last count, just enough to buy a small continent."

"You know something?" Red stretched, taking care not to put too much stress on her injured back. "Right now I wish I could do just what he said. Go home."

"Was it ever a place you wanted to return to?"

"I didn't think so. But you only realise how much you miss things when you know you can't have them any more." She yawned mightily. Waves of fatigue were coming up from her feet, making her feel slightly giddy. She'd overdone things today, she decided. Too much walking, too much grief. Too much soot in the lungs.

"It's nothing, Jude. Pick a planet you like, I'll be fine. Right now I just need a shower."

She lay on the gel bed, staring up at the curved ceiling and studied its intricate carvings. She had seen this view a lot over the past few days, and was getting to know every square centimetre of those carvings.

It was hard to know what to feel. Earth was no happy centre to her memories, that was certain. All she'd known there was misery and loss, hunger and fear. She'd become a Search and Destroy agent, a licensed bounty hunter, in order to escape the place.

She couldn't blame Harrow for being vague. His reaction would have been the same as hers, had someone wandered up and asked her for directions to Babylon, and how about those gardens, eh? As had been said, it was ancient history. A footnote, at most.

She rolled over, burying her face in the pillows. Harrow had told her about the stories surrounding the disappearance of Earth: that it had been hidden by human forces at the beginning of the Bloodshed, to keep it safe from mutant attack, or that it had been utterly destroyed in a horrific weapons test. Dismantled by killer machines. Stolen by aliens.

Fairy tales. No one knew what had happened to the Earth, and no one much cared.

Except Durham Red.

She'd thrown away her life, her career, everything she'd ever worked for when she got into the cryo-tube. She'd lost twelve hundred years to sleep. Then she'd gone a little mad, ran away to Gomorrah and lost another eight months to the Osculum Cruentus.

Now they were telling her she'd lost her home world, too. What was next?

There was a faint chiming from a panel next to the bed. Red groaned into the pillows and rolled onto her back again. "Jude, can't you let me have my nervous breakdown in peace?"

I'm sorry, holy one, but you need to come back up to the bridge."

Red sat up, carefully. "This isn't an excuse to see me naked, is it?"

"What? No!" Harrow was trying to sound indignant, but there was a hint of nervous stutter in his voice as well. Red grinned.

"What then?"

"It's a cipher-transmission. The ship picked it up while we were on Pyre."

"Crap!" Red swung her legs off the bed, waiting for a moment until her head had stopped trying to fly off her shoulders, and then reached for her clothes. "Does the whole damn galaxy know where we are? Change course!" She started to scramble into her things.

"Holy one, it was directed to my crypt-key, not the ship."

"Who knows that?"

"Matteus Godolkin."

For a moment Red wondered if she'd heard right. "It's really him? You're sure?"

"He's on Lavannos – it's a retreat world, a monastic community, outside Accord territory. And Red, he's found something there that you have absolutely got to see."

6. ARCH

Lavannos had a landing field. It wasn't much to look at, just an irregular patch of ground levelled off and faced with ferroplastic, with a few storehouses and fuelling points around one edge. It was, however, one of the only places a ship could set down without the risk of sliding into a crater.

Durham Red watched the surface of the planet scan beneath *Crimson Hunter* as Harrow brought the ship in. She marvelled. "This place looks like the worst Guinness I ever drank."

"Guinness?" Harrow hit the landing key and took his hands from the controls. "Who was that?"

"Never mind."

Crimson Hunter lurched very slightly as its sense-engines picked up a touchdown signal, and took the dampers offline. Red felt the ship wallow under her. Suddenly, she was feather-light. "Whoah! What's that?"

"We've switched from artificial gravity to the real thing. Lavannos is small – the gravitation here is only about point-two standard gees."

Red was lifting her arm and letting it drop. "Sneck, talk about an instant weight-loss programme."

The ship shuddered around her, and there was a whining from under the deck as the landing spine engaged. A few moments later they were down, the drives easing to silence. Red unstrapped and stood up carefully, while Harrow shut down the controls and locked them off.

She felt slightly dizzy and airy, as though if she moved too fast she would simply blow away. "Not sure I like this, Jude. It'll be back to normal when we get inside, right?"

"I believe there is normal gravity within the church, yes."
Harrow went quiet for a moment, standing by the command
throne as Red headed for the door. Eventually he said: "Ah,
holy one? Excuse me for asking, but–"

"Hmm?"

"You are going to change, right? Into something more
suitable?"

Red looked down at herself. She wasn't wearing anything
unusual; a skin-hugging bodysuit of soft black leather, high-
heeled boots, elbow-length gloves. A bodice over the top,
plus a few sundries in silk and black lace. "This is suitable."

"For a monastery?"

"You said dress warm."

He sighed. "Maybe they'll give us robes. Something con-
cealing."

As it angled down, the landing spine had unfolded like an
exercise in metal origami, turning itself into a sloping corridor from the ship to ground level, set with stairs. Harrow
went down them first, with Red close behind. "You remember your name?"

"Alissa Carmine. And you're Mikah Tallon."

"But you won't be saying them because?"

Red huffed. "Because I've taken a vow of silence. Jude,
I'm not sure I like that part."

He had stopped at the exit hatch. "I'm sorry, holy one,
but the longer you can keep your mouth closed, the better
our chances of staying hidden here."

She glared at him. "What did you say? Oh, the teeth!" She
flashed her fangs at him. "Sorry, Jude."

"Hush, Sister Carmine." He put a crypt-disc against the
hatchway lock, and the armoured inner door slid up and
out of sight.

There were breath-masks and thermocowls in the airlock.
With the heavy cowl draped over her shoulders Red began
to feel a slightly more normal weight, but the mask had an
odd scent to it. She didn't like her sense of smell impaired –
it was one of her best hunting tools.

Not that she'd have any need of that here. Both she and Harrow had agreed that, while a place of quiet study and meditation was not exactly Red's usual style, she could do with some downtime. Lavannos seemed the perfect place to rest and hide out.

All the better for Godolkin being here. It would be fun to have the big guy back as part of the team. She wouldn't order him, though. She had decided that long ago. She'd have him by her side willingly, or not at all.

Red vowed to tell him that, when he had showed her what he had found.

The outer hatch thumped heavily as its latches powered free, and then it split and swung open in two halves. Lavannos air, thin and viciously cold, rushed in.

She felt it sting her face, past the heat-flow from the thermocowl, ducked her head against it. Pyre had been cold, but this was almost pure pain. It felt like being scoured.

Harrow was already out of the lock. Red followed him onto the ferroplastic, hearing faint metallic noises behind her as the hatchway closed up. The air on Lavannos was so attenuated it made everything sound reedy and far away.

Her boots crunched on frost.

The sky was three-quarters orange, one-quarter icy blue-black. Mandus hung over her head like a ceiling, stunningly huge, its surface churning visibly as she watched. Most of the light came from the gas-giant, a lambent ochre glow, but a bright star to Red's left threw long shadows across the field. It was a weird combination; everything around her was lit in flat, dead shades of yellow, but given hard edges by the star. It all looked wrong. With the gravity so light, and air so thin and cold, it all felt wrong, too.

The horizon was startlingly close.

Harrow tensed next to her. Red saw figures were moving across the landing field towards them, clad in thermocowls even heavier than their own. "Here we go," she muttered, from the corner of her mouth.

There were five of them. At their head was a thin, angular woman, silver-white hair tugged back from her face. The four men behind her kept their faces down, and carried guttering censers on chains.

"Het Tallon, Het Carmine." The names, and a lot of other false information, had been sent on ahead by comm-linker. Their application to attend the retreat had been processed while they were in orbit. "Welcome to the sacred moon of Lavannos. Be at peace."

Harrow dipped his head. "Prior Rinaud?"

"I am. Het Tallon, we have studied your applications and pronounced them valid. The church accepts you, for as long as you require."

Red tried not to grin. Her mask was transparent. "Our thanks," said Harrow.

"The church follows the rule of Saint Lavann. Will you accept this?" The woman's voice had changed cadence, slightly. Her words sounded ritualistic.

"We will," Harrow responded. They had read the rule while still in orbit – well, Harrow had. He'd given Red the highlights.

The woman nodded. "There is no enmity between human and mutant here. We stand together as God intended. Will you accept this?"

"We will."

"You come to the church with open hands. No weapons are permitted here. Will you accept this?"

Much to her chagrin, Harrow had made Red leave her arsenal aboard the *Crimson Hunter*. Everything she had collected – auto-chetter, laser and plasma pistols, a really sexy particle-magnum – were stowed away under crypt-lock. "We will."

"While you are here, you are bound by these laws. Thank you, Hets. Now let's get inside before I freeze my skinny white ass off, lord pardon my foul tongue."

There was only one way to the monastery from the landing field. The Serpent Path.

It was aptly named, winding sinuously between the rims of several huge bubble-craters. The path was nearly thirty kilometres long, too great a distance to walk in such bitter temperatures. Luckily, Rinaud and her entourage had no intention of making the trip on foot.

They had driven to the field in an ancient ground-rover; a high-sided, glassed-in construction slung between six huge spiked wheels. Any kind of suspension must have been something of an afterthought – it crunched and jolted its way back up the Serpent Path, swinging wildly left and right, sending splinters of black Lavannos stone skittering away in tall arcs as it went. Comfortable it wasn't, but it did afford an almost uninterrupted view of the strange little world's surface.

Red, hanging tightly onto her seat, preferred not to look. There was something about Lavannos that made her feel queasy – probably just the light gravity, but the appearance of it bothered her. It looked like the after-effect of some monstrous biological process, with its pockmarks and blisters and great, open wounds. At times, it reminded her more of flesh than rock.

She wanted to ask how long it would be before they reached the church, but of course she couldn't.

"That one to the left we call the Great Scour," Rinaud was saying, pointing to a vast, shallow depression filled with gleaming white frost. "It's shallow, much more so than the others, so the wind just whistles across it. The Scour is where the church gets most of its weather from."

"What's that on the other side?" Harrow asked. The terrain seemed to fascinate him. He was moving around the rover's empty seats, trying to get better views of the features as they passed. Red, hunched up in the back, gave him the sour eye and wondered if she shouldn't have brought the kid a packed lunch.

"The Hourglass," Rinaud replied. "Two linked craters, very smooth but very deep. One of the brothers fell into it a few years ago, poor beggar. He hit the bottom alive, that was the hard part. Just slid down the slope."

"Did he get out?"

"From two kilometres down?" Rinaud shook her head. "The supply tender only arrives every three months, and we have very few vehicles here. Nothing that could go into the Hourglass and come back up again." She shrugged. "We rolled food down the slope for a time, but after a couple of weeks he stopped shouting. Thermocowls can only keep going for so long without a charge. Oh, here we are…"

The vehicle had rounded the flanks of an unbroken blister. Beyond, shining a piercing white against the blackness of Lavannos, was the Church of the Arch.

Compared to most of the constructions Red had seen in this time, it seemed pitifully small, a roughly U-shaped congress of boxlike structures clad in brilliant white stone. The roofs were steeply angled, presumably to defend against the build-up of frost, and Red could see a broad dome towards the back of the building. Just behind that was a tall, slope-sided tower.

The rover ground its way up alongside the church and shivered to a halt.

Rinaud got up. "Welcome to the retreat, Hets. I have things to attend to, but if you'll follow Samnas here, he'll show you to your rooms and then take you to the abbot. He'll answer any questions you might have."

Red only hoped that was true.

The rooms were small and very bare. Each had a narrow single bed; Red sat on hers for a few seconds and immediately began missing the gel-beds on *Crimson Hunter*.

At least the gravity inside the monastery was something close to normal. Enclosed within the plain white walls of the place, Red started to feel much better. She could probably stand being here for a few days, she decided, as long as she didn't have to look outside. Given that the monastery lacked windows, that didn't seem like an option anyway.

The abbot's room, somewhat surprisingly, was barely more furnished than her own. For some reason she had imagined the leader of the monastery to live in more luxury than his charges, but this wasn't the case. He had more space, and a few rugs on the floor and that was pretty much it. And the tea, of course.

Durham Red hadn't drunk tea for a very long time, and hadn't expected to ever again. Her favourite hot drink was something quite different, of course, but that didn't mean she couldn't enjoy other foods.

"I'm afraid I'm out of Earl Grey," the abbot was telling them. "I only have the one plant, although I have some of the brothers working on cuttings. These leaves are largely synthesised, protein manufacture, but they produce a passable brew."

"This is a strange drink," said Harrow, cradling his cup as though he wasn't entirely sure how to hold it. "But warming."

Red, as one of the silent order, had been given a little dataslate. She scribbled on it with one finger and held it up to show the abbot: Great tea.

"Thank you, Het." He cocked his head to the side, quizzically. "I am told you took a vow of silence before you arrived."

She dropped her gaze and tried to look demure. Harrow, perched in the chair beside hers, leaned closer to the abbot. "My companion took the vow at another retreat. She chooses to keep it, as long as nothing else is required."

"No, no. That is quite acceptable. Many of our attendants have similar restrictions."

"She has suffered much, in the past year," Harrow said quietly.

"I see." The abbot's forehead creased slightly. "Erm, her attire–"

"Covers scars. She was with the Thanatos sect for some time."

"Ah!" The man put his hands together, and if in a moment's prayer. "Poor child. Het Carmine, I hope you find your time at the Church of the Arch more restful."

She gave a nod of thanks, then raised an eyebrow at Harrow. He blinked at her for a second before realising what she wanted.

"Oh yes! Het Abbot, there is one more thing. We were recommended to the church by a friend of ours, a fellow pilgrim by the name of Godolkin?"

The abbot smiled broadly. "Matteus Godolkin, of course. Large fellow, particularly fond of the Earl Grey."

"Would we be permitted to speak with him? We'd like to let him know we arrived here safely."

"I'm afraid Matteus has moved on, Het." The abbot spread his hands. "The supply tender arrived not many days ago, and he chose to leave Lavannos at that time. I fear the peace he sought here eluded him."

"Shit," Red hissed. "Snecking, snecking, snecking shit. We missed him."

They were on their way back to the accommodation block, both draped in grey attendants' cloaks. The abbot, sensing their distress at his revelation, had suggested they spend some time in quiet meditation, perhaps wander the halls of the church for a while. The open areas of the monastery, he said, were open to them, and it was still two hours until Compline.

It was late afternoon and there were few people about; they passed a small number of attendants, and one or two monks. Red had just about managed to contain her outburst until she was sure they were alone.

Harrow winced, and took her to one side. They were just outside the long cloister, to the east of the building. "Sister," he whispered, looking left and right. "Remember your vow!"

"Screw the vow, Jude! Why would he tell us to come here and then scoot? Anyone would think he didn't want to see us, or something!"

"Well, as I recall he still regards you as a blasphemous, satanic demon, the anathema of everything he holds dear, and the creature that stole his very soul. So it's a possibility…"

"Oh, cheers."

"However, I'm not so sure. The abbot is lying to us."

"What, that old tea head?"

"Holy one, I grew up in the cult-temples of the Tenebrae. I have studied under numerous abbots, priors and pilgrims – one gets a feel for their ways." He grimaced. "It is hard to explain, but there is something in his manner that sets me on edge."

Red pondered. "Okay, Jude. You might well be right. I think we should take tea boy up on his offer and have a look round," she winked. "And I mean a good look, you follow?"

He grinned. "Anywhere, holy one."

They split up. It would be faster searching that way, as they only had a couple of hours before the chapel would fill up for Compline. They would be expected to attend, especially on their first day.

Besides, Red wanted some time alone.

She headed back the way they had come, through the refectory, while Harrow went onwards into the cloister. Coming through it the first time she had been so furious at missing Godolkin she had hardly noticed it.

It was the third largest building in the church, beaten only by the great library and the chapel itself. Rows of rough wooden benches and tables were arranged along the walls, leaving the centre open. At the northern end, a raised table was reserved for the abbot and senior members of the church hierarchy.

Red slowed as she walked past the benches; they were very old, worn smooth from use. They could easily have been there for as long as the monastery itself, almost five hundred years. Things in this day, she had learned, were often built to last.

There was no one else in the refectory.

She paused near one table. Deep cuts marred its surface at one end, long scours and gouges out of the wood, smoothed down by time. She found herself staring at them, as though they might reveal some hidden meaning if she looked long enough.

Her breathing made an odd sound in the high, vaulted hall, echoing softly around her. As though she were surrounded by faint whispers, distant chants. She shivered under the cloak, and put her gloved hand down to the scratched wooden table.

If she spread her fingers, just so, her fingernails might fit into some of the grooves.

If someone slightly larger than her scraped a clawed hand across the wood, their nails, just before they tore free, might leave marks that looked a little like–

Behind her, the door groaned softly on its hinges.

She gasped and span around. The entrance to the refectory was empty. The doors were still.

Red had noticed that the doors were very large, and could be locked securely from the inside. Why would anyone need to do that?

Maybe they dated from an earlier time, when the church might have to defend itself from attack. Not that a good set of locks would do much against antimat guns, but her grasp of Accord history was slim, at best.

Red moved on, up past the abbot's raised table. She glanced at it, wondering if similar scratches might show up there, too, but the surface was smooth and well polished. The abbot was more careful with his furniture than his charges.

There was a door from the refectory to the chapel. It was closed, but when Red pushed, it swung open. She stepped through.

The interior of the chapel was deliciously cool.

The main doorway to the structure led into the unpressurised courtyard: Red could imagine ceremonial processions, on high and holy days, lines of monks and attendants making their way under the baleful eye of Mandus and into this silent, vaulted space.

She had come out into the eastern transept. Walls of white marble surrounded her, carved with ridged columns and lofty, gothic arches. Her boot heels clicked softly on smooth red stone as she wandered towards the nave. There was an altar there, a wide block of white stone, raised on a rectangular dais. Steps led to the altar on either side, and wooden pews were ranked before it.

Above her was the dome she had seen from outside. She had to crick her neck back to see it properly. It was gilded, set with painted stars.

The sense of peace here was amazing. It had been a long, long time since Red had been anywhere so tranquil.

There was a doorway behind the altar, covered from behind with a curtain of black satin. Red glanced quickly around the chapel, making sure she was alone, and then peeked behind it.

The Arch of Saint Lavann lay before her.

It was surrounded by walls entirely panelled in beaten gold. The floor was lower than that of the rest of the chapel, and was of uneven, glossy black stone; the surface of Lavannos itself. From this, at a slightly skewed angle, protruded the Arch.

Red ducked past the curtain. The Arch rose above her head by a metre or more, a slender span of dull, silvery metal. As she walked around it she could see that it formed just over half a perfect circle, but was leaning slightly backwards, towards the northern end of the chapel. Behind it was a painted panel, three metres high, coloured discs arranged on a field of flaking gold leaf.

Mandus was there, yellow banded with dull orange, and a bright blue dot among the stars for Shantima. Near Mandus was another disc, small, and painted a glowing scarlet.

Red looked back to the Arch. There were ridges arranged around its inner surface, faint markings along its sides.

Something about it pricked her memory and she reached out to touch it.

"Please don't do that."

She started, and span around. The abbot was standing behind her, his back to the curtain.

He smiled. "No one told you that it's not to be touched, I'm sorry." He walked forwards. "It's very old, you see. We're not sure how old, but it was here before the church. If we had to wipe away the finger-marks of everyone who wanted to feel the metal, it would have worn down to nothing by now."

Red held up her gloved hand and shrugged.

"I know," the abbot said. "But it's something of a tradition." He pointed past the Arch, to the painted panel. "This was done by Lavann himself, before he even came to this system. It was what he dreamed of. He always said that he saw Lavannos in a dream, and came here to find it."

Harrow had said something about this, on the way in. Red gave the abbot a look: go on.

"Well, so the story goes, when he arrived Lavannos wasn't here. Which must have been somewhat embarrassing, since he had all his followers with him at the time." The abbot gave her an almost imperceptible wink. "A misunderstanding on Otor, apparently. Then, as the followers questioned Lavann's sanity, this moon appeared before them, glowing with heat."

He was walking slowly around the Arch. "They had to wait fifty years until it was cool enough to build upon. But his followers were so stunned by seeing the moon appear before them that they never abandoned him, not one of them." He reached out to the Arch itself, not quite touching it. His face was a study of reverence, as if he could somehow feel its age, its holiness, past the millimetre gap between skin and steel.

"This was here when he arrived. No other structure on all Lavannos, just this. He built his church around it. His followers named the moon after him, of course."

Red began to back away, towards the curtain. There was something in the abbot's voice that was starting to bug her, to send little spikes of memory up from the darker places in her mind. Had she been given a similar spiel by the Osculum Cruentus?

On the face of it the abbot seemed benign, his religion no more unusual than many she had known. Untold monasteries throughout the ages had been built around the site of some holy vision or miracle cure. The Church of the Arch should have been no different.

But she was getting some very bad vibes from somewhere.

She smiled at the abbot and tapped the back of her wrist, hoping he'd know what it meant. She'd been away from Harrow too long, been gawking about this cold place listening to fairy tales when she should have been hunting for Godolkin. It was time to be away.

The abbot looked at her blankly for a moment, then grinned. "I'm so sorry. Of course you need to be elsewhere. And I must begin preparations for Compline." He raised his right hand, the fingers slightly bent. "Peace be with you, Het Carmine."

Durham Red returned the gesture, falteringly, and then ducked back past the curtain and away.

On her way out of the chapel she resisted the urge to run.

She headed back through the refectory, past several monks already making preparation for the after-Compline meal, and returned to the cloister. She was hoping that Harrow might be waiting for her at the entrance, but the corridor was empty.

Red paused there for a moment, gnawing her lip. Harrow could be on the other side of the monastery, or he could be around the next corner. Unable to call him for fear of blowing her cover, she was reduced to waiting around for him; never something she enjoyed.

Vow of silence my arse, she thought angrily.

If anyone found her here they might very well wonder just why she was hanging about in a corridor. Red decided to go into the cloister. At least there she could wander back and forward to her heart's content, pretending to meditate. That was what cloisters were for.

She opened the door and went in.

The cloister was a long hall, two storeys high but open to the ceiling. Two lines of white pillars stretched away to the far end, and there were stone benches arranged down the centre-line of the black marble floor. Statues, their heads universally bowed in prayer, lined the walls, and great urns with long-leafed plants provided welcome patches of colour.

She couldn't see Harrow and the cloister was very quiet.

Red walked slowly in, studying the statues. Abbots and priors who had gone before, she guessed. The carving was of a high standard – hand-made, with visible chisel-marks, but skilfully executed and the faces were compelling. Their blank marble eyes seemed to watch her as she walked past. It was hard, in this lonely place, not to feel as if she was under scrutiny.

There was a sound ahead of her, a slight scuffing.

Red almost called out, but the noise might have been from someone other than Judas Harrow. She increased her pace.

Midway down the cloister, she saw him.

He was lying on his side, his cloak spread around him. His eyes were open. A thin line of foam had edged from the corner of his slack mouth to pool on the floor.

He wasn't moving.

Red gasped, and started towards him. As she did, a figure stepped out of the shadows next to Harrow's prone form.

It was an attendant, a woman. Small, very young: Red saw jet-black hair, brown eyes, a smooth face with skin the colour of dark sand. She wore simple, loose clothes under her cloak, unadorned save a heavy, silver crucifix slung around her neck.

There was an expression on her childlike face of absolute horror.

"You!" she hissed, incredulously.

Red stopped. "Me?"

"God is with me," the woman muttered. She reached up to the crucifix and tugged it free. Tiny links of metal chain fell from it to the floor, bouncing off the marble.

She did something to the silver cross with her fingers. Abruptly it blossomed from either end, splaying out to a ridged tube in one direction and, with a complicated metal sound, a long blade in the other.

A silver blade. Red had seen such a weapon before, in other hands. When Godolkin had tried to take her head off with one, it had been two metres long and as wide as her thigh. This was on a different scale entirely: half the length, two fingers wide at the base, wickedly sharp.

But there was no mistaking an Iconoclast's holy sword.

7. INTO THE DARK

Judas Harrow was alive. Red could hear his soft, ragged breathing. But his eyes were not moving.

The small woman was standing dangerously close to him. She had dropped into a strange, fluid crouch, the blade held horizontally over her head, both hands around the grip. She must have attacked him while he waited for Red in the cloister and paralysed him with toxin.

Red looked her up and down. She seemed so young, so small. Compared to the other Iconoclasts she had seen, this woman was a child. She had none of the sensory implants the shocktroopers sported, no mesh of charm-tattoos that mutated her skin into a living circuit board. Her eyes looked like normal eyes, not milk-white data-feeds. On the street Red would have passed her by without a second glance.

Maybe this is what troopers start off as, she wondered, before they end up like Godolkin.

"Aren't you a little short," she said, "for an Iconoclast?"

The woman narrowed her eyes. "I'll be taller than you, Blasphemy, when your head lies chattering on the floor."

"Cute." Red folded her arms. "Listen, kid. I don't know who you are, or what you're playing at. But I told the Tenebrae and now I'm telling you: I'm not part of your stupid little war. Never have been, never will be. So put the toy sword away and I might be persuaded not to slap you around this place for poisoning my friend."

The woman's eyes flicked down. "Your what? You and–" She shook her head. "No, I'll not be trapped by your lies,

Blasphemy. The Lord has sent you to me, and this is where your journey ends. Make your peace with God, monster!"

She charged.

Red didn't even have time to back up; the woman was stunningly fast. The blade whined through the air at neck level, coming within a hair's breadth of her throat. Red twisted sideways, slapped the sword up with the back of her hand and tried to follow with a kick to the woman's ribs, but the Iconoclast's knee was already slamming with incredible force into her sternum.

She felt herself whirling backwards. The marble floor hit her in the back and she slid, fetching up hard against a pillar.

The Iconoclast was in the air, coming down at her.

Red snapped sideways, punching across hard. Her blow caught the Iconoclast in the side of the head, but didn't even slow her. The blade snapped up again, whipping out to Red's face.

She blocked it with her forearm, knocked it away, used her other hand to chop out at the Iconoclast's neck. She felt the blow connect – the woman let out a cry and twisted away, but before Red could follow up she had lashed out with her foot, a flurry of perfect kicks that took Red in the knee, the thigh and the hip.

Red's leg went out from under her. She span on her back, darted up again, smashing the heel of her hand into the woman's chin, bringing her elbow around and up to connect with stunning force into the left side of the Iconoclast's jawbone. The woman dropped to one knee, but her sword was suddenly in her left hand, her arm up and behind her, the blade singing towards Red. She had to block it with her hands; the left, the right, the left again, before she was able to draw a breath and jump away.

She was panting, sweat beading her brow. This wasn't right. She was weaker than normal, she knew, still recovering from the Glow and all its effects, but she was still more than a match for any Iconoclast she'd seen. She'd taken Godolkin minutes after waking from the cryo-tube.

This woman, with her smooth face and her childlike form, had come damn close to taking her head off her neck.

Red wiped her mouth with the back of her hand. "Not bad."

The woman was back on her feet. She rolled her head around on her neck, as if getting kinks out of her shoulders. The sword was still in her left hand, but as Red watched she flung it lazily back to the right, twirled it around and back to upright.

She smiled. "Is that all you've got?"

"Out of practice." Red linked her fingers and cracked her knuckles, then shook her hands loose. "But it's all coming back to me."

"Oh good." The woman brought the sword back up above her head, the two-handed grip again. "Iconoclast Special Agent Nira Ketta. Just so you know the name of the one who kills you."

"Pleased to meet you, Nira. I'm Durham Red!"

And she leaped.

She flipped herself up, high over the Iconoclast's head, turning a perfect somersault and kicking out as she did so. Her boot caught Ketta in the shoulder and slammed her across the floor, into a stone seat. The sword span away.

Red was on Ketta in a second, punching down with all the strength she had. But Ketta wasn't there. She'd already ducked out of the way, and Red's fist punched a kilo of stone out of the seat instead. Ketta's fist took Red in the stomach, knocking her back, then the Iconoclast's foot came up and around, kicking high, taking Red in the side of the face and spinning her one-eighty in the air.

She came down hard, jumped up again as Ketta dived past her, going for the sword. For a second or two the women could do nothing except exchange a blistering series of punches, each blocked by the other, until Ketta mis-timed fractionally and Red got her twice in the head.

She reeled back.

Red barrelled into her, shoulder-smashing her around, then got her arms tight around Ketta's head. "Sorry," she said, and twisted hard. The woman's head went around front to back, with an ugly cracking noise. She slumped.

Red let her drop, and let out a long breath. That had been damn hard work. She hadn't had anyone fight like that in a long time – any one of the blows she had landed would have smashed the bones of a normal opponent.

Her leg really hurt.

She went over to Harrow. As she crouched by him, his eyes moved fractionally towards her. "Sneck, Jude," she whispered. "What did she do to you?"

"He's alive," said a voice behind her. "So it should be obvious I did nothing."

Red's eyes went wide. "You've got to be snecking kidding…"

Ketta was rising from the floor.

Her head was still twisted almost entirely the wrong way, but as Red watched in horror, she reached up and swivelled it smoothly back on her shoulders. The Iconoclast tilted left and right, as if testing the way her skull sat, then assumed another fighting stance, this one obviously designed for unarmed combat. She smiled. "You can submit now, if you wish."

"You can piss right off, if you wish." Red got back to her feet. "I told you, I'm not part of your games any more."

"Even if that were true, monster, an Iconoclast lies dead upon this world. And you'll pay for that."

Red gaped. "What? An Iconoclast? Where–"

Ketta blurred towards her.

Red leapt out of the way, but she wasn't quite fast enough. Ketta's hand clamped down onto her ankle and yanked her back in range of a whirling kick to the ribs. Red felt the breath go out of her, lashed out reflexively with her left hand, hitting nothing but air. She staggered back, took two more blows to the face, then kicked up, high and true, catching Ketta under the nose and flipping her onto her back.

The woman bounced up, hammering another blow into Red's skull.

Red snapped clear around, kicked back hard into Ketta's kneecap, slammed her elbow back and felt the impact as she found the Iconoclast's ribs. Ketta went back slightly and Red ducked under her next blow, lashing out in another kick that took Ketta in the temple. As the woman reeled, Red grabbed her by the side of the head, whirled her about and into a pillar.

Ketta cried out. Red yanked her head back and slammed it, with all her strength, into the marble.

The stone shattered.

Ketta's head went halfway through the pillar in a cloud of dust and stone fragments. She snarled in fury, battered Red's hand away and hit her with a straight-arm punch just below the throat.

Durham Red skated backwards across the floor and into an urn. It exploded, showering her with soil and foliage.

She coughed and spat blood. Ketta was staggering away from the pillar, shaking chunks of marble out of her hair.

"Wait," Red gasped. She got up.

Ketta shook her head slowly. "No, Durham Red. We finish this now."

"You think I killed an Iconoclast? Here?"

The woman's reaction surprised her. An awful expression crossed Ketta's face, a kind of sick horror. "Him, and the others," she whispered. "Blasphemy, you truly are a monster. To have done such a thing."

"Eh?" Red straightened up. "I've been here half a day, you dipstick! I came here looking for an Iconoclast."

"You found one." Ketta was breathing hard, and she wasn't smiling any more. Red would have taken that as a good sign, a hint that she could take this girl in the next round, if she didn't herself feel as though she'd been chewed up and spat out.

"Are you saying," she said quietly, "that you've seen a dead Iconoclast on Lavannos?"

Ketta looked at her for a long time. Then she reached into her clothing and took a small metal pod from a pocket there. "See for yourself," she replied.

She threw the pod at Red.

"Crap!" Red dived aside, heard the pod skitter past her and fetch up in the pile of soil from the smashed plant. It was bleeping. She covered her head.

Nothing happened. Eventually she looked up, from under her crossed arms.

Ketta was gone.

Red went over to the urn, warily. The pod was still there, bleeping plaintively. A small circular screen on one face was showing a blinking green dot. "Sneck. A tracker."

She pocketed the pod and walked back over to Harrow, feeling more than a little foolish. "Don't look at me like that, Jude. It might have been a grenade."

"Mwrr," he replied. His eyes were following her, now.

"Somebody got you pretty good, didn't they?" She got him up into a sitting position, and wiped the foam from his lips. "Come on, Jude. We can't stay here. They'll want us to sweep up."

It took some effort getting Harrow back to his room without being seen, but Red managed it. Just.

By the time she laid him down on the narrow bed he was starting to get some voluntary movement back and trying to speak. "Bubburr," he kept saying.

She smiled down at him. "Jude, you know I've not got a clue what you're saying. Put a sock in it until I get back, okay?"

"Ba. Burrbr."

"I've got to do this. You heard what she said. Maybe it's him and maybe it isn't, but I've got to know."

She went to the door, taking Harrow's breath-mask and thermocowl from a hook, and ignored his incomprehensible mutterings. The door could be locked from either side, with a mechanical device so primitive it had taken her some time to work out how it was used. She turned back to Harrow and held the key up.

"I'll lock you in, okay? That way you'll be safe until I get back. In the meantime, just chill out and practise those buburs."

Out in the corridor, she checked Ketta's tracker over. It was a flattened egg of black metal, not much bigger than the palm of her hand. There were a few control studs ranged along one side, but she didn't want to touch those and risk losing the signal. Instead she cradled it carefully, turning around to see how the dot moved.

It was pointing roughly northeast with a distance marker that Red took to show about five kilometres. Not far, she thought. She could get there on foot, if she had to.

There was still some time until Compline would take place, so there was a risk of being seen in the monastery if she hung around. She had to remind herself that the case against the place still wasn't proved – all she had were some odd feelings and the words of a crazy little Iconoclast who was sworn to kill her. But the more she thought about it – about the refectory with its massive doors and scratched tables, the oddly-familiar Arch, the over-friendly abbot and his tea – the more she wanted to leave the weird moon.

The best way to go, she decided, was outside.

There were heat-locks in several positions around the courtyard, the closest of which lay just to the east of the main gate. Red found it without too much trouble, only having to hide once or twice, and put the thermocowl and breath-mask on. Once the integral heaters were up to speed, she keyed the heatlock and went through.

Moments later, she was in the courtyard.

The gravity was light out here, and the thin air stunningly cold. Red had forgotten what it would be like outside, and wondered for a moment whether she should go back and find another way to track down the signal.

"Sneck, girl," she hissed to herself. "It's just a bit of weather!"

Once outside the gates she hugged the side of the monastery as long as she could; partly to avoid being seen, partly for shelter. It was only when she reached the north-eastern corner that she realised the route she would have to take.

The tracker was guiding her along the rim of the Eye of God.

Red cursed to herself. The Eye of God was as breathtaking as it was unnerving, a crater so vast it reached to the horizon and beyond. It was impossible to see it as a shape, it was just a hazy wall in the distance, and a cliff dropping away from the front of the monastery, so deep that light never reached the bottom.

She began trudging along. The wind, fast and icy cold as it was, didn't have much force behind it. There wasn't enough density in the air. It didn't slow her, but every now and then its gentle pushes made her realise how close she was to the sheer drop dozens of kilometres deep.

"It's a plot," she snarled into the mask. "That little bitch is trying to get me to trip and fall off the edge, let this place do her dirty work for her."

The rim of the Eye wasn't level or smooth, despite how it looked from the air. The edge of the crater was ragged, torn. Great shards of glassy rock still speared up from it like broken teeth, the remnants of the titan blister that had once stood here, and in other places the ground was shattered and scoured into great gullies. There were rock fragments and frost everywhere.

Hard going.

After a while, Red noticed that the width of ground she had to walk on was becoming steadily less. The double crater Rinaud had called the Hourglass almost touched the Eye at a point ahead of her, and the flat space between them was being drawn into a point. Red wondered if she would reach the source of the tracker signal before she ran out of ground.

She remembered Rinaud's story about the monk who fell into the Hourglass. Had he been making this same journey?

He was probably down there, freeze-dried, his screaming face frozen forever, looking up at her right now.

Red swore and shook the thought away. The trip was tough enough without trying to scare herself silly.

Just before she reached the point where the Hourglass touched the Eye of God, the tracker started to whine. Red took it out of her cowl and saw that the green dot was almost at the centre of the screen. The distance marker was down to a few metres.

She glanced about. Just bare, gleaming rock, frost, terrifying drops. No sign of a corpse, Iconoclast or otherwise.

"Great. Snecking great. What the hell am I looking for?"

She moved forward and risked a glance back towards the monastery. It was mostly concealed by upright shards and boulders, but what she could see of it looked very small indeed.

"Fine place to hide a body, if there is one. What kind of dipstick would come out here?" She shivered. "Except me. Christ, what am I doing?"

There was nothing here. It was some kind of trick, to get Red away from the monastery. Maybe Ketta had some other target.

Maybe she was after Godolkin, and wanted to throw Red off the scent.

It was time to go back. She turned, began to make her way back along the rim, and as she did so she noticed something to her right. One of the great gullies, the one she had most recently had to climb into and back out of again, had been modified. She hadn't spotted it on the way out – she'd been facing the wrong way. But the wider end of the gully, where it met the Eye, had laser cuts on the western face.

Red scrambled back down into the gully, at the shallow end, then began to walk towards the Eye. As she got close to the edge, she saw that there was a step there, leading down.

She peered over the edge. "Bollocks," she whispered.

The drop soared away from her. Red had never seen anything so impossibly far down and not be empty space. The crater was hemispherical, she knew, but from her scale it was just a sheer cliff, straight down forever. There wasn't a hint of curve.

But set into the wall, for about ten metres, was a set of steps. They were narrow, barely wide enough to walk down even if you weren't wearing a thermocowl that reached down to the ankles, and rimmed with frost. The prospect of setting foot on them was awful.

But someone had. There were depressions in the frost, bootprints. Small ones.

Ketta?

Red took a deep breath, and lowered herself onto the first step. She wished she had taken Harrow's advice and worn sensible shoes.

She went down, a stair at a time, hugging the wall.

By the time she got to the bottom, her heart was hammering worse than it had during the fight with Ketta. If there was nothing at the bottom, she decided, and she had to go back up, she'd have to do it backwards. No way she was going to risk turning around on the bottom step, with the thermocowl dragging her about.

There was an opening at the bottom of the stairs, a round tunnel leading into the stone of the Eye's rim.

Red ducked in. The tunnel sloped downward, shallowly, and Ketta's bootprints were here, too. The tracker, when she took it out to look at it again, was whining and blinking wildly.

It was very dark; Red took an emergency flashlight from the cowl, and shone the beam around. From what she could see, the tunnel went for about a hundred metres before ending in complete blackness.

Not for the first time, she wished she hadn't left all her blasters on the *Crimson Hunter*.

She scrambled along the tunnel. It wasn't high, and she had to stoop. The edges of the thermocowl kept catching on the walls.

Partway along, she almost slipped on something on the tunnel floor, something frozen onto the rock. She shone the flashlight at it, scraped some frost away with the toe of her boot.

It looked an awful lot like vomit.

Red suddenly felt very alone. She had seen things no one should see in a thousand lifetimes: she'd been shot, stabbed, beaten up, kidnapped, drugged, bled and worse. She had drunk the blood of hundreds, had hunted men down for money, and killed more times than she could count. But here, in this freezing, glassy tunnel, staring at a patch of frozen sick, she was afraid.

"No gun," she said quietly. "Note to self: never, ever go anywhere without a gun."

The tunnel opened out not long after that. Red stood at the edge and stared. No wonder she had seen nothing but blackness at the end of it.

There was a cavern ahead of her. It was immense.

The whole monastery could have been housed in that vast space. It was wider than it was high, smooth-sided where the beam of her flashlight fell, made of the midnight glass-stone of Lavannos. A bubble, trapped under the surface, she realised.

The tracker was emitting a solid, thrumming whine. She took it out and pressed the control studs until it went silent.

Red scrambled down onto the floor of the cavern. There was a lot of frost build-up: her boots went in it up to the ankles. Which was how she managed to trip over the corpse before she saw it.

She managed not to drop the flashlight, but her collision with the body had her legs from under her. Red lost her footing and tumbled, rolling onto her back. "Shit!"

It took a moment or two to get upright again. The thermocowl was so large – it practically ungulfed her – so heavily padded that it was like walking around under a cupboard. She fought her way upright, feeling like an idiot, then turned the flashlight on the corpse.

It was a man, naked to the waist, sprawled out under the frost. He was frozen solid, eyes open, mouth full of snow. His face and shoulders were daubed with glittering, crystallised blood.

It wasn't Godolkin.

Red looked closer. "Sneck," she muttered. "How did he get out here?"

There was something strange about the man's head. Red reached down, grabbed the body's frozen arm and hauled it out of the frost.

And came face to face with the inside of its open skull.

She gave a yelp of horror and leaped back, letting the corpse topple back. The man's head had been cut completely open on a line just above the eyebrows. The top of his head was missing, and the contents scooped out; there was nothing left inside but frozen scraps of vein and tissue. Red had seen right down to the base of his brainpan.

"Goddamn!" No wonder there was a pile of vomit in the tunnel. Red might have lost her own lunch, if she'd had any. She took another step back.

Something crunched under her boot. She looked down and saw frozen fingers skittering away. "Aw, crap," she moaned.

There was another body behind her. A woman this time, perhaps in her mid-forties. No visible injuries, save the shattered hand and the fact that her skull was opened and emptied in the same way as before. Gazing blankly through a mask of blood.

Red swallowed hard and scanned the flashlight beam across the floor.

There was another carcass. And another. Two more.

Several, lying in a heap, skulls full of frost.

The edge of a great pile of corpses spreading from halfway along the floor of the cavern to its distant edge – rising up metre after metre – a tangle of arms and legs and slack faces and severed skulls. A mountain of corpses, freeze-dried, denied the dignity of decay and rot. Stacked like logs. The ones she had seen first were just the few that had rolled off the pile.

Red could barely take it in. There were thousands of them. It was a charnel pit, a nightmare.

Every corpse had been skulled, the brain removed.

"Godolkin," she whispered. "Don't tell me you're here too."

"Is that who you're looking for? That heretic?"

She snapped the flashlight beam up. Major Ketta was crouching in the shadows, to the side of the cavern, hidden under the folds of a black thermocowl.

Red hadn't heard her in the thin air, hadn't been able to smell her through her breath-mask. "Is he here?"

Ketta shrugged. She seemed sullen, beaten, as though the horror of this place had stripped all the fight from her. "I've not seen him."

"You said an Iconoclast was here." At that, Ketta pointed to one of the corpses, a few metres behind Red.

She turned the flashlight on it. The man was on his side, eyes staring blindly into the cavern, his skull gaping. He was quite small and slender, his skin dark. A little jet-black hair still remained around the edges of his opened cranium. "One of yours?"

"Major Gaius. My predecessor."

Not Godolkin. There was still a chance, then... Red grimaced, looking closer at the Iconoclast agent. Something inside his skull was flashing, a tiny light in the bone of his head.

A tracer-implant. Red suddenly felt sick. She snatched the tracker out of her cowl and flung it away. "Sneck, what the hell is going on here? Did your people do this?"

"Hardly Iconoclast style, Blasphemy." Ketta straightened. "We don't hide our actions away in the darkness. That's a mutant thing to do."

"Not this mutant." Red gnawed her lip for a moment.

Where had all the bodies come from?

Red turned the flashlight beam on the corpse-pile again. She couldn't believe they had been carried all the way down those treacherous steps, not when it would have been far easier just to toss them into the Eye of God.

The circle of light climbed the mound of bodies, and above.

There was an opening in the stone, the lower edge fanged with crimson icicles. "There," she muttered, mostly to herself. "They come from up there."

She started forwards, and began climbing over the frozen bodies.

The Iconoclast was staring at her. "What in the name of the Holy Patriarch do you think you're doing?"

Red glanced around at her. "I'm going to find my friend," she said simply. "You can come along if you like."

Ketta glared at her, not moving.

"Suit yourself," Red muttered. And kept on climbing.

8. THE WHEEL

Climbing up to the opening was probably the most ghastly thing Durham Red had ever done.

The bodies she clambered over were frozen hard, their limbs like brittle wood. She could hear flesh cracking away from bone whenever she put a foot down, could feel the soft crunch of desiccated tissues through her gloves. Some of the carcasses that had been thrown down from the opening were connected to each other; joined as one by slivers of blood that had frozen together. Others were loose, alone, moving treacherously under her as she scrambled over them.

Partway up she knew she'd never make it with the thermocowl on. Its weight was too much, even in the light gravity, and she couldn't get her legs free of it properly. Eventually she gave up on the thing.

She found a relatively stable place to perch for a few seconds, and stripped the seal. The cowl's heating fans whirred to a halt, and freezing Lavannos air rushed in through the opening: Red gasped, feeling the cold hit her like a punch to the senses, squeezing the breath from her lungs.

The cowl came off in one fluid movement. She flung it away from her, down to the floor. It landed next to Ketta. "If you can't do anything more useful, kiddo, look after that for me. I'll be back for it later."

The Iconoclast didn't reply. Red shrugged, and began to climb again. It was easier without the cowl and the exertion soon warmed her. A human would have frozen to death in minutes, she knew, but Durham Red was much more than human in a lot of ways.

The last few metres were almost flat; she had reached the top of the pile. She scampered up, wincing as her fingers found purchase on the lip of an open skull, and pulled herself upright. The opening, a round tunnel big enough to drive Rinaud's rover though, gaped in front of her, its lower edge a razored mass of overlapping icicles.

All the hanging ice gleamed in dark crimson.

Red shone the flashlight up the tunnel. "Steep slope," she reported, calling down to Ketta. "Looks like a drain: they just slide the poor bastards down it."

"Shout louder, monster. If the killers are here they might not be able to hear you."

The Iconoclast's voice hadn't come from the bottom of the pile of human corpses. Red glanced around, and swore under her breath. Ketta had discarded her own cowl, and was scaling effortlessly up the pile of corpses.

Within moments she was standing upright at the top.

Red turned to face her. "If you were going to take another pop, you'd have done it down there."

"Don't count on it."

"So?"

"I'm sworn to destroy you, monster. Make no mistake about that. But my primary orders are to find and take – alive if possible – the killer of Major Gaius." Ketta nodded towards the opening. "Amazingly, that seems not to be you."

The Iconoclast was very close to Red now. If she lashed out without warning she could slam the girl right off the pile, be on her before she hit the floor. There was a good chance she could have Ketta's throat out before she could react.

But...

If Godolkin was alive, he would need help. If he wasn't, his killers would find out what it felt like to be ripped open. In either case, an extra pair of fists would be no bad thing.

Besides, Ketta seemed like a smart cookie. If she could convince this one that she wasn't the monster she was portrayed as, perhaps the news would spread. Maybe, just maybe, she could get these clowns off her back.

It was a slender hope, but better than none. "Okay, major. Looks like we both want the same thing right now. So until this is over, we call a truce, okay?"

"Why not? By not killing you when I had the chance, I've signed my own death warrant anyway."

Red raised an eyebrow. "The chance?"

"Monster, in case you'd forgotten we are standing on top of a pile of mutilated corpses!" Ketta pointed angrily past her, to the opening. "Is there any chance we could get on with this?"

The drain-tunnel ended in a metal door.

Red, bracing herself against the curving wall, the pointed heels of her boots sunk deep into frozen blood, scanned the flashlight beam around the frame. "No controls," she growled. "Bugger. How are we going to get through this?"

"Prayer?" Ketta scrambled up next to her. "This is designed to be opened from elsewhere, possibly some distance away. No reason there'd be anything on this side."

"Great."

"Have faith, monster." Ketta reached down and slid a small panel from her belt. She placed it against the frame.

Red saw the panel light up, a faint green in the darkness. "You know, Godolkin insists on calling me 'Blasphemy'. I'm not sure I like 'monster' much better."

"Do you not?" Ketta was sliding the panel over the frame. It was some kind of deep-scanner; as it moved, Red saw a window through the metal and into the systems beneath. "There."

The panel was over a junction box. It chattered softly and, under the metal, relays in the box flipped over. The door groaned, and began to move aside.

"That," said Durham Red, "is a very nice toy."

Ketta gave her a look, and ducked past her through the door.

Red followed with the flashlight. As soon as she was in she could see that there was an identical door a few metres further up. "Airlock?"

Ketta didn't answer. She was using the panel again. In a few seconds the door behind them had closed, the one in front was grinding open.

Dull light filtered through the widening gap.

Red tensed and killed the flashlight. From the corner of her eye she saw Major Ketta drop into a fighting stance.

She dived through, into the room beyond, and ducked under a flare of plasma fire.

The shot screamed over her head; she felt the heat of it scour her back, heard it explode against the metal door. She rolled, came up right in front of the man who had fired. He tried to bring the pistol to bear but he was too slow, the barrel too long. Red grabbed the gun, wrenched it out of his grip, and backhanded him across the room.

He slammed against the wall, headfirst. Blood exploded as he struck.

There were two more men in the chamber. Red flipped the gun into the air, caught it by the grip as it came down and blew the furthest man in half. As she did so, something blurred past her and slammed with incredible force into the last attacker. It was Ketta – there was a massive sound, two blows so fast and hard that they were effectively one, and the man spun away, his body sliding back across the room with a carpet of gore behind it.

Abruptly, the chamber was silent, but for the sound of blood dripping off the ceiling and spattering onto the stone floor.

Ketta reached down to the upper half of Red's second victim and plucked the blaster from his clenched hand. Red examined the gun she had taken from the first man, and noticed that it still had a finger in the trigger-guard. She made a face and flicked the grisly thing away. "Three down."

Two of the dead men were mutants. One was human. All were dressed in pale grey coveralls. None of them had been wearing breathing gear.

Red took her mask off and sniffed. The room smelled much how she would have expected it to – scorched metal and flesh from the plasma shots, blood and shit from the dead men. Candle wax. But there was something else, something older.

Ketta was looking at the walls. "Oh my God," she whispered. "What is this?"

The chamber was roughly rectangular, with the airlock door behind them and a smaller door – thankfully still closed – ahead. The walls either side were set with what appeared to be long stone troughs. Above those were hooks, some with metal implements dangling from them.

The metal things were all the same, metre-long complex constructions of black iron, handles, levers and two vicious, curving blades. They looked like huge tongs, or pincers. The stone beneath them was washed with blood and tissue.

Red peered into one of the troughs. It was full of rancid water, dark and scummy, with fragments of matter bobbing in it. "Oh sneck. Major, I think these are what they use. You know…" She mimed lifting the top of her own head off.

Ketta screwed her face up, then turned away. "Let's go. Somebody must have heard this."

The door wasn't locked, but it was quite thick. Red opened it up and stuck her head around, saw only empty corridor beyond. "We're clear. Come on."

They went through together, guns outstretched. Red felt happier with a powergun in her fist, but she was suddenly a lot more wary of Ketta. Luckily, the Iconoclast seemed more intent on the job at hand.

Despite her talk of orders, this was personal. Red could see that a light-year off.

Ketta stopped and raised a hand. Then she tapped her ear: listen.

There was a machine working just around the corner. Something big, metal and primitive. Red heard cogs meshing and the clink and clatter of heavy chain. She took a deep breath and rounded the bend.

What lay beyond was something she would remember for the rest of her days, especially when she was alone and the nights were dark.

The corridor terminated at the entrance to a circular chamber – another bubble-cavern, although smaller than the corpse pit on the other side of the airlock. The floor had been levelled off with wooden decking and a massive construction filled the remaining space almost to the ceiling.

It was a wheel.

A vast, spoked wheel, tipped on its side, the rim set with gleaming spikes. Its axle was a column of black stone wider than Red was tall; giant gears were set beneath, taking power from a riot of chains and pulleys that criss-crossed the deck. Men in coveralls were straining at the chains, bringing the wheel around another notch. It looked ancient, rusted and stained. It stank of blood and thick black oil.

There were people slung between the spokes.

She could see four from where she stood; two men, two women. They lay on their backs, arms and legs spread and cuffed to the framework of the wheel. They wore the bloodied remnants of attendants' cloaks.

They were all dead.

The head of each attendant lolled backwards, emptied, drooling gouts of blood onto the wooden floor beneath.

As Red watched, the wheel turned to its next notch; it rotated a few metres and then halted with a grinding metallic squeal. The motion brought a new attendant into Red's line of sight. She saw his body shudder in its cuffs as the monster wheel stopped.

This one was alive.

Suddenly she felt a hand on her shoulder, pulling her back. It was Ketta. She glared back at the Iconoclast, then saw what she had seen and took the girl's mute advice, easing further back into the corridor.

Someone was on the deck, walking around the wheel.

It was another grey-clad man, this one tall and powerfully muscled. He was probably human, although unlike the others his head was shaved bald and covered with odd, spiralling tattoos. To Red's dismay, she saw that he carried one of the long iron tools she had seen before.

He had stopped under the furthest attendant. She heard the chained man moan, and struggle weakly. He must have known what was coming.

Durham Red knew what was coming. She didn't want to see it, but it happened before she could look away.

With one sudden, swift movement the man in grey lifted the iron tongs high, and clamped the blades around the attendant's skull. He squeezed.

The man between the spokes screamed, long and high, the sound only cut off by a sickening crunch of iron blades tearing through scalp and bone and the layers of tissue beneath. Another blade snickered out between the handles, severing the convulsing victim's spinal cord, and in a spattering heave of blood and watery fluid, his brain slopped out of his head and disappeared into a trough set into the axle.

The body went limp. The top of his skull bounced off the wooden floor and rolled away. Red saw it spin to a halt among the gears.

She slumped back, her stomach flipping. Ketta was further back down the corridor, away from the sight. She had her back to the wall and was taking in great gulps of air, her eyes staring wildly.

Red heard someone spitting a constant stream of whispered obscenities, and realised it was her. She clamped her mouth down over the words.

Back in the chamber, rusted metal ground against metal. The wheel was on the move again.

Red gritted her teeth and looked back at it. She saw it lock into its next position, bringing its next victim into view.

This one was a human male. He was big, his skin corpse-pale, his short hair a colourless thatch. He was naked from the waist up, and the skin of his torso was covered in a complicated mesh of tattoos.

Ketta was crouching at Red's side. "The heretic!" she gasped, as the shaven man beneath raised his bladed tongs to clamp down on Matteus Godolkin's skull.

Durham Red had never moved so fast in her life: she went across the wooden deck like a comet, hitting the bald man at waist level and knocked him flying across the chamber. The iron tongs span away, shattering a head-sized chunk of stone from the wall when they hit.

Red bounced to her feet, snarling. The bald man was lying still, but his companions had dropped their chains and were racing towards her. Plasma fire ripped out across the deck.

She dived aside, behind the axle, letting off two shots as she went. Each shot hit a man in grey; superheated blood and bone fragments exploded back into the walls. Red peered back around the stone column, just in time to see Ketta blur out of the corridor and into the surviving attackers.

There was a sudden cacophony of screams, blows, and breaking limbs. It ended mercifully quickly – in five seconds, maybe less – until all the grey-clad men were dead. Red didn't even see it happen. She was already looking up at Godolkin, trying to see how the cuffs would come off.

A heartbeat later, she was flying back into the axle, her face a mask of pain.

The stone slammed into her spine and the back of her head, sending sheets of light through her vision. Past the colours she could see the bald man, striding towards her, swinging the tongs. He'd smashed her in the jaw with them while she was distracted.

Once, he might have got away with that. Not twice. Red launched herself from the axle, leaping at the man and slapped the awful implement away. She had hit him hard, and he went over, flailing. Red grabbed his head as he hit and slammed it over and over against the deck. On the third blow the wood gave way, and then her teeth were at his throat, puncturing the skin.

Warm blood poured into her mouth. She sucked it down, feeling the heat of it roaring and filling her, sending sparks of raw pleasure through her veins. The man beneath her convulsed once, and then his heart misfired on empty chambers. He stilled.

Red flung her head back and hissed in pure, animal joy.

She stood up, wiping her mouth.

Ketta was watching her, eyes huge. The woman's face was aghast with horror. "Monster," she whispered. And then she was gone, flinging herself back down the corridor.

Red let out a long breath. That could have been worse: Ketta could very easily have started shooting.

She looked up. "Godolkin? You still with me up there?"

The Iconoclast tried to crane his head further back, to see below him. "Blasphemy," he slurred. "Hear you. Real?"

"As real as I'll ever be. Hold on." She reached up to grab the nearest spoke and pulled herself up. "See?"

He raised his heavy head to her, then let it fall back. "Tired."

"I'll bet. Let me get these cuffs off."

It didn't take long to get Godolkin free, but it was more of a job lowering him down to the floor without dropping him. He seemed to have been dosed with something much like Harrow had fallen prey to, although his altered biochemistry was doing a better job of fighting it.

While he gathered his wits, Red checked the other spokes, but there were no more survivors on the wheel. The thought chilled her – another few seconds arguing with Ketta, and Godolkin's thoughts and feelings would have ended up rolling into the axle like all the others.

How many times had this wheel spun? How many brains had ended up sliming their way down that awful trough?

Godolkin was on his feet by the time Red had completed her search. "Mistress," he growled. "You should not have come here."

"You're welcome." Red took the breath-mask from where she'd slung it on her belt, and slipped it on. "There's got to be another one of these somewhere. Grab a couple of guns while I find one. We're getting out of here, and fast."

As before, she had forgotten how cold Lavannos could be. The chill of it went through to her bones as soon as she was out of the airlock, despite the hot blood in her belly. She had a moment's panic that Ketta might have stolen her thermocowl on the way out and flung it down into the Eye of God, but thankfully it was where she left it. The hum of its fans as she sealed it back up was a welcome sound indeed.

"You had a companion," Godolkin said, as they made their way across the cavern floor. Neither had spoken while they were climbing down the pile of bodies. It had seemed wrong to do so, somehow. "I heard another voice."

"Her name's Ketta," Red told him. "Iconoclast Special Agent. Mad as a snake but bloody good in a fight. Think I gave her a bit of a shock drinking that bald guy, though."

"Did you drink from her?"

"What? No!"

"And yet she fought at your side?" Godolkin shook his head. "The universe has gone mad while I was away."

Red chuckled, clambering up the sloping floor of the cavern and into the entrance tunnel. "Let's just say we wanted to kill the same people. Careful here, these steps are damn narrow, and you don't even want to think about what'll happen if you trip."

She felt better once she was up on solid ground again, away from the dark chill of the caverns and their awful secrets. "Want to tell me what happened?"

Godolkin glowered. "I was caught off-guard, mistress. My mind was otherwise engaged. They used toxin shells."

"Ouch." Red had seen the three puckered wounds on his torso. She had wondered how he'd received them. "But the message, that was from you, right?"

"I must confess it was. And the find is genuine."

"Wow..." She'd almost forgotten about that. "Thanks for letting me know. I hope we get to see it before we get off this rock."

Godolkin cleared his throat. "You should not thank me, Blasphemy. My intentions were not benign."

Red stopped and turned to face him. "What do you mean?"

He bowed his head. "The find was an excuse. Had the circumstances been different I would have left it where it lay and not made contact. Your orders on Gomorrah had already given me some of the freedom I craved."

"Yeah, about that..."

The Iconoclast raised his hand, brushing her words aside. "I dreamed of you, mistress."

"Really?" Red's eyebrows went up. "In a nice way?"

"No."

"Oh."

"In the foulest way imaginable. I dreamed of sickening acts with you, mistress – cannibal feasts so depraved as to drive a man insane. I believed your influence was behind it." He closed his eyes. "The message was an attempt to lure you into confrontation."

Red suddenly found it difficult to speak. There must have been something wrong with the breath-mask.

After a time she stepped closer to Godolkin, until her nose was almost touching his chest. She craned her neck back to look at him. "Let me get this straight, buster," she growled. "You dragged me all the way to Lavannos because you thought I was giving you nightmares?"

He met her gaze. "You have my soul, blasphemy," he grated. "I want it back."

I could tell him, she thought.

All it would take would be a few words. She could let him know that she had no real power over him, that his beliefs

were no more valid than an evening of Bela Lugosi vids.
That all she had taken when she had bitten his neck on
Wodan was a litre or two of rather odd-tasting Iconoclast
blood.

And if she did, he'd most likely pick her up and toss her
into the Eye.

She whirled and began stalking away. "I haven't got time
for this," she snapped. "We're going to have a look at this
relic of yours, pick up Harrow, and then get off this shitty
little planet forever."

"Is that an order, mistress?"

"Snecking right it is! And then you and I, Mr Godolkin,
are going to have very serious words."

The monastery looked deserted by the time Red and
Godolkin reached the gates. There was no one in the courtyard, or near any of the separate outbuildings. Red began to
panic, until she realised that, in local time, it was a little
past midnight.

Matins was at five in the morning. The monks and attendants, those that hadn't had their brains ripped out on a
giant wheel, would be getting an early night.

They headed for the reliquary, the closest heatlock to the
main gates. Not to mention the resting place of Godolkin's
find. The Iconoclast went first, as he knew the territory.
Red followed up with her blaster primed and set to full output.

Once through the heatlock and inside, Red dumped the
thermocowl, glad to be rid of it. The mask was no great
loss, either: she'd had enough of breathing her own recy-
cled air, flavoured with a delicate mix of plastic and sweat.

Godolkin, of course, had been wandering about in a
minus-thirty chill with nothing but a pair of leather trousers
to keep him warm. When Red thought about it, she realised
that Ketta hadn't let the cold bother her much, either. Iconoclast bloodwork.

She found herself envying the pair of them, just a little.

They walked past rows of shelves packed with dozens of artefacts. Red paid the dusty finds little attention, but was intrigued to note that a few of them seemed to be robot parts. Droids had been common enough in her day, but there were none in the Accord. The trick of making them had been one of the many branches of knowledge lost in the Bloodshed.

No one made intelligent machines any more.

Godolkin had moved on ahead and stopped near a long workbench. There was something on it, draped with a silvery sheet of fabric-metal. "Here, Blasphemy."

He pulled the sheet away, revealing the object beneath. The one he'd found embedded in the wall of a cavern, right under her feet.

It was a long, flattened cylinder of dark metal, ridged and fluted, the ends subtly rounded. It widened at one end into a broad dome, set with panels and indicator lights. It was two-and-a-half, maybe three metres long, massively built. Impossibly old.

Durham Red recognised it immediately. She had climbed into one exactly like it, more than twelve hundred years ago.

It was a cryotube.

And it was intact.

9. PAST TENSE

Not for the first time that day, Durham Red found herself without words.

She ran her gloved hand over the ridged surface of the cryotube, feeling the faint vibration of its systems, the vast strength of its construction. If it wasn't the exact same model she had slept in for twelve centuries, it was damn close. She couldn't see any differences that she could remember.

Chunks of brittle Lavannos stone still adhered between some of the ridges. She prodded one and it fell away, thumping softly onto the carpeted floor of the reliquary.

"I came a long way to see this, Godolkin," she breathed.

There was no chance she could have stayed away from Lavannos. If Godolkin's intention was simply to bring her here, to engineer their final confrontation, then he couldn't have picked a better way to do it. Once she knew the retreat-world harboured an intact cryotube she would have walked barefoot through lava to get her hands on the thing.

She had woken into a universe unimaginably different from her own. A dark age of insanity, ignorance and despair had swept the galaxy clean of everything she had experienced. She was adrift in this strange, violent time. Even her world was gone.

All her roots had been severed.

Until now. This one object, ripped from a cavern wall under the melted, glassy surface of Lavannos, was a direct link to Earth. If nothing else it gave her a chance to touch, one last time, a little piece of home.

As for its contents, she hardly dared hope.

She didn't know how long tubes like this had been in service when she had gone to sleep, but her day was one of constant improvement and innovation. She couldn't imagine that this cryotube could be much younger than her own. Which meant that whoever lay inside was very probably a product of her world.

It might even be someone she knew. More than one Strontium Dog had opted out of the world. "Godolkin? I know you didn't have my best interests at heart when you called me about this. But thanks anyway."

He seemed mildly embarrassed by the sentiment, and she wasn't surprised when he changed the subject. "Were such devices common in your day?"

"Well, they were around if you had the money. Cryofreezing was never cheap. It took all I had just for a short break."

"Under the circumstances, it would appear you ended up with a bargain."

That was a matter of opinion, but Red wasn't about to press the point. "It still has power, at least," she said, gesturing towards some of the indicator lights scattered over the tube's surface. "Micro-fusion core. It's good for about three thousand years, or so the guys at the freezer bank said."

"So it may yet contain a living soul?"

"That's kind of what I was hoping." She paused, staring intently down at the tube, trying to picture what lay inside, as though Ketta's magic panel lay on it. "Godolkin, I'm not sure we should open this."

His expression told her that was not the reaction he'd been expecting. She hadn't quite been expecting it herself. But now she was here, with the cryo-tube in front of her, she wondered if she actually had the right to open it up.

Godolkin looked nonplussed. "I'm not sure I understand, mistress. Didn't you travel to Lavannos in order to do just that?"

"That and a vacation, yeah." She sighed. "But Godolkin, look around you. This galaxy isn't exactly the nicest place someone could wake up in: ask me, I should know. Now I'm a big girl, I can take care of myself. But what about the poor bastard in here?"

The Iconoclast glowered. "Mistress, you did not intend to sleep twelve centuries away. I find it hard to imagine anyone else would, either. Do you not think that whoever lies in this sarcophagus has rested long enough?"

She never got to answer, because at that moment they both heard the outer door of the heatlock sliding open.

"Crap!" she hissed. "What now?"

Godolkin was draping the fabric-metal sheet back over the tube. "Concealment," he replied. "We hide."

He ran around to a space between two shelves, did something to the panels there. Red watched them slide away, leaving a rectangle of blackness. "In here, Blasphemy. Hurry!"

She darted across the reliquary and into the opening. There were stairs beyond so she had to grab the wall to avoid tumbling down them, then trotted down a few to let Godolkin squeeze in behind. A second later he slid the panel closed, leaving the steps in total darkness.

Past the panels, she heard the inner lock door opening.

Godolkin gave her a gentle shove. She took the hint and headed down the steps, working entirely by feel. Her night-vision was very good indeed, but even she relied on a photon or two. No light was reaching the stairs at all.

After a minute or two she reached the final stair and stepped down onto a smooth, faintly curving floor. Another bubble cavern, like the one full of corpses back at the Eye. Lavannos must have been riddled with them.

Red wondered where all that gas came from. She'd seen some weird and wonderful planets in her time, but none that was basically a giant sponge made of black glass.

She felt Godolkin step down next to her. "Why are we hiding?" she whispered. "If it's the bad guys, we can take them."

"It might be the abbot," he said. "The reliquary, this cavern, are passions of his."

Red scowled in the darkness. "I don't trust the abbot."

"The abbot is a good man. Whatever crimes may occur on this world, I'm certain he's not a part of them."

"Harrow thinks he's a liar."

Godolkin snorted. "Harrow thinks you are a saint. His judgement of character cannot be described as expert."

Red glanced across at him, and was surprised to see his outline. There was a tiny amount of light coming into the cavern from somewhere. Even her phenomenal eyes were having difficulty adjusting.

But there should have been no light here at all.

She turned her head, trying to find the source of it, using the edges of her vision as if she were trying to locate a faint star by looking slightly to one side of it. Sure enough, there was ghostly, infinitesimal luminescence coming from one side of the cavern.

She followed it, and within a few metres found the wall with her outstretched fingers. "Godolkin? Come and have a look at this."

"The wall is glowing," he confirmed. "Could there be phosphorescent chemicals in the stone, perhaps?"

"Maybe." The dim light was outlining objects in the walls, a random scattering of shapes. "These are abbot's finds, eh?"

"Some of them."

On an impulse, Red took her right glove off. She placed her bare hand against the rock.

It was cool and slightly damp – condensation from her own breath, probably. She leaned close, putting her nose almost against the cold surface of it. There was something about the light that bothered her.

Godolkin walked into her from behind.

It was only a nudge, but in the almost complete absence of light it took her by surprise. She just managed not to make a sound as she stumbled into the wall.

As she fell against it, it moved.

The motion was tiny, barely there at all. She'd never have felt it though the gloves. But as her weight fell against the cavern wall she felt it shiver in response.

"Sneck," she said, very quietly. Things as big as caves were not supposed to move. Not even a little.

There was a long, low groaning sound, as of vast stresses held in check for centuries, and suddenly released. "Godolkin? This is where you pulled the cryo-tube out, yeah?"

"It is."

"And you pulled it pretty hard, didn't you. Just snapped it out of the wall, I'll bet."

"You could say that."

As if in response, the cavern wall cracked from top to bottom.

It happened in an instant. There was a single, ear-splitting report, and a tiny puff of dust that hit Red in the face. When she next looked at the wall, she could just see a vertical line in it that hadn't been there before.

She heard the panel into the reliquary slide open.

Scant edges of light filtered down the steps, into the cavern. There was the sound of footfalls; someone was coming down, probably to investigate the noise.

Red hauled the blaster from her belt and checked the charge. She smiled grimly. It was rather low on fuel, but even on full power it was good for a few shots yet. To her right, Godolkin was levelling both the guns he had taken from the wheel room.

The footsteps stopped. Light, blinding and powerful, erupted into the cavern.

Red yelped in pain and fired wildly, covering her eyes with her free hand. After so long in the darkness her eyes were fully adapted to the gloom, her pupils completely dilated. Whoever had walked down those steps had shone a simple hand-lume into the cavern, and almost taken her retinas off.

Plasma fire ripped towards her, horribly loud.

She had moved as soon as she'd fired, knowing she hadn't hit anything and having no intention of being a stationary target. The shots screamed past her into the wall.

Red hit the floor, sliding, bringing the gun up again. Before she could pull the trigger a sear of yellow fire lanced directly out at her; there was a gigantic impact, smacking her right hand back so hard it almost dislocated her shoulder, spinning her over backwards. The blaster had been blown clean out of her grasp.

She lay crumpled for a moment, blinded by the gunfire, her hand singing with pain, electric jolts crackling from her wrist to her shoulder. She realised that she was a sitting duck a fraction of a second before Godolkin's guns thundered, and there was the ghastly sound of a human body taking two plasma shots simultaneously.

Burning offal spattered the walls.

Red rolled onto her rump, sitting up, cradling her hand. Through watering eyes she saw Godolkin hammering across the cavern towards her.

Behind her, a thin, high whine from her blaster became a sputtering hiss.

And then a memory, unbidden, bubbling up through the dark swamp of drug-induced amnesia. Cold metal at her back, the sound of gunfire, Judas Harrow stabbing a little plasma derringer with a knife. He was rigging it to explode.

Just before it did, it made the exact same noise that her own gun was making now.

Godolkin grabbed her by her damaged shoulder, and wrenched her up. She screamed, and then she was flying through the air.

The gun detonated.

The cavern went white-hot, white-bright. Red hit the ground hard, sliding and tumbling away. Her eyes were closed, but she was still dazzled through her own eyelids. The noise was incredible. It sounded like half the cavern was coming down around her, a cacophony of falling stone, shattering glass, the hissing impacts of dust and sand.

Very quickly after that, the cavern turned silent and dark.

"Ow. Sneck. Ow!" Red was trying to get to her feet, but she felt as though she'd been through a grinder. She only managed it on the third try.

She could barely see. There was light in front of her, but her vision was an agonised blur, her eyes streaming. There was rock-dust in the air, so much she could taste it as she breathed. Fragments crunched under her boots as she stumbled forwards. "Godolkin?"

There was no reply. Red blinked rapidly, wiping her face with the one hand that still worked. Her fingers came away wet, whether from blood or just tears and snot she couldn't tell. Her vision wouldn't clear.

"Godolkin! Sound off – that's an order, you big lummox!"

There was an answering groan. Rock slid against rock. He must have been buried; now he was fighting his way free of half the cavern wall. If they had done nothing else this trip, Red reflected, they'd certainly given the abbot's archaeology habit a twist.

She reached down to her bodice and ripped part of it away, used it to wipe the fluid from her eyes. That helped a little, enough to let her see a haze of bluish light in front of her. And a massive shape, rising from a pile of broken wall. Godolkin.

She gave a small sigh of relief.

"Godolkin? I can't see too much. Are you hurt?"

"I am–" He coughed hard, and spat. "I am uninjured. Largely."

"Great." She shook her head, trying to clear it. "I hope you're going to look after me, now I'm blind."

He walked over to her, his footsteps crunching over rock and dust. She felt him looming over her. "Your sight will return within minutes, Blasphemy. You are merely dazzled."

Red sniffed. "Bloody plasma guns. No wonder everyone's buying particle…"

He was right, however. She could see more clearly with every passing moment, although her ears were still ringing. Her right arm hurt like hell, too. She flexed it experimentally, wiggling her fingers. There didn't seem to be any permanent damage. She wouldn't be playing any racquetball for a few days, though.

The cavern was flooded with soft blue light.

Godolkin was standing beside her now, looking at the source of the light. Red wiped her eyes one last time and followed his gaze.

"Holy shit," she whispered.

The faint glow they had seen earlier hadn't been part of the rock, it had been filtering through a thin part of the wall. Weakened by Godolkin's violent removal of the cryo-tube, the stone there had fallen prey to stress, time, and finally the explosion of Red's blaster – the cavern wall, in a section maybe five metres high and the same distance across, now lay in razor-sharp fragments scattered across the floor.

There was a room beyond it.

Red padded warily forwards. The room was like nothing she'd seen on Lavannos, or anywhere in this time. Instead of the intricate churchlike architecture of the Accord, or the sepulchral white stone of the monastery, this was metallic, hard-edged, cleanly functional. The walls were muted silver and flat grey, the flooring a kind of rubberised mesh, and cool blue light radiated from the ceiling panels. There were discreet display screens set into the walls, a couple of integral seating units on one side, storage on the other. The room looked neat, efficient. Expensive.

It was also canted over at several degrees from the vertical, the far right-hand corner of the floor as the lowest point.

She had reached the threshold now, the point at which rock became metal. The open end of the room was shattered, she could see now, ripped in half by the formation of the cavern. Chunks of it had been flung up and out, then frozen in the solidifying stone.

This was the source of the abbot's sacred relics.

Red stepped over the lip of broken rock and into the room. The floor around the lip was smeared with solidified rock, and there were truncated spears of the stuff adhering to both floor and ceiling. A long track of black glass trailed down to the low corner, pooling there. The rubber mesh under her boots was scorched and burned through in dozens of spots and tracks.

"Godolkin? Did you know this was here?"

"I did not." He clambered over the edge to join her, running his great hands along the broken edges of rock. "I cannot imagine anyone knew, otherwise the abbot would have been in here with a fusion lance." He reached down to one of the broken stalagmites, snapped it free with a twist of his arm. "Blasphemy, this structure was here when the crust of Lavannos melted."

A whole room, trapped in the glassy stone like a fly in amber. How much else? There was a hatchway at the far end of the room, an octagonal metal door that could lead anywhere.

"What do you think it is? A ship?"

Godolkin was studying the display panels. They were intact, but blank. "This looks like no space vessel I have ever seen, Blasphemy."

"Yeah, well. Where I come from, starships don't look like cathedrals on wings. Guess times change." She prodded the seat cushions with a finger. Dust puffed up as the foam crumbled.

The room looked brand new from a distance, preserved perfectly in the rock. But that, she could see now, was an illusion: the silvery walls were mapped with an infinity of tiny cracks, the mesh squashed beneath her boots and didn't spring back up, the seating had gone to powder.

Whatever this place was, it was incredibly old. She could easily imagine it existing before the crust of Lavannos had turned to foam. Especially if it had once housed the cryotube.

And where there was one tube, there might be more.

She walked past Godolkin, towards the door. There was a flat metal pad next to it, some kind of control, but the ceiling lights must have been running on emergency power only. Nothing else worked.

"Help me get this door open."

"Mistress, we should retrieve Harrow."

She couldn't think about that now. "He'll be okay, I locked him in. Now get a grip on this thing and heave, okay?"

With the Iconoclast's strength working at it, the door came open with a minimum of fuss. Red peered through, into a corridor maybe ten metres long. It had a strange cross-section, eight-sided, like a broad coffin. Looking at it made her feel vaguely uneasy.

The far end of the corridor was level. It bent in the middle, the walls there crumpled and flaking.

Red stepped through the door. The corridor branched halfway along, to her left. The position of that branch struck an odd chord in her, something she couldn't immediately identify. She trotted along and rounded the bend.

"Oh," she said. "Now I get it!" She looked back, and beckoned to Godolkin. "Come and see this."

The bend wasn't a right angle. The corridor that joined there slanted off at about forty-five degrees, carrying on for some considerable way. The end of it was crushed, wrenched upwards by some seismic cataclysm, the light-panels failing in ones and twos until the full ruin of it was lost in darkness. But what Red could see, just ahead of where the light failed, was how the outer structure of the shattered corridor was braced with wide, circular rings of gleaming metal.

"You know where that is?" she asked, pointing. Godolkin frowned.

"Under the chapel."

"And Godolkin scores extra points for spatial awareness."

She grinned. "That mess is right under the Arch! There's Saint Lavann's holy artefact – a busted ring-girder!"

The Church of the Arch was built on wreckage. Saint Lavann had founded his monastery on nothing more than a discarded piece of bracing.

It made a bizarre kind of sense, now that she thought about it. That the abbot had so much archaeology right under his feet was no coincidence at all. The church had been constructed right on top of it, centred around the one part that had been sticking out of the ground.

Durham Red wondered if anyone else in the monastery would appreciate the irony of that as much as she did.

The intact part of the corridor had another door at the end, identical to the hatch in the first room. Despite Godolkin's misgivings, she at least had to see what lay beyond that.

"If there's nothing here we'll quit, okay? I promise. Back up the stairs, shoot our way out if we have to, and grab Harrow. But this place!" She spread her hands. "Godolkin, this is what things looked like when I went to sleep. I've got to see if there are more cryo-tubes nearby, if nothing else."

"I am your slave, Blasphemy. You only need order me, and I shall follow you into the core of this moon, if necessary." He glared down at her, his data-eye gleaming malevolently white. "But you have my protest on record: I believe this to be a waste of time, an unnecessary distraction, and very possibly a trap."

She prodded his bare chest. "You are so paranoid."

"Yes," he nodded gravely. "I requested that feature during my last upgrade."

"Just open the damn door, Captain Paranoia."

As with the last hatch, there was a small panel that concealed a recessed handle. Godolkin got a grip on that, put his shoulder to the door and wrenched it aside. This one put up more of a fight, however: Red winced as the hatch emitted a piercing metallic screech, while flakes of corrosion and bright peelings of steel rattled onto the mesh.

The hatch resisted Godolkin's attentions up to about halfway, then slid easily open. Some kind of locking mechanism had sheared under the Iconoclast's strength. Red was presented with a sudden view of the next chamber.

"Oh no," she whispered.

Whatever the structure was, it had not been entirely unoccupied when it was buried.

This chamber was much larger than those they had seen before. It was a broad, angular space, built on three separate levels, each linked by shallow ramps. Workstations were set along the walls, shelving control boards with bucket seats and overhead displays. A big, glass-topped desk, like a digital map-table, occupied the centre of the chamber, down on the lowest level.

There were bones everywhere.

Two skeletons lay on the floor just inside the doorway. Ragged scraps of fabric clung to them in threads and the floor was discoloured around them; ancient stains, dark pools of rot and blood turned to foul dust over the centuries. Red crouched next to them for a moment, smelling their musty age, seeing the strange way that they were entangled.

Had they been embracing when they died?

She looked closer and saw flaking scratches on the skull of one body, the wrist bones of the other. She shuddered. These men had died tearing at each other's flesh with their bare teeth.

Elsewhere, more evidence of horror. A skeleton that had been blown apart, the lower half of it still sitting at a workstation, the remainder reduced to great shards of bone embedded in the station's control board. Further away another carcass lay with a rusted pistol lying among the scattered bones of its fingers, its own skull carbonised shrapnel. Near the map-table, a skeleton whose finger-bones were thrust into its own eye-sockets.

"Blasphemy," growled Godolkin. "These men died mad."

She nodded dully. "They killed each other, didn't they? The ones that didn't kill themselves. Christ, what a nightmare."

There were other doors leading away from this room, but Red had no desire to go through them. "I've seen enough. Godolkin, if your abbot is as nice a guy as you think, I pray he doesn't ever come down here."

Godolkin was studying a skeleton slumped over one of the second-level workstations, one that had a corroded knife-blade sticking out of the back of its skull. He lifted the corpse away, and Red saw that the blade went right through, into the board itself. "Ouch," she hissed.

The corpse had been lying across something. Godolkin lifted it carefully free; it looked like a thin slab of metal a handspan across. He handed it to Red. "Mistress?"

She took it, gingerly. As she turned it over a wad of pulpy dust slid out from between the two sides of it and shattered against the floor. She coughed as the musty stuff stung her throat. "Yech. It's a book, I think. Or was…"

The covers of the book were formed from some kind of metallic plastic. They had survived the years far better than the pages and the writing on the front cover was still quite legible.

"Oh my God," Red gasped. "It's in English."

Operations Manual, she read. Then, in smaller letters beneath, *Luna Translation Centre Tycho-Alpha – Do not remove from ops room.*

"Godolkin, how did this get here? How did this book get all the way out here?"

"What do you mean?" He must have seen the stunned shock on her face. "Mistress? What's wrong?"

She took a deep breath. It was suddenly hard to get air in the ancient chamber. "Earth had one moon," she told him. "We called it Luna. Tycho was a crater, one of the biggest – there was a city on it, back in my day. So either this book is a snecking long way from home, or..."

She looked up at him. "Godolkin, I think we're on the Moon!"

10. DRIVE

It was well after Compline and the monastery was in darkness. All the candles had been snuffed out. Where lumes provided light, they had been turned to their lowest setting by automatic timer.

Major Ketta sat on the hard little bed in her room, with every lume she could find blazing around her.

She usually preferred the dark. Perhaps a predilection for the shadows was part of the entrance requirement for the Iconoclast Special Forces, or maybe such a preference had been instilled in her as part of her conditioning. She had so little memory of what she had been like before recruitment that anything was possible.

It was true that her work often required her to operate in as little light as possible. Unlike the open brutality of the Iconoclast regular armies, her successes tended to rely on being hidden, unheard, unseen. While the shocktroopers were burning cities to bring wayward planets to heel, Ketta had, on more than one occasion, achieved the same effect with a climbing line, a data-pick and a slim-bladed knife.

Hers was the silent world, the shadow world. It was in darkness that she became truly alive.

On Lavannos, though, things were very different.

Here, the dark brought only terror. She had given up trying to sleep during the night, after the first few nightmares. Never, in all her days, had she been subject to such awful visions as those she dreamed in the Church of the Arch. Even before seeing what lay in the cavern, on the edge of the Eye of God, she had been in fear of her sanity.

She had seen worse sights in her time, that was the strange thing. She had stalked the cities of worlds blasted by hunger-guns, sifting through steaming human wreckage for survivors on which to practise her singular methods of information-gathering. She had witnessed mass executions, ritual decimations, scourging, disembowelling. The limits of suffering, both human and otherwise, were no new territory for her.

But Lavannos frightened her. Something about this tiny world, she had decided, magnified terror.

When she had last contacted Admiral Huldah Antonia, that terror had almost overcome her. Despite the darkness outside her room, and what she had seen in the lair of the monster wheel, she resolved to be more dignified this time. She had a reputation to uphold, after all.

Ketta would never have been able to keep a transjump comm array openly in her room and maintain her cover story. A simple pilgrim would never have access to such specialised equipment. Besides, comm-linkers of any kind were frowned upon in the retreat, as a distraction and a barrier to peace. An Iconoclast Special Agent, however, had access to equipment most soldiers of the Accord only dreamed about. Earlier that evening, she had taken various innocent belongings scattered about the room and built a comm-linker out of them.

The power-cells, slender and incredibly powerful rods of self-fusing polymer, were hidden in the spine of a book of scripture. The coder and input cascade were hidden in the picture-panels of a holy triptych; a rosary twisted just so became the signal-guide. The datastream transmitted by the array was very narrow, but it could go a long way without the need of Iconoclast relay stations.

The linker was already set to Antonia's crypt-key. Ketta tapped out a carrier code, activated the transmitter and sent the datastream leaping through jumpspace. Seconds later the code was picked up, verified, and returned with a comms signal on its tail. Antonia's voice scratched out through Ketta's earbud. "Datakey confirmed, Major Ketta. It's good to hear from you again."

"Het Admiral." Ketta prodded the earbud a little further in, trying to get a bit more volume. "I'm picking up more interference than usual. Is there a problem?"

"No, major, nothing that need concern you. You're probably getting some noise from the drives. *Othniel* is in jumpspace – we'll be with you very soon."

Ketta closed her eyes momentarily in relief, and was quite glad the signal wasn't strong enough for video. "That's good news, admiral. I'll not be sorry to leave this place."

"I'll send a landing craft before I turn Lavannos inside out, have no fear."

At the moment, fear was pretty much all Ketta had. "Admiral, how secure is this line?"

"Level three encryption," Antonia replied. "Why do you ask?"

"I have some vital information, for your reception only. If there is anyone with you, I suggest you send them away."

"There isn't."

"Good." Ketta squared her shoulders. This was going to take some explaining.

"Blasphemy," said Godolkin levelly. "You are raving."

Red was stalking around the map-table in circles. "It's not impossible. I don't see how anyone could do it, but it's not impossible."

"Contrary to popular belief, Durham Red, some things *are* impossible." Godolkin had his arms folded implacably, his chin stuck out. He looked like a statue carved from white marble, massive and unmoveable. "Shifting planets is one of them. What do you think happened? You really think someone attached a line to this world and dragged it two hundred light years?"

"I don't know!"

"Earth is gone, Blasphemy. I know that fact is hard, but it must be faced. The planet of your birth has vanished from the cosmos. Surely it is more likely that this book, and *only* the book, made this journey?"

Red stopped pacing. "Okay, that is more likely. But this looks a lot like an ops room to me." She saw him open his mouth to speak and held up a hand. "Yeah, maybe I have got a screw loose. Maybe this whole set-up is a fake, or a trap, or whatever. I don't know! But I've got to find out."

"How?"

"I'll let you know. In the meantime, you need to get back to Jude. Ketta's drug should have worn off by now."

Godolkin looked uncomfortable. "Mistress, if you are intent on pursuing this deranged quest, my place is at your side."

"Judas needs you more than I do right now." She took the key from a pocket and held it out to him. "He's in room eighty-five, end of the hall, upper floor. It's a mechanical lock so you have to put this into the hole and twist, okay?"

He frowned. "I'm not sure…"

"You don't have to be. Just be quick."

"Very well, Blasphemy." He took one of the guns from his belt and passed it to her. "Try not to make this one explode."

She watched him stride out of the room, then turned back to the bone-scattered ruin around her.

This was completely irrational, she knew that. If she was sensible she would be going with Godolkin right now, picking Jude up and flying *Crimson Hunter* off this rock and away. There was almost no chance she was right, a much greater chance of running into more brain-scooping maniacs. Not to mention Major Ketta. Now an Iconoclast knew she was here, it could only be a matter of time before the missiles started flying.

She knew all of this, but she couldn't bring herself to leave this mystery behind.

"Sensible is for wimps," she muttered.

A quick search of the room revealed no more clues. Red wasn't too surprised at this: any sufficiently advanced set-up would have all the relevant documents filed away on computer. The operations manual would be in hardcopy form, just in case an emergency took the computers down.

She just wished they'd made the pages from something a bit more durable.

There were three other doors leading off the upper level. One of them was jammed fast: Red knew she'd never move it without Godolkin's help. The next slid a quarter of the way and then stopped, but Red was slim. A quarter was all she needed.

The room beyond was smaller by far. It looked like an office, with a desk and what had been a comfortable chair. In a small adjoining chamber there was a narrow bunk, and next to that a fresher with a shower unit. A skeleton was crumpled in the shower, skull battered to pieces, a long metal bar lying next to it.

Red stood looking at the skeleton for some time, then sighed to herself and walked back into the office. She searched there for a few minutes, but found nothing of value or interest in any of the desk drawers. Most of the contents had rotted to dust anyway.

She went back into the larger space, the place she could only now think of as the ops room.

This excursion was looking more like a complete bust with every minute that went by. Red gnawed a fingernail nervously. If she didn't find something soon, it probably meant there just wasn't anything to find. She'd leave Lavannos never knowing what had happened here.

That would eat her away from the inside.

There was one more door to try, at the far end of the upper level. Red yanked and hauled at the hatch for a minute or two, without any more success than she had at the first door. It felt like it was close to coming open, but some ancient part of its locking mechanism was resisting her.

Godolkin could probably have done it. Red was strong, strong enough to tear a man's arm out of his socket one-handed, but she couldn't match Godolkin's muscle. It looked like she was stuck until he got back.

Unless…

Red groaned, leaned back and then slammed her forehead against the hatch. "You prat!" she snarled. "Christ, Durham, for a smart girl you're not all that bright, are you?"

She walked briskly back along the upper level, into the office, past the desk and into the fresher. When she returned to the door, she had the metal bar in her hands.

It made an effective pry bar, giving her all the leverage she needed to break the hidden lock and slide the hatch aside. Cool air rushed out at her as the door came open.

She had been hoping for another room, perhaps one with shelves laden with sturdy, time-proof documents. Instead, she saw another corridor, this one so straight and long that it seemed to dwindle away to nothing. She cursed under her breath.

A glance over her shoulder confirmed that there was still no sign of Godolkin.

The corridor looked intact. It was at least twice as high and wide as the ones she had seen so far, with a different, more hexagonal cross-section. The floor of it was bare metal, not rubber mesh, and there were open braces every few metres that seemed designed to trip up anyone who walked too close to the wall.

Red stepped through the hatch and began to run along the metal floor.

Her footsteps gonged, echoing up and down the tunnel. For a while it didn't look as though she was going anywhere, as brace after brace, panel after panel passed by in constant, identical succession. It was only when she had jogged about two hundred metres that she saw anything different: a small service hatch, set against the left-hand wall. Other than that, the features of the corridor seemed endlessly similar.

As it turned out, the tunnel was over a kilometre long. Red was quite out of breath when she arrived at the far end, and wondering why anyone would build such a long, dull corridor in what otherwise seemed a practical and efficient complex.

It was only when she got to the far end that she found out.

The tunnel wasn't a corridor. It was a maglev track.

There was a mag-car at the far end of the tunnel, resting neatly on the protruding braces. It fitted the cross-section perfectly, and had a metre-wide hatch on its flat, hexagonal end. Presumably the door from the ops room would only open when the car was there waiting: anyone wishing to get to the other end of the tunnel would step in, be whisked along, then step out of the opposite hatch. Simple, if the base had anything other than the barest wisps of emergency power.

Red tutted, and hauled herself up to the car's hatch. It slid aside easily, almost as if it had been oiled.

There were little bench seats inside, and places where grab-straps had once hung. Red walked between the seats and tried the far hatch. That opened without fuss as well. She was glad to finally find a door or two that did.

She jumped down from the car into a short hallway. There were lockers on either side of her, doors hanging forlornly open, rags and rot on their floors. And above a massive double-hatchway at the far end of the hall was a large metal plaque, the paint it had once sported now just flakes and coloured dust on the floor, but the words etched into it still legible after so many, many years.

Tycho-Alpha Translation Drive Chamber
Authorised Personnel Only
Warning! Radiation Hazard! Radmeters must be worn at all times
Have you checked your rads today?

Red gaped up at the sign. There it was, written into a metal slab four metres across, fixed and solid and undeniable. The proof she had been looking for. The book, and the complex of rooms and corridors she now stood in, belonged together.

Whatever murderous excesses the ill-fated occupants of this place had committed, at least none of them had taken the manual out of the ops room.

So this was the Moon. Not just *a* moon, orbiting an alien gas-giant in the middle of nowhere, but *the* Moon. Something had happened to it, back in the distant past, something that had rendered it unrecognisable – this complex, these rooms and systems and the crewmen they contained, had been here, under the Tycho crater, when the cataclysm had occurred. They had died here, trapped and insane.

Red walked slowly up to the double hatch, placed her hand flat against it. It was all starting to fall into place, she realised, the last pieces of the mystery sliding and locking around her like the components of some titan puzzle-box.

The key to it all was the translation drive.

She had heard the words long ago, before she had gone to sleep, back when she had hunted men for a living.

She had been on the trail of a rogue scientist, a defector from an industrial corporation whose size and wealth were matched only by its ferocious protection of intellectual resources. For an employee to leave the company was unthinkable. For a senior technician to escape the corporate arcology with a slug of project data in his pocket required nothing less than a death sentence.

Red had initially balked at killing a man for trying to change jobs, but her opinion changed when details of the scientist's expertise were revealed to her. The man, she had been told, was a bio-weapons expert. He had already tried to sell viral agents to both sides in a planetary war, and was working on a delivery system for tailored cancers. Obediently, Red had found the scientist in hiding on Rotin's World, and had carried out her mission with extreme prejudice.

It was only later that she discovered the truth. The man had nothing to do with bio-weapons research at all. His field was advanced theoretical physics; Morris-Thorne wormholes, exotic matter, quantum inseparability. Methods of moving a starship between distant points without actually travelling through the intervening space. A translation drive.

Red had been duped, well and truly. It wasn't the first time and it wouldn't be the last, but that didn't make her like it any better.

She'd forfeited her fee by ripping the throat out of the man who'd lied to her.

It was all coming back to her now. A translation drive, the sales pitch went, would make conventional superlight travel obsolete. Comparing conventional phased transfer with quantum-translation was like comparing flights of stairs to high-speed elevators. In one case you had to slog laboriously from one floor to the next. In the other you got into a box, got out of it again and you were somewhere else.

It was a nice idea. But to Red's knowledge, not one that had ever gotten off the back of the dead physicist's notepad. Some trivial thing about the amount of energy needed to translate a small paper cup being greater than all the power generated by a galaxy over a million years, or some such bizarre calculation.

If Durham Red was right, a couple of centuries after she'd climbed into her cryo-tube, someone had cracked the problem.

Big time.

They'd built a translation drive powerful enough to move the moon two hundred light years. Although it looked like they had managed to melt the crust in the process.

She rapped the hatch a couple of times with her knuckles. There was no way she was going to get those mighty doors open, Godolkin or no Godolkin. Without powering up the whole base, the last piece of the jigsaw was going to stay well and truly out of sight.

Red didn't like that, but she thought she could probably live with it. After all, she'd just been given the first clue as to what might have happened to the Earth.

She turned away from the hatch and climbed back into the mag-car, wrapped in her thoughts. She was just about to open the door when she heard footsteps on the other side of it.

Her eyes widened. The footfalls were close, very close: she'd been so lost in thought she'd not heard them until they were almost on top of her. For a second she wondered if Godolkin had found her, but that wasn't his steady pace on the other side of the mag-car, nor Judas Harrow's catlike pacing. This was, from what she could hear now, at least twenty people. Some of them were carrying something heavy.

Red darted back through the car, closed the door silently behind her, and realised that she was trapped.

There was only one place to go. She dropped to the floor and rolled under the mag-car, folding herself into the gap between the electromagnets and the conductive metal floor. There was a brace stopping her going all the way under, leaving her only about half a metre to play with. She sucked her breath in, trying to think small thoughts.

The car door opened above her head, and people began climbing down and into the hall.

Red had been right about their numbers – when they were all past her, lined up between the lockers, she'd counted twenty-two pairs of feet. A couple of them were carrying a long, heavy object between them. Red couldn't see where it was, as her field of view only extended a couple of handspans above the floor, but it had a rich, bloody smell.

Nothing in the least bit appetising, not even to her.

There was no talking going on, just a breathless silence. Red heard a faint bleeping, as of some piece of electronic equipment, and then a series of heavy, metallic impacts. The floor shivered under her. A second later, with a whine of ancient motors, the giant hatch split.

Green light spilled out from the widening gap.

Red squinted, trying to see past the feet. The hatch took almost half a minute to open, during which time the hall's occupants waited patiently. Only when the doors were firmly seated into either side of the frame did they begin to file in.

When they were past, Red squeezed out from her hiding place and scampered to the side of the hatch. She peered round, blaster raised and powered.

The drive chamber was vast.

There was a massive construction at the heart of it that could only have been the translation drive: a glossy sphere of black metal wider than *Crimson Hunter* was long, studded with panels and power feeds and huge, snaking coolant pipes. Only the upper half of the sphere was visible from where Red crouched, the rest was below ground level. The drive sat in what must have been a massive cylindrical shaft, held in place by slender-looking braces. From the gap between the sphere and the shaft walls, vomitous green light poured up.

There was a narrow deck around the shaft. On this stood twenty-two monks of Saint Lavann.

There wasn't anyone there she recognised, but there was no mistaking their attire. Apart from the two that were burdened, everyone else had spread out around the drive, a gap of several metres between each monk.

They had started to make a noise.

It was a low, sonorous chanting. Red couldn't make out any words, but it was a discordant, unearthly sound, a fractured register that beat at the ears. There was something familiar about it, yet at the same time it was horribly alien. She winced, and looked a little further around the edge of the hatch, trying to see what the two monks had been carrying.

She was half expecting a body, but it looked like a silver tray, as long as a coffin and high-sided, covered with a grey cloth. As she watched, they set it down on the deck between them and stepped away.

The sound of the chant was beginning to give Red a headache. The floor seemed to be vibrating in time to it, the air shivering around her. She swallowed hard. Her heart was pounding, and sweat beaded her brow, soaked down between her shoulder blades under the leather. Her hands were shaking, fingers slick around the blaster's grip.

Something awful was about to happen here. She could feel it, the breath of it, like the clammy pressure before a thunderstorm. She found herself edging back.

Suddenly, the chanting stopped. One of the monks had thrown back his hood and had stepped up to the silver tray.

He raised his hands. "Mighty one!" he roared, his voice bouncing crazily around the chamber. "Take and receive this offering!"

In response, the other monks chanted a single sentence, in no language Red could name. It didn't even sound as though it had been designed with mouths in mind.

The first monk spoke again, his hands still raised. "Take these memories, these thoughts and souls, grey lilies harvested by we, the devoted! Seed of the Harbinger, hear us! Ia! Awaken, Mighty one! Feed, and rise to glory!"

At that, he reached down and pulled the grey cloth free of the tray.

Red couldn't see what it contained at first; it was a mounded, irregular mass, gleaming slickly in the green light, smeared with dark fluid and dripping greyish chunks over the lip of the tray and onto the deck.

Suddenly, she realised what it was she was looking at, and had to suppress a cry of disgust. Everything that had spilled from the skulls of those poor victims on the wheel, everything that had slopped down that horrible trough, was piled on the tray just a few metres from her.

For a few seconds Red wondered if she was going to be sick. Her nostrils were clogged with the fleshy reek of human brains.

The chanting had started up again. As if in answer, something under the floor moved.

Red had been on an ocean trip, once, in her previous life. On the way back to port it became apparent that the navigator, having enjoyed slightly too long a party with some of the passengers the night before, had mis-set the course. Before anyone could correct the mistake the ship had scraped twenty metres of hull plating free on a submerged rock. That feeling, of a huge and totally destructive object grinding past beneath her feet, was almost exactly what she felt now.

Something was coming up out of the shaft, between the translation drive and the deck.

At first she thought it was liquid, some pale oily stuff oozing up out of the green light and sliming towards the monks. But within a few beats of her hammering, panicked heart she saw that this was no liquid: a pulpy tendril was probing blindly across the deck, colourless and as thick as her forearm, heading for the tray. As she watched, she saw the slender tip of it caress the silver, then reach up to lick the surface of what it contained.

A thousand more tendrils boiled instantly up from the depths.

Red moaned in horror. A forest of lashing tentacles was erupting from the gap, some as thick as her waist, some as fine as hair, all wetly translucent and impossibly long. In seconds they had covered half the drive, coiling and squirming like decapitated snakes. They brushed at the panels, the coolant tubes, even the monks, but the full weight of their frenzy was centred on the tray.

Hundreds of the loathsome things were hammering at the mound of tissue, flicking chunks of grey in every direction. The larger tendrils were sucking the mass down. Red could see slicks of fluid and matter inside them, gulped down and out of sight by some awful peristalsis.

God help her, the things were feeding...

She jumped to her feet, levelled the blaster and began pumping shot after shot into the tentacles.

Plasma slammed into the mass. The tentacles detonated, dozens of them with each shot, blown to spray and fragments and superheated steam. In seconds her side of the drive chamber was an opaque fog of smoke and exploding tendril.

Half the monks were running for cover, others were belting towards her around the deck. A few were levelling blasters: Red dived back behind the hatch as return fire began howling out towards her. Plasma shots and frag-shells filled the hall, blowing the lockers to pieces. She was surrounded by clouds of burning foil.

It was chaos.

There were too many enemies, and every time she incinerated one mass of tentacles hundreds more billowed into view. She leaned around the hatch, blasted one monk in half as he ran towards her, took another one's head off with a glancing shot, then ducked back as a frag-shell screamed fragments off the hatch next to her head.

She wasn't going to be able to blast everything in the drive chamber that was trying to kill her, not before one of the shots coming back ripped her open. It was time to go.

The hall was a mess, a blazing ruin of shattered lockers and smoke. She bolted back towards the mag-car, using the mess as cover, keeping as low as she could. Shots ripped past her, but she managed to get up and into the car without having her spine punched out through her guts.

She scrambled through the car, hauled the far door open, and came face to face with another army of monks.

Of course the ones back in the chamber would have called for reinforcements. She just hadn't expected them to arrive so quickly.

They were on her in seconds, dragging her down from the car. She lashed out as best she could, crushing a skull here, ripping a jawbone away there, but there were too many of them. Then something cold and sharp slammed into the side of her neck.

Blackness flooded out from behind her eyes. Her last thought, before the world fell away entirely, was the hope that they would not wait until she woke up before they ripped the brain out of her head.

11. THE GATHERING STORM

Othniel was ten hours out of Shalem when the explosion occurred.

Antonia was on the bridge at the time. She was up on the command gallery, leaning on the rail, watching the bridge crew at their work beneath her. Two hundred men and women, seated behind vast banks of workstations, watching their boards or the massive holographic icons that hung in the smoky, incense-laden air. Fans whirled under the vaulted roof, and prayer-chants piped in through audio panels formed an edgy counterpoint to the chattering of the controls, the muted hum of conversation, the constant background hum of the jumpspace drives.

It was a wondrous sight. Antonia gloried in it. It made her feel strong.

Sub-captain Erastus was at the command board, in control of the ship during the superlight jump. Antonia had been at the rail for almost an hour, watching. She had relaxed into the rhythm of the ship.

Perhaps too relaxed. When the explosion went off she took almost a second to react.

The vibration was distant, but significant. The prayer-chants stuttered for a moment, and Antonia felt a ripple of concern sweep through the crew below. A killship was five kilometres high and massed a hundred thousand tonnes. A vibration you could feel through the deck meant that something very bad was happening.

Antonia straightened. "Hold steady!" she barked. "Sensor ops, report!"

"No hard returns," the operator replied. He tapped at his boards, bringing up a tactical schematic; a huge grid-marked globe sprang to life over their heads, wrought from threads of green light, a model of *Othniel* at its centre. It rotated wildly for a moment before settling. "Nothing from the sense-engines or precog units. We're alone out here."

"That's a bonus."

The tactical globe shrank to one side, while the *Othniel* model moved and grew to fill the space it had left. It turned sideways to Antonia, showing her the fishlike profile of the vessel; the hangar cut out in the prow, the drive arrays, the enormous dorsal and ventral spines.

Red spots were blinking at the ship's centre, just down from the hangars and slightly aft. Antonia cursed. "Maintain course. Throttle back ten factors. Looks like a damper's blown."

She turned away from the rail and headed for the exit gates. "Erastus, I need to see this. Keep me appraised."

"Thy will be done." Erastus bowed his head as she went past him.

Thankfully, only one of the dampers had failed, and when it had exploded most of the blast had been channelled out through the weakened hull plating on the starboard side. Some damage had been done to the decks above and below, but they were unoccupied. Omri hadn't had time to repressurise them.

Looking at the twisted wreckage, Antonia found herself breathing a sigh of relief. If the blast had funnelled through into any of the other dampers there could have been a cascade failure. *Othniel* would have had to drop out of jumpspace and limp home.

That would have crushed her. She needed to see Lavannos, and those who had killed Gaius, burn.

She found a grav-lift and headed up a hundred decks, to the communications vault.

The vault was a low, disc-shaped chamber, devoid of furniture or any overt decoration. Only a circular keypad on a stand and a glowing ring of holo-projectors in the concave floor marred its perfection: in all other respects the room was featureless.

Antonia could just have easily made her communiqués from the bridge, or the linker in her cabin, but there was something about the vault that helped her to think.

She went to the keypad and typed in a request. The air above the projectors filled with a hazy column of static. She waited for a minute, then another.

She was about to tap out her request again when Tech-Prime Omri appeared in the column. "My apologies, Het Admiral."

"Not a problem, tech-prime. I know how busy you are."

Omri's eye-lenses whirred. "These have been interesting days, admiral, but work has been progressing. Is there a problem?"

Antonia nodded. "We lost a damper. Aleph-twenty."

"Just the one?" Omri paused, and a ring of static darted through his image. "Give me a tactical readout."

"Of course." Antonia went to the keypad and began tapping through the available files: ship status data, internal scans, damage reports. She selected the relevant icons and touched "send".

Omri vanished. The column became a blur of images, blueprints and diagrams and sense-engine output, a chattering succession of light and colour that moved too fast for her to follow.

The images halted abruptly, and Omri's holographic form scanned back into view. "Your appraisal?" asked Antonia.

It would have taken her days to go through that amount of technical information. But then, she wasn't a tech-prime. "There is a continued weakness in the principal charge-capacitor array. Overheat in the ventilation ducts. Microfractures in seventeen vanes of the dorsal heat-sink. The un-pressurised decks above and below the blast dampened the explosive effects, but the mountings on three more dampers must be considered suspect. You were lucky."

Antonia didn't feel all that lucky. "Your recommendation?"

"Continue with your mission, Het Admiral. Then return to Shalem immediately, at a speed no greater than eighteen factors. And try not to antagonise anyone on the way home."

A speed of eighteen factors would get *Othniel* back in about a week. "I'll transfer the flag to *Despoiler* upon my return." She smiled. "Thank you, Omri. I needed your reassurance."

"It is my duty to serve, Het Admiral. I look forward to your return."

The holo-ring went dark. Antonia stayed where she was for the moment, pondering, tapping lightly at the edge of the keypad with a fingertip. She wondered, not for the first time, if she was doing the right thing.

She shook herself. Doubt wasn't something that had any place in the mind of an Iconoclast admiral.

Lavannos had enjoyed the ignorance of the Accord for too long. Something had been allowed to fester there, something that had taken the life of a great warrior and respected agent of the patriarch. Antonia, as admiral-commander of Shalem, had enough autonomy from high command to make punitive strikes on any world she considered a threat to the security of the Accord.

Besides, according to Major Ketta, Durham Red was on Lavannos. Yet another reason to scour the place.

Antonia turned to go. As she did so, the holo-ring sprang back into life.

She whirled. The image of a man had appeared there: tall and muscular, his lined face grimly handsome. Clad in black armour and white face-paint, his hair covered by a sensory skullcap.

Fleet Admiral Trophimus.

Antonia snapped to attention. "My lord!"

"At ease, admiral." Trophimus was Antonia's direct superior, lord of the battle-fortress Noamon and commander of the fleets of twenty entire temple-stations. He reported only to the patriarch himself. "How fortunate to find you here at such an hour."

Fortune, Antonia thought despairingly, had nothing to do with it. Trophimus had been trying to reach her for days, and with her reports still uncompleted she had been going to ever-greater lengths to avoid talking to him. He must have placed a priority order with the entire relay-station network, telling them to look out for signals to or from her crypt-key, and to piggyback a parasite signal onto any call she made. He'd simply taken over control of the vault as soon as her conversation with Omri had ended. "Indeed, my lord."

Trophimus steepled his fingers. "I'll come directly to the point, admiral. I know your time is precious." He raised an eyebrow. "Too precious to spend completing Curia's reports, in fact."

"About those–"

He waved a hand. "Don't concern yourself, Het. I've got an approval already written. Just get them to here at Noamon and I'll stamp them off." He smiled. "Believe me, I know what a bane paperwork can be."

Antonia felt as though a balloon, inflated behind her ribs for weeks, had just been popped. "Oh," was all she could manage.

"That's not the reason I called, Het Admiral." His smile faded. "I understand you are en route to Lavannos."

"That's correct."

"A punitive strike?"

Antonia nodded. "Yes, my lord. A threat to the Accord has been detected there, and the taint of evil. It must be eliminated before it can spread."

She decided, against all protocol, not to mention Durham Red for now.

"Hmm." Trophimus frowned. "This judgement is based on the reports of Major Gaius?"

The name, spoken by other lips, sent a blade through her. She stiffened slightly. "My lord, Gaius had been investigating rumours of a blood-cult on the fringes of the Accord for some weeks. He was convinced it was not connected to the Tenebrae, but was linked to some other, far older form of worship." She took a deep breath. "He believed that the cult might centre on the retreat-world of Lavannos, sacred moon of Mandus. It appears he was right."

"He was killed during his investigation."

"Yes, my lord. There is another agent on Lavannos, Major Ketta. Her report indicates that Gaius was butchered by the very cult he sought to expose."

"I see." Trophimus made an odd kind of grimace, as though he was wrestling with some internal dilemma. "I have had a request, Het Admiral. Archaeotech division would like a stay of execution on Lavannos."

"Archaeotech?"

"They also have heard rumours, apparently. Something about important pre-Bloodshed artefacts."

Antonia gaped. "Fleet admiral! We are discussing a dangerous cult here, the murder of an agent of the Accord! How can those imbeciles at Archaeotech even consider trying to stay my hand for the sake of some worthless trinkets?"

Trophimus spread his hands. "My thoughts exactly, Het Admiral. I don't expect for a minute that you will honour their request. I just wanted to make sure you knew about it."

Something in his tone gave Antonia pause. "Why?"

"Admiral, your methods polarise opinion in high command. There are those who consider you an innovative and honourable commander. Others hold a less charitable view."

That was no surprise. It was an open secret that Antonia was regarded as a dangerous throwback by several other admirals. "I see."

"I hope you do." He leaned forwards, and lowered his voice. "I beg you to tread carefully, admiral. There are things happening here, things I cannot discuss. Suffice to say that great changes will face us soon. Do not let yourself be overwhelmed by them, Huldah Antonia."

"I understand, fleet admiral. And thank you for your concern."

"The prompt completion of future reports would be nothing if not a help, Het Admiral." He winked at her and then vanished.

Antonia stared into the space he had left. "Goodbye, father," she whispered.

She got back to the bridge with only minutes to spare. *Othniel* was decelerating from superlight speed.

The holo projectors had been slaved to a forward tactical view: a massive panel of light hung in their air, filled with the raging fires of jumpspace. As Antonia reached the rail, *Othniel* returned to the universe.

There was a lurch. The jump-shaft vanished, the searing flare of it scanning away to either side as the killship emerged from the tunnel. The prayer-chants changed cadence immediately, becoming strident battle-hymns.

Mandus, the titan gas-giant that gave Lavannos shelter, grew to fill the panel, orange light washing down over the bridge.

A disc of pure black hung at its centre.

"Orientate all antimat batteries for ground-fire," Antonia snapped. "Launch daggerships, Alpha and Beta shoals. Make sure the hunger-guns are woken and active."

She turned to Erastus. "Sub-captain, keep that world in your sights. I want it razed on my command."

"Thy will be done, Het Admiral." He grinned wolfishly. "Just give the word, and I'll burn it apart for you."

"I look forward to that." She put her hand on his shoulder, glaring at the black disc of Lavannos. "In the meantime, have my landing craft made ready, with a platoon of shock-troopers on board. I have a few things to attend to on the surface."

Not long now, my love, she thought grimly.

Not long at all.

12. OPEN

Durham Red had thought that the worst place she could wake up would be on the wheel, chained to the spokes, head back with a pair of blades around her skull. She was wrong.

She was on her back, lying on something hard and smooth. It was cold. She was shivering uncontrollably, her limbs shaking with the chill, and there was a terrible pain in the side of her neck. Whatever the monks had injected her with had burned through the skin as it had taken her down.

There was a bright light above her. It glared through her closed eyelids, so painful that she had to put up a hand to her face. Moving the arm hurt quite a lot, but the pain began to fade as control returned to her.

When she caught up with the ones who had dosed her, she resolved, very bad things would happen to them.

She turned aside, away from the light, and opened her eyes. For a moment all she could see was white, and wondered if something had happened to her eyes, but gradually a few details began to resolve in the glare. A wall, a few metres away. A small table or trolley, with bright things gleaming on it. The edge of what she was lying on. Her own bare arm.

Red sat up, hard. She didn't have her clothes on any more.

The bastards had stripped her. She wore nothing except a shapeless gown of grubby white fabric, tied loosely at the neck. No wonder she'd been cold.

Very slowly, she swung her legs around and down.

She was on a long, smooth slab of metal, indented like a shallow sink. There was a rusted drain at one end of it, a stained, bundled towel at the other. Her head had been resting on that. She reached back to the back of her neck, and her fingers came away wet.

What in sneck's name was going on here?

She clambered down off the table and looked around. The light above her was from a bank of lumes, extending from the ceiling on an adjustable arm. The walls of the room were bare, the smooth white stone of the monastery, and the floor was cold tile under her feet. There was a rough wooden table against one wall, a closed door opposite.

The trolley by the table was covered in implements.

Red prodded them gingerly. There was a saw, scalpels and syringes, a heavy-bladed butcher knife. A long, jointed thing like the leg of an insect, a handle at one end, a vicious point at the other. Everything was grimy and stained with rust.

Red pulled the front of the gown forwards, looking down the neck-hole. She breathed a sigh of relief. Whatever loathsome operation had been scheduled for this room hadn't happened yet. Maybe she'd woken too early, but a squad of monks and surgeons could be trooping towards her at any minute, itching to open her up and see what made her tick.

Let them try. She picked up the butcher knife, taking a moment to wipe off the handle on her gown.

The door wasn't locked. She pushed it open and looked outside. There was no one in sight, just a white-walled corridor stretching away in either direction. Doors, just like the one she was clutching, were set into the walls every few metres and they were all closed.

She had to be in the accommodation block, at the eastern side of the monastery. It was the only place big enough to house this corridor. And there she had been, in her room on the floor above this, never knowing there was an operating theatre under her feet.

Dear God, she'd left Judas Harrow here.

She walked out into the corridor and closed the door behind her. Both ends of the passage disappeared around corners, quite some distance away. She began to pad silently along the tiled floor, the knife held blade downwards in her fist.

After a few metres she stopped and listened hard. She could have sworn she had heard something ahead of her, around the corner.

There it was again. The sound of something heavy being dragged along the floor.

She was too open here, too exposed. If they had guns she'd be a sitting duck, and all she had was a butcher knife. It wasn't even balanced for throwing, too heavy in the blade. If she lugged it at anyone she'd be lucky to stun them with the flat of it.

There was a door alongside her. She turned the handle and pulled it open, glancing inside to make sure it was safe.

And realised, in one awful instant, that safe wasn't a word she could apply here.

There was a man in the room. He was upright, leaning slightly forwards, bound by the arms and neck to a heavy wooden frame. He was naked, and his shaved head drooped forwards.

From throat to groin, he was open.

Red clapped a hand over her mouth. The man's ribcage gaped at her, the skin and flesh of his chest sliced and peeled back, fixed to the frame with rough metal nails. His ribs had been spread exquisitely, separated from the sternum and bent to clutch at the air like the petals of some monstrous flower. The organs they had once protected had been teased from their moorings to hang on an intricate collection of wire hooks.

Worst of all, he was still alive. His organs pulsed and throbbed. As Red stared, he lifted his heavy head to her.

He was trying to scream, but his mouth had been sewn shut.

Red slammed the door and backed away, her stomach churning. Was this what had been scheduled for her?

The dragging was getting closer.

She gritted her teeth and headed towards it. No matter if there was an army dragging a body along that corridor, she decided, she would rather face it with a rusty knife in her hand than open another one of these doors.

It was very close, now. The dragging was wet, laboured, mixed with a dull scraping. Hoarse, wheezing breath, and a sudden slapping sound. Two slaps, then a drag. A breath. And then the same, but closer.

There was nothing being dragged. Whatever it was, was dragging itself.

Red moved back from the corner. She couldn't look, couldn't see what that awful, tortured thing might be. She turned away.

The corridor was full of tendrils.

They were on her in seconds, billowing around her, slimy and corpse-cold. Before she could bring the knife up dozens of them were knotted around her arms, her legs. More wrapped around her head, forcing it back until her vertebrae cracked with the strain. She howled.

There was one tentacle bigger than the others, as thick as her arm. It levelled a viscous end at her, stayed waving, hovering, curled like a cobra ready to strike. Red tried to turn her head away, but the other tendrils held her tight, tearing her hair out by the roots. Fluid dripped from the big tentacle, sliming down her face.

Teeth erupted from its sides, saw-blades of pale bone, and it snapped forwards. Red felt it hammer into her mouth, past her jaw, the teeth ripping into her throat as it wormed its way down...

And screamed herself awake.

"It's this place," said Godolkin dully. "It makes you dream."

Red looked madly about, panting. There was no monastery around her, no tentacles. She had her clothes on, or what was left of them. She didn't have a knife in her hand.

The real situation, if indeed this *was* real, was not much better.

She was bound, chained, heavy cuffs clamped tight around her wrists, locked to what felt like a cold metal bar that was lying along her shoulders, behind her neck. It was forcing her head forwards, so she couldn't see much of what was around her, but what she could see was black Lavannos stone. Behind her was a wide pillar and it was to this that she – and Godolkin, at least – were tied.

Her ankles were cuffed to another bar, joined to the top one by a vertical beam. The bonds were very, very strong.

She rattled uselessly. "I guess you've tried to get out of this," she growled.

"I have."

"Bugger."

"My sentiments exactly," muttered Harrow, from some-where to her left.

Red twisted, trying to see him, but her head was too far forwards. "Jude? Are you okay?"

Harrow snorted. "Apart from being drugged, locked up in my room, then hauled out, beaten up and drugged again, I'm doing quite well, thank you."

"Godolkin?"

The Iconoclast shook his chains experimentally. "I have seen better times, Blasphemy, but I am unharmed. How-ever, I do feel the situation is unlikely to improve."

"That's right," Red grated. "Keep your chin up." She yanked her head around, working her shoulders under the bar until she could see a little more to her right. There wasn't much to see: just stone walls, a low, wide doorway, some candles. "Anyone know where we are?"

"You are very close to immortality, Durham Red."

She knew that voice. "Well, if it isn't the abbot of Earl Grey. Have you come to let us out?"

"I'm afraid not." He came through the doorway, stooping slightly to get through. "I hear you've been having bad dreams."

"No more than usual." She wondered if he would get close enough for her take a bite out of him, but a second later more monks began filing through, all of them carrying frag-carbines. Which put paid to that notion.

"Really? It sounded quite unusual to me." The abbot smiled warmly. "It's quite an honour, you know. He doesn't speak to everyone." .

Red blinked at him. "Who?"

"The Mighty One. The Mindfeeder. Him."

"Oh, I see! That brain-eating monster you've got in the drive chamber."

"In the drive chamber." The abbot seemed faintly amused at that. "Yes, my dear. Him."

"I didn't dream at all," said Harrow.

Godolkin had, thought Red, although she thought it probably wouldn't be a good idea to say it. "So, now me and tentacle-boy have had a chat, do I get to be a monk?"

The abbot raised his eyebrows and nodded to her. "Very perceptive. That is how we are usually chosen, yes. But I'm afraid in your case, that won't be possible. After all, I've gone to very great lengths to get you here, holy one."

"Abbot, it was I who called the Blasphemy to this world, not you."

The abbot sighed. "Godolkin, my old friend. You, with all your dreaming, would have made quite a good brother. Just not a very bright one." He walked around to face the Iconoclast, partly out of Red's limited view. "Getting her here has been something we've been working towards ever since the fall of Pyre. We couldn't find her, but we found you. On Cassita Secundus."

Godolkin made an exasperated hiss. "The pilgrim who recommended the retreat to me. He was one of yours."

"Of course he was. Actually, he was going to fill you full of drugs and have you shipped here, but you came so willingly of your own accord that he didn't have to bother. Once you were here, we knew you'd never be broken into revealing Durham Red's location, so it was a matter of getting you to call her." He was walking around the pillar, back towards Red. "I have a certain connection with him, you see. I can influence the dreams a little."

Red flailed a foot in the abbot's direction, but didn't even get close. "What about the cryo-tube, you snecker?"

"That, my dear, is called 'baiting the trap'." He rapped the wall with his knuckles. "This stuff flows like water if you get it hot enough."

"You planted the tube," said Godolkin quietly. It was probably starting to dawn on him how badly he'd been duped. "Everything else?"

"Everything else."

"The reliquary?"

"A store room."

"I have been a fool."

"Yes, yes you have. But console yourself, Matteus Godolkin. It took a very long time for you to fulfil your purpose. I had almost given up hope of you ever reaching out to her. The cryo-tube was my last chance."

"Where did you get it?" Red asked.

The abbot faced her. "Strangely enough, I do have a passing interest in archaeology. It's what I did before I came here. The tube was one of my prize finds."

"Pity you didn't find mine first. Then I'd have had your throat out, and saved everyone a lot of snecking trouble!"

"Temper temper..." The abbot gestured to two of the other monks. The men scurried out of Red's view and came back holding several long bars of the same metal she was chained to. She watched as they eased one bar through the one behind her ankles. She hadn't even realised that one was hollow.

Another bar slid behind her head. Once Godolkin and Harrow had been put through the same treatment, there was a heavy, metallic sound from deep inside the pillar. Red felt something unlock behind her, releasing the bars and frame from the pillar's surface.

The full weight of the construction was suddenly hanging off her shoulders. She groaned, and felt herself tipping back. Before she could fall, four monks had darted forwards and grabbed the ends of the long poles. In seconds they had hauled her up, carrying her between them.

With gravity no longer pulling her down, her head was able to tip back, which felt good for a moment. Then it hit her.

Her head could go back. Sneck, they were going to put her on the wheel.

"No! Get me off of this thing, you snecking bastards!" She flung herself about on the frame, or tried to, but the chains were so short she couldn't get any momentum. The monks staggered a little, then laughed among themselves and set their feet a little wider. Red felt herself being lifted into the air.

The abbot was going out through the doorway. The monks began to follow, taking Red with them. She could hear Godolkin and Harrow being carried the same way.

The doorway led into the wheel room.

Red was dragged up the side of the thing, between the spikes set into the rim, and over onto the spokes. The poles locked down into braces, fixing her firmly in place. Her head lolling back, she got an upside-down view of the abbot watching her. "You sick bastard!" she snarled. "Did you come up with this thing?"

"Oh no. This has been here ever since Saint Lavann. He saw it in a dream, I believe." He reached out of her view, and when he came back he was holding a set of the horrible, bladed tongs. "It's only fitting that I give this gift to you, Durham Red," he told her calmly. "It's your mind that will wake Him, you see. He's asleep right now, dead and dreaming, but when your thoughts join with all the others He has fed on, He'll wake up." He leaned towards her, and whispered. "You really are a lucky girl. Oh, the dreams you'll have!"

"I'll dream of kicking your arse all the way to hell, you scumbag," she hissed.

He smiled, and raised the tongs. "Yes, I'm sure you very probably will."

The monk next to him exploded.

The man had been hit with a plasma charge, set at full heat. His body fluids flashed into steam, blasting his body apart in a shower of blood and pulverised meat, painting the abbot crimson from head to foot and blowing him across the decking. Red heard the tongs fly from his hands.

The wheel room was suddenly bright with gunfire. Red twisted wildly, trying to see what was going on – she caught a glimpse of a massive form, clad in multiple layers of black armour, firing a huge weapon bolted over its right forearm. The weapon chugged and flashed and Red heard the unmistakable sound of staking pins slamming into flesh.

The staking pin was part of the sacred trinity of weapons used by Iconoclast warriors.

She had been on the receiving end of them before, back on Wodan. The staking pin was a needle-sharp metal bolt the size of a baby's arm. The burner cleansed the staked victim with holy fire and then the silver blade, unfolding like metal origami from its grip, would sever the neck. Stake, burn, behead; the traditional ways of killing a vampire.

Conveniently, they killed pretty much everything else, too.

The wheel room had become a battleground. Frag-shells were going everywhere, razor-sharp shrapnel screaming off the walls and the metal workings of the wheel itself. Red felt an impact and a sharp pain as a chunk of steel embedded itself into the vertical part of her frame, and realised just how close she had come to having her spine bisected.

Stakes were hammering out in return: Durham Red, her view still upside-down, saw a monk get hit by one and go flying back through the air, smacking into the axle and staying there, sagging around the gleaming end of the pin. Impaled.

The monks fought hard, but they were swiftly overwhelmed. From what Red had been able to gather, overwhelming numbers and superior firepower were what passed for tactics in Iconoclast warfare.

Within a minute or two it was all over. There were a couple of meaty impacts from somewhere below her – beheadings, she guessed – and then the room fell silent.

Red kept quite still, waiting.

Footsteps sounded below her. Two sets, one an easy, leisurely pace, the other an almost silent padding.

"This is the one." The voice was a woman's and not one that Red knew of. "Take him and bind him. He will spend a long time dying."

Couldn't happen to a nicer bloke, Red though to herself.

"Admiral?" That was Major Ketta. "Over here."

The heavier footsteps returned. "Well, what do we have here?" The first woman again. "Saint Scarlet of Durham, the heretic Matteus Godolkin, and a mutant. Ketta, what a nice present you've given me!"

"Gift-wrapped, too," said Ketta.

Admiral Huldah Antonia was a striking-looking woman. Red judged her to be in her mid-thirties, quite tall, very slender with a muted, almost boyish figure. Auburn hair swept back under a tall headdress. Clad entirely in black, body-hugging rubberised armour, her face painted white with a crimson stripe across her eyes.

Haughty and superior as hell, too. A typical Iconoclast officer.

The troopers had taken Red and the others down from the wheel, but had been careful not to unchain them. The abbot, still unconscious, had been cuffed securely.

A lot of the shocktroopers had their guns pointed directly at Durham Red. "Please," one of them said eventually, "let us burn her!"

"Hold your fire, soldiers." Antonia raised a hand and the troopers lowered their weapons. "Fear not, she'll burn soon

enough. But it needs to be public. Slaughtering her here
would be satisfying, but half the enemy wouldn't believe
she was dead, and the other half would celebrate her mar-
tyrdom. This needs to be done carefully and it needs to be
done properly."

"Whatever," Red muttered, glaring. "Better that than having my brain fed to a monster."

Antonia looked puzzled and glanced at Ketta, but the
agent could only shrug. "I see only one monster here," she
replied.

"In the drive chamber. It's what they were feeding the
brains to."

At that, she was interested to notice, Admiral Antonia
paled just slightly under her war paint. "I'll have that inves-
tigated, Blasphemy," she said quietly.

"Yeah, why don't you. In fact, why don't you go and
investigate it yourself? I'm sure he'd love to meet you!"

Antonia smiled. "Keep talking, Blasphemy. Every quip
from now on earns you another day in the Chapel of
Agony." She turned to her soldiers. "Carry the others out,
into the courtyard. Fit them with breath-masks too. We
don't want them dying before their time."

Shocktroopers hauled Harrow and Godolkin up, and carried them away, still bolted to their frames. Harrow lolled,
seemingly unconscious. Godolkin whispered to her as he
was dragged past. "Forgive me, Blasphemy..."

She wanted to answer him, but he was gone before she
could speak.

"I take it there's no point saying: 'You can have me if you
let them go,' is there?"

Antonia shook her head. "Not when I can have all of you,
no. Ketta?"

"Het Admiral?"

"Take the remaining shocktroopers and wait ten minutes
outside, then return." She slipped a long, slim knife from a
sheath at her wrist. "I wish to have a short conversation
with our guest."

Ketta looked unsure, but nodded. "Thy will be done."

Red watched the Iconoclasts file out. She eyed the knife. "Where are you going to stick that?"

"Back in here," said Antonia, and put the knife in its sheath again. "I'll not tell you why, Blasphemy, but you've done me some favours on this world. The soldiers must continue to believe you are the epitome of all evil. All I see is a mutant with long teeth."

"So?"

"So, I'm prepared to deal with you."

"Deal with me how? You're going to let us go?"

"No, I'm going to torture you to death live on galaxy-wide holofeed. Your friends will be executed too, but if you co-operate I'll make their ending a swift and painless one."

Red shifted uncomfortably in the frame. The piece of shrapnel was still digging into her back. "Aren't you committing some kind of terrible crime just by talking to me?"

The woman shrugged. "I'm not. I'm sticking a knife into you for fun, in all the places it won't show." She glanced quickly over her shoulder. "And anything you say to them will be deemed automatically untrue, oh princess of darkness and mother of lies."

Red sighed. "Okay, you've got me. What do you want?"

"I want you to tell me exactly what you mean by 'drive chamber'."

13. SCREAM

Antonia thought about using some of her shocktroopers to take the monastery room by room, but had decided there was no need. In a short while the entire surface of Lavannos would be molten anyway. No one would remain alive.

She had one more task to perform before she left this place forever. She needed to see the resting place of Major Gaius.

Durham Red and her companions were taken into the monastery's courtyard and held under guard there. They were given breath-masks and draped with thermocowls, although Godolkin had refused the latter. Some of the shocktroopers had balked at giving the Blasphemy and her heretic companions any form of succour at all, until Antonia had explained to them that freezing to death was actually quite a painless way to expire.

While that was being done, she had wandered out of the main gates and stood for a time, watching the great roils of cloud moving slowly across the face of Mandus.

Ketta joined her a few minutes later. She was wearing battle-armour brought in specially aboard the landing-craft, and breathing comfortably through its integral mask. "Het Admiral? The prisoners are secure."

"Thank you, Ketta."

"Some of the shocktroopers are still unsure about letting them live, even for a while. Some of them are, well…"

"Afraid?" Antonia shivered. "Nothing to be ashamed of there, Ketta. Believe me, I'd like nothing more than to put a blade through the neck of that bitch right now. But I saw what happened when she was resurrected. I was at Broteus when the Tenebrae came out of hiding, and as a result I've got two undamaged ships out of forty. If their saint dies in a simple execution, what then?"

"Can't we just kill and leave her here? The Tenebrae would never find out and she'd just pass into legend again."

"The idea of Saint Scarlet as legend terrifies me almost as much as she does in reality, Ketta." Antonia wandered a few paces away. "Rumours of her reappearance are already on the loose. She's too big, too dangerous. You almost don't dare kill her. You know something, major? I don't *know* what to do with the Blasphemy! The only thing I can do is to deliver her alive to the patriarch, and let him make the decision."

Ketta was silent for a long time. Then she said: "Admiral, may I speak freely?"

"Always, my friend."

"I believe you think more than any Iconoclast I have ever known."

Antonia smiled grimly. "I shall take that as a compliment, Ketta, even if it was not intended as such."

She leaned back. *Othniel* was poised in the sky above them, fifty kilometres up. It held steady, using braking thrusters to keep position between the pull from Mandus and the pitiful gravity of Lavannos. As she watched, flickers of light showed briefly around the vessel's prow. Another correction.

Swarms of daggerships, super-fast interceptors, darted around it.

"Everything you said about this place is true, Ketta. The things the Blasphemy told me. If I can give thanks for anything, it is that I do not have to stay here long enough to sleep." She turned back to the agent. "I am going to see Gaius. Will you walk with me?"

"If you wish. I'll arrange a guard."

Antonia nodded. "Make sure they keep their distance. We have things to discuss."

· · ·

When Antonia told Ketta about the origin of Lavannos, she almost fell into the Eye of God. "Admiral, that can't be!"

"It could just be a lie concocted by the Blasphemy for some foul purpose of her own, but I don't know. A faction within Archaeotech division tried to stay my hand while I was on my way here. Fleet-Admiral Trophimus told me himself."

"Your father?"

Antonia gave Ketta a look. "Please don't say that out loud again, major."

"Forgive me, Het Admiral. But how would Archaeotech know about this place?"

"I can't imagine." She thought about giving her the warning Trophimus had given her, but decided to keep it to herself for now. "But if this story about Earth's Moon is true, if ancient humans somehow were able to shift an entire world, no wonder those Archaeotech fools wanted me to hold fire."

She'd never been able to see much point in the Archaeotech division anyway. Many forms of technology had been lost in the Bloodshed, it was true, and perhaps some of them might have a use in the Iconoclasts' continued suppression of the Tenebrae. She had often wondered how many bridge crew she might need if a killship's systems could be run by the fabled artificial intellects of old. Four or five, probably, but where would the joy be in that? A war fought between machines would be no war at all. It was humans that mattered, not cold circuitry.

To the untutored eye it might seem that the Iconoclasts were a homogenous, united force, all striving towards the common goal, the greater good. To anyone who could see the broader picture, nothing could have been further from the truth. Every officer had his or her own agenda, every division and department their own vision of how things should be. If it wasn't for the holy patriarch, the whole unruly lot of them would dissolve into anarchy, of that Antonia was sure.

God forbid she ever saw such a day. "How far now?"

"Just ahead, Het Admiral. This next gully."

The steps were just as Ketta had described them. Antonia told the guards following them to take up position around the gully and wait until she returned or signalled for assistance.

Ketta went down the steps first, hugging the wall. Antonia followed close behind, staring down with some shock into the Eye and wishing she had brought a gravchute.

The steps were mercifully few. Before long they were into the tunnel, stooping to climb along it. Both their suits of armour contained integral flashlights, turning the gloom in the circular passageway as bright as day.

As they reached the end of the tunnel, Ketta paused. "Het Admiral, be warned. This place is... foul. It damaged my soul to be here, and I lost no one I was close to."

Antonia put out a hand and touched the agent's shoulder. "Your soul is in no danger, Major Ketta. Rest assured of that."

She stepped past her and down into the cavern.

Gaius lay to one side of the awful space. She crouched next to him, brushed the frost from his eyes. "My poor man," she whispered.

She would shed no tears for him, not in this frozen hell of a place. She would not dishonour him so – he was an agent of the Accord, who had died doing his holy duties. And, in so doing, had led her to Lavannos. A dangerous cult had been wiped out and the blasphemous Saint Scarlet, the walking disease whose very existence promised such ruin to humanity, had finally been brought to heel.

"You have done well, my love. So very well. No one could ask more of you." She stood. "Time to sleep." She walked back to the tunnel entrance. Ketta had stayed there, crouched just inside. "Thank you, major. We'll go back now."

"Are you not taking his body?"

Antonia shook her head. "I have something else in mind. I think he would have appreciated it."

It took them the same amount of time to return to the monastery as it had to walk to the cavern, but this way seemed far longer. The journey was conducted in silence. Neither woman felt much like talking.

When Antonia reached the monastery she took a moment to check the situation in the courtyard hadn't changed. Durham Red and her pet heretics were still under guard, thankfully, and everything seemed as it was.

She left Ketta in charge for a moment, then went back out through the gates and onto the Serpent Path. When she had walked far enough to get a good view of the Eye, she halted, and took the comm-linker from her belt. "Erastus?"

The screen lit up, an image of the sub-captain's grizzled face filling it. "Right here, Het Admiral. Your orders?"

"It is almost time, sub-captain. First, I'd like you to practise your precision bombardment techniques." She used the linker's keypad to type in a series of digits. "These are the coordinates of a subterranean cavern some ten metres below the surface. Be so kind as to vaporise it for me."

Erastus grinned. "Thy will be done." His image vanished.

The sub-captain probably thought Antonia had a cave full of prisoners she wanted executed in a hurry. Let him think what he wanted. There was no way she could have taken the frozen carcass of Major Gaius back with her, not with his skull the empty goblet it had now become. Cremation seemed an acceptable compromise. Besides, he'd always enjoyed fireworks.

She looked up at *Othniel* in time to see one of the forward batteries spit out a stream of antimat fire. Even through the thin atmosphere of Lavannos she heard it coming down, a dry ripping sound, like someone tearing old cloth.

The energy bolts struck the ground, right over the rim of the Eye. Instantly an area half a kilometre wide bulged upwards, flashed into fire, and blasted up and out in a vast fountain of pulverised rock. Under the awesome power of the shot the body of Gaius and every other unfortunate soul in the chamber would have vaporised in an instant of time too small to measure.

Raw energy was blowtorching out of the ground. Most of the debris cloud was still in the air. "Resquiat in pace," Antonia murmured.

A secondary explosion flared upwards, smaller but still awesomely violent. The wheel room, Antonia guessed, connected to the cavern by the drain tunnel. The pressure build-up must have taken it apart. As she watched, a great section of the rim of the Eye fractured away, a thousand tonnes of noisome black Lavannos stone carving off and sliding in a cloud of smoke and fragments down into the crater.

Antonia could imagine how much Erastus had enjoyed that. In a few minutes she'd let him have some more fun.

She headed back to the monastery to join the others. Ketta was at the gate, waiting for her. "That was good shooting."

"Wasn't it?"

"Admiral, some of the attendants tried to leave the monastery. They had to be dissuaded."

Antonia shrugged under her armour. "Pay them no heed, major. They are obviously tainted and cannot be allowed to leave this place. Besides, some of them might be monks in disguise. We can't take the risk."

"Of course. Shall I bring the landing craft in?"

Antonia's dropship was too big to set down anywhere but the landing field. Her assault against the Church of the Arch had begun from the air, with her and the shocktroopers entering the courtyard in grav-chutes. "I think it is time for that, yes. Tell the pilot to engage the landing spine on the way in so we can get the prisoners up the cargo ramp."

She went back into the courtyard. The prisoners, three still chained to their frames and the abbot cuffed in Iconoclast restraints, had been lined up against the west wall.

The abbot's hands were together as if in prayer, but not of
his own choice. The restraints had a third ring that went
around the neck, and the wrist-cuffs were held a certain distance away from it on a solid bar.

The shocktroopers were in formation opposite the prisoners, weapons raised and ready. "At ease," Antonia told
them. "Get ready to move the captives onto the landing
craft."

The abbot, she noted, had woken up. She wandered over
to him. "Hello," she said flatly. "I'm going to hurt you."

"You might think that," he replied. "But something's
going to happen."

He seemed perfectly calm, quite happy in fact. Antonia
had seen defiance before, but this was something else. This
was conviction.

"What do you think will happen, abbot?"

"Well," he said. "If an insect scratches you, you brush it
away, don't you? You might even swat it down..."

As he spoke, the ground moved.

It was slight; less than the vibration Antonia had felt on
Othniel's bridge, but it went on for longer. At first she
thought it might be a seismic quake, some shifting of the
ground caused by the cavern's demolition. But it was more
than that. Some vast object, deep beneath her feet, was
moving past her.

"Oh crap," said Durham Red.

Antonia grabbed the abbot by the shoulders. She was
suddenly very afraid. "What have you done?" she gasped.

He grinned. "Wait."

And horror was born from the ground.

There was no other way to describe it. It flooded up
around her, through her, a titan wave of raw mental
anguish. It hammered her down, and she tumbled to her
knees, clutching her head as though the pressure inside
would blast her apart. She was screaming, but she couldn't
hear herself, because something else was screaming too.

A scream that was tearing her mind apart.

Dimly, she could hear that everyone else was howling too. She lifted her head, the effort almost stopping her heart in her chest, and saw shocktroopers rolling on the tiles with their heads in their hands, Durham Red shrieking and Ketta curled in a foetal position and slamming her head repeatedly against a wall. Only the abbot had his mouth closed, and he was standing where he had been chained, his eyes rolled back in his head, face twisted in a fierce, insane joy.

It was all she could bear to see. The walls were rippling around her, the very air shaking. The scream was still ripping up around her, and it was getting worse. It was the deafening shriek of a million babes in arms, thrust into searing fires. It was the howl of a billion men as their brains were torn from their heads. It was the death scream, the birth scream, terror, pain, loss and mourning. It was unbearable.

It was gone.

As suddenly as it had begun, the scream was over. Antonia collapsed, as if a puppet with cut strings. She couldn't stop shaking.

Her throat was a column of pain. She'd been screaming so loudly that she'd torn it inside.

She panted, trying to get her breath back, to spit the taste of blood from her mouth. Some of the shocktroopers were still screaming, and the sound beat at her ears. She got to one knee, then hauled herself upright.

"What did you do?" she hissed.

The abbot had his head down, but he was glaring at her under his brows. His mouth was stretched in a wide, vulpine grin. There was blood oozing from between his teeth. "He wasn't even aiming at us," he laughed. "All we got was the edges of it. Don't you see, he's still not awake yet!"

She slapped him across the face, hard, but it didn't stop him laughing. Then she remembered what he had said before.

You might even swat it down...

She ran across the courtyard, and began searching the sky. When she saw *Othniel* she almost let out another scream of her own.

The flagship was tilting over.

Antonia pulled the comm-linker from her belt and flipped it on. "Sub-captain!"

The image on the screen was wavering, shot through with static. She heard what sounded like a riot in the background – instead of battle-hymns, the bridge echoed to a chorus of shrieks.

"Erastus! Sub-captain, come in!"

At that, he fell into view. He had his back to her, and he sounded as though he was sobbing. "I heard Him!" he howled.

"Iconoclast, pull yourself together!"

"I heard Him!" Erastus span around to face the pickup. His face was a mask of blood, gouts of it pouring down his cheeks like the tracks of vast tears. "I don't need to see! I can hear!"

The man had torn out his own eyes.

Antonia hurled the linker away, so hard that it hit the wall and shattered. Above her, *Othniel* was still tilting. Lights flickered over its hull, but these were not the staccato flares of manoeuvring thrusters. Those spots of brightness were centred on the weapons emplacements.

The hunger-guns were blowing themselves up.

She could hear them past the shrieks of the troopers and her own hoarse breathing; distant thumps, as the sentient weapons tore themselves apart. The daggership shoals were dissipating, ships spiralling out of control. She heard a lash of engines as one snapped past the monastery and into a nearby crater, followed by an explosion that sent fragments of metal and black glass whipping into the air.

Some of the daggerships were attacking *Othniel*. Antonia saw one, its drives flaring at maximum thrust, dart straight towards the killship's flank. It hit the weakened hull plating, where the dampers were.

The entire deck exploded.

The hull vomited a horizontal sheet of fire and debris, flames blasting out port and starboard, from prow to stern. It cut the ship in half. Just as the noise of that awful detonation reached Antonia, the decks above and below the dampers exploded too. And then the ones above and below those.

Every deck exploded in sequence, up and down, the entire ship consumed by a series of shattering blasts that filled the sky with metal. For a second she saw the framework of the dreadnought keep its shape, but it was nothing more than a blazing skeleton that broke apart a moment later, shedding vast plates of metal and ceramic, daggership hulls, corpses. *Othniel* came down like lightning falling from heaven, like a comet, a melting storm of steel and fire that plummeted down into the centre of the Eye of God and was gone.

Antonia slumped back against the wall. She could still hear daggerships thundering overhead, colliding in mid-air, crashing down into craters.

One of the shocktroopers wouldn't stop screaming.

Durham Red was twisting in her frame. It looked like she was having convulsions. Matteus Godolkin was sagging against his cuffs, the mutant Judas Harrow was trying to shake the mental scream from his head. Ketta was still curled in the corner, alive or dead, Antonia couldn't tell. Some of the shocktroopers were lying still in crumpled, ungainly heaps, some were up and trying to help their fallen colleagues. It was chaos.

There was the sound of a fusion engine, drawing closer; the landing craft. Antonia sagged in a kind of relief, and then heard a sudden report; a metallic shearing noise.

Saint Scarlet had snapped her frame in half.

Antonia dropped her hand to her pistol, but it was gone. She saw, as if in slow motion, the Blasphemy break free of one leg-cuff, the lower beam of the frame already broken, her hands still bound to a long T-shape that extended partway down her back. She was running towards Antonia, ignoring the fractured metal bar that was still cuffed to one ankle.

Above her, the landing craft slid sideways through the air and crashed into the roof of the monastery.

It was obviously out of control, the landing spine still raised, the wings part-extended. The sound of the drives had risen to a deafening whine, and Antonia felt the down-draft rip at her as the vessel hammered sideways into the church. Hugely armoured, it took off the entire upper storey without trying.

It was coming down right on top of Antonia.

There was nothing she could do, nowhere to run. The great slab-flat side of the craft was tilting down at her, bringing down a sea of masonry. The wall below it angled out, breaking up as it did so, falling in a storm of bricks and pipe work and white stone cladding down into the court-yard.

Durham Red hit her at a full run.

She didn't even try to move. They were both going to be pulped by the landing craft in moments – at least like this, she would take the Blasphemy with her.

The vampire hit her hard, bowling her over, swiping her sideways with the metal bar still chained to her arms. The impact was amazing, the pain sudden and incredible. She felt her left arm break, armour or no armour, and then she was rolling across the courtyard tiles.

Under the landing craft.

Its shadow covered her, enveloped her. The noise of the drives was absolutely deafening.

Then the craft, the wall, the upper floor of the monastery and all it contained, came down on top of her.

And everything went dark.

14. GOING UNDERGROUND

Not for the first time that day, Durham Red awoke in quite a lot of pain.

It took her a few seconds to work out where she was, and how she'd managed to get there. It was dark, for one thing, very dark indeed. She wasn't even quite sure which way was up.

The last thing she remembered was the courtyard.

She had been chained to the abbot's frame, stacked up like firewood and reeling from the after-effects of that awful psychic shriek. She'd seen Antonia, the Iconoclast admiral, across the courtyard and decided that her most dangerous enemy was right there. None of the other troopers had regained their wits, and even Major Ketta was out of it.

The admiral must have been hard as rocks to have been on her feet after that.

And then, against all hope, the metal frame had bent.

It was only the slightest movement, but Durham Red knew from past experience that once something bends, getting it to break is only a matter of strength and time. She remembered being up on the wheel, during the Iconoclast attack, the chunk of frag-shell shrapnel that had come so close to embedding itself in her vertebrae. It was still halfway through the vertical part of the frame, poking into her back. For a time, she'd thought of it as nothing more than yet another hardship. As if she didn't have enough to put up with.

A few good pulls, however, and that sharp little piece of metal had helped her snap the whole frame to pieces.

The bar above her shoulders was still intact, but the chain around her left ankle had failed at the same time as the lower bar sheared into two unequal parts. Suddenly, she could run. She had begun barrelling across the courtyard, hoping to take Antonia out first, then somehow get hold of a weapon and start blasting.

Okay, she thought, it wasn't much of a plan. But it was better than waiting around to be loaded onto an Iconoclast landing craft.

Red shifted in the dark and groaned. Oh God, the landing craft. It must have taken some of the same psionic pounding she had. It had come down right on top of her.

Why was she suddenly back at the wrong side of the courtyard? She couldn't remember. That was her trouble, she did things without thinking, sometimes. Her reactions tended to be faster than she was.

Abruptly, there was light. Red squinted against the glare, and turned her head away. All she could see around her was rubble.

Someone next to her coughed.

She looked back, past the source of the light. She wasn't alone.

Admiral Huldah Antonia was right next to her.

"Well," Red muttered, not long afterwards. "Looks like we're both pretty much snecked."

From what she could gather, she and Antonia had been under the monastery wall together when the landing craft had come down on top of them. The courtyard had collapsed under the impact. Half the monastery was lying on top of them.

The space they were in was actually quite large: above them was a hundred tonnes of assorted rubble, below and to the sides a mixture of courtyard tiles, masonry and black Lavannos stone. There had been a void under the tiles, far enough underground to have supported the courtyard for decades, but unable to withstand the massive force of the landing craft coming down on it. Red wondered if it would have given way as soon as the ship had put its landing spine down, sending them all into the pit.

"How far down do you think we are?"

Antonia shifted painfully, as much as she could. "Halfway to hell," she replied.

The Iconoclast was trapped, and in far worse shape than Red. Great chunks of stonework lay across one arm and one leg, pinning her down to the floor. The leg didn't look to be in too bad shape – the foot was still moving at the end of it – but the woman's arm was definitely broken.

Red had done that. The rubble was just adding to her woes.

Durham Red, for her own part, was able to get up and walk around, in the space she had. But the rest of the frame was still on her, the wide bar above her shoulders, forcing her head forward, the piece of lower bar dangling off her right leg.

She tried to roll her head around. Her neck was stiff as a board. "I feel like James Dean."

Antonia didn't venture what she felt like. A pancake, probably. Red began looking around for a suitably sturdy piece of masonry. She found a slab of marble that looked like it weighed about half a tonne, and began edging sideways towards it.

"What are you doing?"

Red glanced over at Antonia. "Gonna try and bust this frame." She nodded at the flashlight in the Iconoclast's armour. "How long's that going to last?"

"Weeks."

"Cool." She jammed the end of the frame into a gap under the marble, and heaved down. There was a crunch of stone and the gap gave way, pitching her over backwards. "Ow! Sneck!"

She got up, and tried again, making sure she was more solidly wedged this time. The metal bent fractionally behind her. "Oh yeah…"

Antonia was watching her intently. It was staring to get on her nerves. Eventually she rounded on the woman. "What the hell are you staring at?"

"At you."

"Well don't."

"Forgive me, Blasphemy. But here I am, trapped alone with the creature I have had nightmares about since I was a small child, the ultimate enemy of humankind. Can you blame my fascination?"

Red sagged against the frame. She'd used all her strength for the moment, and pulling down on the thing didn't seem to be having much more effect. She'd try pushing in a minute, when she had her breath back. "Look, admiral, I'm not anyone's ultimate enemy, okay? I just took a wrong turn."

"Shall I be more clear?" the woman scowled. "To the human race, which I am sworn to protect using any means necessary, you are a danger of unimaginable proportions. Don't you see, you yourself are completely unimportant! You are just a mutant, a woman out of time. But what you *represent*, that's where the danger lies. Saint Scarlet is a far more potent force than Durham Red can ever be." She twisted under the slabs, obviously in some pain. "That's why you must be destroyed, publicly humiliated. The Tenebrae have to be disabused of the notion that you are their Messiah."

"I've already told them that."

"And they didn't believe you," Antonia replied quickly. "They retreated back into the shadows for a time, but they will return, with your name on their lips as they slaughter billions. Durham Red, you were on Pyre. You have seen what they are capable of."

"Yeah, and I was on Wodan too! Guess what, you bastards are both as bad as each other!" She gave the bar an angry shake. "No, you know what? You Iconoclasts are worse! You don't see them stealing every scrap of food from mutant planets, letting whole populations starve!"

"Those are tithe worlds," Antonia snarled. "They were permitted to settle there on condition they redeploy ten per cent of their planetary output for the support of poorer worlds. That's what 'tithe' means – a tenth."

"Screw a tenth! You take it all!"

Antonia rolled her eyes. "Yes, Blasphemy, in a perfect universe there would be enough ships to take their tenth every standard year, but there aren't – mainly due to the actions of your Tenebrae friends. So we take everything once every ten years. If they had the wit to plan for it there wouldn't be a problem."

"Ah, sneck it!" Fury gave Red a sudden burst of strength. She heaved, planting her boots as hard as she could and forcing herself upwards. Her legs shook with strain, the marble slab shifted warningly, and then the metal gave way.

The upper bar exploded, fragments of it whining away and spinning off the rubble. Red found herself sprawling, her back singing with pain.

But she was free. She dropped her arms for the first time in hours. "Oh sneck, that feels good!" She collapsed backwards, landing hard on her rump, then slumped against the nearest wall. The cuffs around her wrists and one ankle remained, but she would deal with them later. Just for a minute or two, she wanted to luxuriate in not walking around as though crucified.

After a short time she sat up again. Antonia was still looking at her. "Face it, admiral. You hate mutants. I'm a mutant. We're never going to see straight on this."

"I hate the Tenebrae. Not every mutant is Tenebrae, just as not every human is Iconoclast." Antonia sagged back. "You are a woman of some honour, Durham Red. I have a request."

Red raised an eyebrow. "Oh yeah?"

"When you bleed me, take it all."

"Erm, look, that 'vampire bite' thing–"

"Is childish nonsense, I have no doubt. But everyone else must continue to believe it." Antonia closed her eyes. "Faith is a powerful weapon. There may come a time when it is the only thing humans have left."

"Well, until that day…" Red used a piece of the metal bar to stab down between the links of the ankle-chain, shattering it. "You're not getting off so lightly, admiral."

It took some effort to get Antonia out from under the rubble. Red probably could have shifted any one of the slabs on her own, but each one tended to be trapped under something else, forming an interlocking puzzle of weight and tension. If she levered the wrong one away, the entire roof might fall in, flattening the pair of them.

Eventually she used some of the metal frame to heave the largest slab up a few millimetres, enabling Antonia to get her leg free. The stone across the admiral's arm was smaller and loosened slightly by her actions on the one below. Red shifted that one much more easily, although she was careful to remove the knife from Antonia's wrist sheath before she did. "Sorry, Het Admiral. It's not that I don't trust, you. I just don't trust you."

"Do you honestly think I would be in any condition to take you on, Blasphemy?"

"No. But I think you might try anyway."

While Antonia attended to her injuries, Red began to explore the void. There was no way up through the roof of the cavern, that was for sure. It looked like they had fallen several metres at least, with most of the monastery filling in the gap. She wondered if anyone was left alive above ground. Whether, if there was, they had the slightest notion that Red and Antonia might have survived. "You've not got a comm-linker at all, have you?"

Antonia was modifying part of her armour, strapping her broken arm down across her chest. "I'm afraid mine broke."

Red started to probe some of the rubble. At one end of the cavern she had seen some shards of Lavannos stone that didn't look like they had come from the roof. "Toni? Come and check this out."

The Iconoclast glared at her sideways as she limped closer. "What have you found?"

She pointed to one of the shards. "If this had come from up there, it would be flat on both sides, yeah?"

"But that's curved on both sides. Do you think there were two voids here?"

Red nodded. "Yup. In fact, this planet's full of them. It's a sponge. We can't be too far from the one under the reliquary – if we can get there, we might be able to climb back out. Or into the drive complex."

They began pulling at the rubble. Antonia, despite only being able to work one-handed, was surprisingly strong. Within a few minutes they found a gap. "Bingo," Red grinned. "Shine me a light on that, admiral."

It wasn't big enough to climb through, not yet. Red had to lie on her back and kick chunks of it away. She kept half an eye on Antonia as she did, but the Iconoclast seemed to have little interest in attacking her. Maybe she was grateful not to have been bitten.

Abruptly, the gap widened. The rubble above it shifted, making a kind of stuttering groan. Dust sifted down. "Toni, go through. Now."

"Blasphemy–"

"Christ, just go through!" She grabbed the Iconoclast and flung her bodily through the hole. She heard the woman yelp, tumbling away, and then she scrambled into the gap behind her. There was a drop in front of her, a metre or two, and more rubble. She twisted to come down on her shoulder, brought her legs out of the hole and as she did so the entire wall of rubble shifted down half a metre.

Red stayed where she was for a moment or two, puffing. When she stood up, she almost fell over. The rubble wall had sheared off one of her boot heels.

She snapped off the other one. "Toni? How are you doing there?"

"Blasphemy, you have entombed us."

Antonia was standing a few metres away, illuminated by the glow of her own flashlight. She pointed upwards. "This void is intact. There is no way for us to leave this space."

"Oh ye of little faith," Red joined her. "Switch your light off."

"Why do you–"

"If you're going to question every single thing I ask you to do, we are going to be down here a really long snecking time! Now switch the pissing light off, okay?"

Antonia scowled, but in a second they were standing in darkness. "Wait," Red told her.

"There appears little else to do."

"All right, wait and shut up."

Red forced herself to relax, letting her pupils grow wide in the darkness. She remembered being down in the relic cavern, just before the abbot's fake wall had given way under her touch. If they were anywhere near part of the complex, there would be a–

"Light!" hissed Antonia. "Over there!"

The Iconoclast was right. A faint blue glow was issuing from one side of the void. "Thought so," said Durham Red, and kicked the wall hard.

It cracked. Antonia put her light back on, and together the two women subjected the stone to a torrent of vicious kicks. It gave way inside half a minute.

The admiral gave her a long stare. "How did you know?"

"We're at the right level. The complex has got to be big – what I saw of it must only have been a small part. I reckon we can't go too far under the church without hitting part of it."

"You were lucky."

"I often am."

The way into the complex wasn't easy. The gap Red had found was the fractured corner of some kind of under-floor duct, full of wiring and pipework. She had to squeeze into that, then crawl far enough until she found a panel that came up when she pushed it.

It took Antonia longer, with a broken arm, but after some effort the two women were standing in a wide, blue-lit corridor. "Have you seen this part before?"

Red scratched her head. "No, we went in the other direction. Not even sure if I could get to the ops room from here. Of course, that might not get us out; I think the reliquary got squashed."

"Then are we any better off than we were?"

"We will be if we can get some kind of communicator working." Red began stalking off down the corridor, towards the nearest turning. She heard Antonia limping after her. "I think this place was built about two hundred years after I went to sleep. That makes it advanced for me, but well in advance of you, too. The Bloodshed robbed you of all this."

"So if we see a communications device, will we recognise it?"

"I'll let you know if I see one." She stopped, and frowned. "Did you feel something?"

Antonia opened her mouth to speak, then closed it again with an audible snap as the entire corridor trembled around them. "That, you mean?"

Red looked back along the corridor, just in time to see the floor erupt.

The foam mesh exploded upwards, panels of it flying around the corridor as a mass of tendrils slammed up and into the air. In seconds they had slimed up the walls, over the ceiling, turning an entire section of corridor into a writhing, squealing forest of grey coils, as pale and wetly translucent as raw squid.

Tentacles lashed out towards Red and Antonia, boiling up through the floor.

Red jumped back, stamping down hard on a rope of slime that was slithering along the mesh towards her, feeling it burst sickeningly under her boot. Antonia was scrambling away from the awful mass, but her damaged leg was slowing her up. The first tendrils had already wrapped around her ankle, and were tugging her off balance. She toppled, howling.

There was no way Red could let her be swamped like that, even if she was an Iconoclast. She launched herself back to where Antonia lay and began slashing at the tendrils with the admiral's knife. They parted easily, like strings of mucous, but there were thousands more of them whipping towards her, reaching for her head.

Abruptly, the mass drew back. It retreated into itself sharply, like the eye of snail, dozens of individual tendrils, some as fine as wire, corkscrewing back on themselves. The centre of the mass, where the tendrils were thickest, seemed to solidify.

Forms vomited out of it, fluid and half-made, spilling out of the mass for mere seconds before being pulled back in and re-digested. Polyps of what looked like armoured brain tissue, thick, greyish tubes, veined and gut-like. Oddly-jointed limbs, identical to the chrome implement she had seen in her nightmare. Part of an eye.

Around them, the air rippled. Red saw it, just for a fraction of a second before a deafening shriek of raw fury blasted into her.

She span away into the floor, clutching her skull. The scream was like nails being driven into her head, a relentless, pounding wave of pure agony. She was crushed by it, torn apart by it. She had never felt such anger, such pain. It was splitting her mind.

And past the rage, past the pain, Durham Red felt something else. It brushed by her, like the whisker of a tiger touching her skin in the dark – the barest, most teasing glimpse of a vast and terrible awareness – and was gone.

As suddenly as it had started, the scream faded again. Red collapsed, rolling onto her back, seeing the tendrils sliding back and away, down the gaping hole they had made in the floor.

Antonia was curled up in a ball on the other side of the corridor.

Red rolled up and onto her feet. Her head was gonging. "It's waking up," she gasped. "Sneck, I felt it! It's waking up."

"It was looking at me," Antonia breathed into the wall.

"It was looking at everything…" That awareness, just for a fraction of a second, had been horribly focussed. Red had felt it like the naked stare of a billion eyes, looking everywhere at once and at the same time looking right at her. She reached down and helped the Iconoclast to her feet. "You okay?"

"I am. Blasphemy, we have to get away from this place. Call in the fleet and have them blast this moon to ash."

"Great plan, Toni, except that this thing took out your kill-ship just by snoring loudly." Red slid the knife into her belt. "I don't know about you, but I got the impression just now that it's hitting the 'stretching and scratching itself' stage. What do you think it'll be like when it wakes up completely?"

Antonia squared her shoulder. "You are right, Blasphemy. Congratulations: you have just been downgraded to the *second* greatest danger to humankind."

They moved more warily, now on edge for the slightest sign. A shiver in the air, a movement beneath the ground, anything.

"That last time I saw it," Red told Antonia," it was in the drive chamber. It must be moving around under the surface. Maybe busting through the voids to get about."

"That will make hunting it down difficult."

"Maybe. Or, we could bust open the abbot's head and use him as bait."

Antonia appeared to mull this over for a few moments. "Actually, I quite like the way you're thinking."

"Not much use until we can get some guns, though. It'll just yell us to death. Hello, what's this?"

The corridor ended in a large, circular chamber, heavily panelled, with a round seating area set into the centre. Five other tunnels stretched away from it, set equidistantly around the wall like the spokes of a wheel. "Grand Central," Red muttered.

"Blasphemy, these corridors are labelled." Antonia had found a plaque set into the wall, covered in crumbling paint. She brushed the flakes away with a gloved hand, revealing letters etched into the metal. "Accommodation?"

"I've got power and systems over here," Red replied, doing some brushing of her own.

Antonia moved to the next plaque along. "Operations."

"Ops? Thank sneck!" Red grinned. "That'll get us back into the monastery, when the time comes."

"Time? Blasphemy, the time for me to be off this ghastly little moon came several hours ago!"

"Came and went, admiral. Look, we've got to stop this bastard, right? Who knows what it'll do when it wakes up. Or who it'll fancy for breakfast." Red jerked a thumb back towards the first plaque she had uncovered. "If we can get the power up and running, we'll have the upper hand. Sensors, communications, maybe even weapons. We can call your people on the surface and get them to come down all guns blazing, cook the son of a bitch in its sleep!" She slapped her fist into her other hand. "But we've got to move fast."

Antonia took a deep breath, then nodded. "You are right. At the cost of my eternal soul, Durham Red, I agree with you."

"Souls," Red grinned. "Who needs 'em?"

The power core wasn't close. When Red forced the door open, they were confronted with another maglev track. "Nuts," she snarled.

She turned to the Iconoclast. "How's that leg of yours? Up to a run?"

"Honestly? No."

"I didn't think so." Red gnawed a fingernail for a few moments. "Okay, here's the plan. I'll take a jog down here.

You get to the ops room and wait for me to get the power up. Either it'll be easy or it'll be impossible, I'm not sure which yet. In either case, I'll join you there in a few minutes."

They parted company. Red sprinted away down the track. She always felt better when she had a plan, a path to follow. A purpose. Her purpose now was erasing this sleeping monster before it woke up and swallowed them all, if only to see the look on the abbot's face when she did.

Maybe it wasn't a very good plan. It did rely on doing some very tricky things, not least of which would be getting the power online.

As Red had told Antonia, there were two ways that would go. Either the power was down because someone had switched it off, in which case she might well be able to switch it right back on again. In her years as a professional bounty hunter she had taught herself to use thousands of machines, from computer systems and door locks to tanks and starships. More than once her life had depended on being able to get her hands on some technical device and making it work, there and then, with no time for fuss. After a while, it became almost second nature.

Not many of them had been from two centuries into her own future, of course.

There was a second reason the power might be off. It might be broken. In which case Red would hightail it back to the ops room and bug out. How she could do so without falling back into the clutches of the Iconoclasts would be something she'd work out later. There was no point making a plan too complicated, after all.

The mag-car was waiting at the end of the track, just as it had at the drive chamber. Red had to force the door open. It hadn't been oiled and kept unlocked by a troop of deranged monks like the one she had passed through before.

The second door was a little easier to wrench aside, and after that Red found herself in almost an exact copy of the locker-hall on the other side of the complex. The only immediate difference was in the big sign above the door, which this time told her she was entering the Tycho-Alpha Fusion Core. Even the radiation warning was the same.

Thankfully, the massive double hatch into the power core was open.

Red suddenly felt quite foolish. If the door had been closed, like the drive chamber hatch, she wouldn't have had any monks to open it for her. They much have used a portable power-supply to trigger the motors, but she didn't have one.

She stepped through.

The fusion core had been built on a similar scale to the drive chamber, although in a different configuration. The shape of it was more complex: a kind of truncated hexagonal pyramid, the walls studded with glass-fronted observation booths. The floor of the chamber stepped down in several wide levels, and in the centre was a vast cylinder of gleaming metal so tall it reached the ceiling.

A faceted torus halfway up the cylinder was the fusion core itself.

Red looked around. For a moment nothing gave her any clues, until she noticed that one of the booths – the largest – was still occupied. She could see the silhouette of a man's head and shoulders inside.

She ran across the floor of the chamber and climbed quickly up the mesh step that led to the booth. The door was locked from the inside, but it wasn't strong. Red kicked it open.

As she'd been expecting, the man in the booth had been there for a very long time indeed.

She moved the desiccated corpse aside, and laid it out on the floor. The skeleton's hands had still been on a set of control boards, the metal beneath them stained with dust and rot. Red brushed away a last couple of finger bones and studied the board.

Most of it was taken up with the same glass-panel control surfaces as everywhere else. Alongside that was a smaller panel, set with a couple of press-button switches and a small lever. A label next to the lever read "prime".

She snapped it down, and when the buttons lit up she pressed them, too.

There was a thump under the board, and a soft whine. The glass panel went black, then filled with diagrams, touch-sensitive controls, instructions, warnings.

It was all here. She could do it.

She got back to the ops room with a few minutes. She'd not had to run back down the maglev track, as the car had been working.

Antonia was still there waiting for her, surrounded by active display panels. The room seemed to have changed entirely since she'd last seen it. Then, it was a gloomy, blue-lighted boneyard. Now, with everything working, it seemed alive. "All right! Now we're cooking!"

The Iconoclast shook her head, dully. "Blasphemy, we are lost."

"You people give pessimism a bad name, you know that?" Then she caught a glimpse of the look on Antonia's face. "What is it?"

"The demon. The creature that inhabits this moon."

"What about it?" Red walked up to the admiral. "What have you found?"

"I ran a sensor sweep. The controls were... difficult. But usable." She pointed at the board in front of her.

The panel was showing a diagram, a cross-section of the Moon. For a moment Red couldn't work out what she was seeing, until she saw a small rectangular label on the display key. It was blinking bright, then dark, and written inside it were the words "Unknown Material".

According to the diagram, almost the entire mass of the moon was taken up by unknown material. Only a thin crust remained.

"It hasn't been moving beneath the surface," whispered Antonia. "It is *everywhere* beneath the surface."

Red stepped back, feeling a sick horror rising up inside her. It was under her feet, that nauseating mass of tendrils, just metres below, but stretching for thousands of kilometres down and in every direction.

It was gigantic. And it was hungry.

15. DUST-OFF

Out of thirty Iconoclast shocktroopers, two full squads, only seven remained. It had been eight, but although the other trooper had been alive, his mind was broken. He couldn't stop screaming, and his fellows had to hold his arms to prevent him ripping the eyes from his head.

Eventually Ketta took a pistol, set the charge low, and aimed it at the man's forehead. "Resquiat in pace," she said, and blew his head off.

The mission was a complete disaster, she thought, turning away as the shocktroopers let the spouting corpse drop. The flagship of the Shalem fleet was utterly destroyed, along with its full crew complement of over four thousand. Admiral Huldah Antonia was dead, crushed beneath hundreds of tonnes of masonry. There could be no hope of her survival: her armour was officer-class, built for mobility over protection. They had pulled a shocktrooper out from under that mess and the man had been pulped.

If there was any consolation, it was that Durham Red had died in the same way.

Her companions lived. They were still chained to the frames, although that situation couldn't continue. Ketta would have had the pair of them staked out like that for the whole journey back to Shalem, if she'd had her way, but the landing craft was no longer capable of taking cargo aboard. They'd have to be shipped back cuffed and under guard, like the insane abbot.

Ketta was wondering about the abbot. Now Antonia was dead, it might be better just to kill him where he stood. The mutant Harrow, too. Matteus Godolkin was a different matter, though. The Ordo Hereticus, the Iconoclast division that concerned itself with those turned by evil, were eager to get their paws on him.

The landing craft was still resting on top of the rubble-pile it had made of the monastery, surrounded by heat-haze as warm air spilled from the ruined building. The dropship was basically undamaged, its armour capable of withstanding far more punishment than a few tonnes of bricks and mortar could dish out, but the landing spine had been partway down during the crash, and had suffered a fatal torsion. Engineer-helots were working around the vessel now, trying to free parts of it before the ship tried to lift off again. She had warned them, quite rightly, that the dropship was their only chance of getting off Lavannos. If the story of *Othniel*'s fate broke before they were away, any further Iconoclast involvement would have the planet melted while they were still on it. Just to be sure.

Even if she did get off alive, Ketta would have to undergo decontamination, both physical and mental. She wondered if she would survive it.

She took a comm-linker from its pouch and flipped it on. "Pilot?"

"Still here, Het Major." The dropship pilot wore heavy biodressings on his left shoulder and the side of his face. He hadn't been too affected by the psychic scream, but his co-pilot had gone insane and attacked him with her bare teeth. He had been shooting the madwoman dead when the landing craft had hit the monastery.

"Have you run the systems checks I asked for?"

"They are just completing now, Het." She saw him studying his readouts. "All primary systems are online. Once enough of the rubble is clear of the intakes, I can be away."

"What about the landing spine?"

The pilot shook his head. "I'm sorry, major. The gyros are down. I can hover, just, but if I try to set down there's a better than even chance of shattering the primary bearing." He turned aside to touch a control, then came back into view. "Which, according to the internal sense-engine, has a status of 'Moribund'."

"Acknowledged. Do what you can."

"Thy will be done."

Would it? wondered Ketta. Her will would be to get off Lavannos in the next minute, fly home to Shalem and spend some time not being afraid any more. She wasn't used to fear, it wasn't an emotion she usually had any truck with. But this place, and whatever alien nightmare the abbot and his monks had been growing, had her chilled to the very bone.

She hoped, when she was finally away, that she would be able to sleep again, and not relive the mind-tearing horror of that scream.

The heretic Godolkin was looking at her. She walked towards him.

It was a pity he had been enslaved by the Blasphemy. He had, by all accounts, been a most exceptional shocktrooper, rising to the rank of Iconoclast First-Class by battlefield prowess alone. He must have seen vast amounts of conflict – his skin, beneath the charm-tattoos, was a mass of scar tissue. His body was powerfully muscled, his face imperious and his unmodified eye a deep blue.

He was, Ketta decided, quite attractive. If you liked that kind of thing.

"Iconoclast-First Class Matteus Godolkin," she said, as she approached. "Surely you must have known your heresy would catch up with you sooner or later."

"Always." His voice was a deep growl. There was a trace of accent to it. She wondered what world he had once called home. Whether or not he remembered it.

She couldn't remember hers.

He looked broken, hanging there on his chains. Ketta found that, despite everything she had vowed, everything she believed, she couldn't hate this man.

He had been bested in combat by a being so lethal that Ketta herself had almost died fighting it. Enslaved by a supernatural power beyond his control. When he had finally escaped her he had come here, to this place, in search of peace. Instead, he had found a living nightmare.

Now, after all these months, the Blasphemy was no more. Godolkin was utterly free of her, only to be taken prisoner by his own people.

It was a horrible irony. Godolkin had never, and would never, be free. He was a slave from start to finish.

"Godolkin," she began. "In a short while the dropship will be flight-capable again. We cannot get you and your companion aboard while you are chained to these frames because the landing spine has been damaged. So we will need to free you."

"And your point is?"

"My point, Het Godolkin, is that if you or your mutant friend try anything funny, I'll have you both staked through the legs. The landing craft has no light-drive, as you well know. We might get picked up on the way back to Shalem, or we might not. Six weeks is a long time to spend with staking pins through your thigh-bones."

Godolkin raised his head. She heard the metal frame creaking. "And do you think that you will be able to get away in time, agent? You felt the second psychic attack as strongly as I did. You know the Mindfeeder is waking up. Do you wish to be in the air when the next attack comes?"

"And where would *you* rather be?" she snorted. "This creature is nothing more than an alien with psionic powers. If it's been given a taste for human brains by these fools, that only makes it all the more pitiful. We'll get away from here whether it's awake or not, and then return with enough firepower to turn this moon molten again. Deal with it like the Accord has dealt with every other alien species." She put her face quite close to his. "Goodbye Mindfeeder. Goodbye Saint Scarlet."

"And goodbye Admiral Antonia, it would seem," said Judas Harrow brightly.

That stung. Ketta had lost more than one friend on this forsaken rock. "Have a care, mutant. You might well be staying. I've not made up my mind yet."

"Hmm, a choice between being murdered here, or being taken back to Shalem for public execution. I'm afraid I don't see much benefit in either, Het."

"Depends on the state I leave you in. I might simply stake you to a wall and leave you to starve. Or fall prey to the monster when it awakes. Tell me, Judas Harrow, do you think it will get hungry enough to open your skull on its own, if there is no one to do the job for it?" She turned away, abruptly tired of browbeating prisoners. It wasn't worthy of her.

Sickened at herself, she stalked away to check on the dropship again.

Within a few minutes, the pilot called Ketta on the comm and told her that he was ready to try taking off. "I'd get everyone into a safe area, Het Major. If there is one. This could go badly wrong."

"Please try to assure it doesn't, pilot. For all our sakes."

She had two of the shocktroopers burn through the chains holding Godolkin and Harrow to their frames, while the rest covered them. One false move, and the heretics would have been crippled by bolter fire. Luckily for them, they had decided to go quietly. Her threats must have been enough.

Little of the courtyard remained and Ketta had seen the way it collapsed. She decided to get everyone outside, through the main gates and onto the Serpent Path. She'd told the pilot to extend the landing spine as much as possible and remain hovering with it close to the ground: a difficult piece of flight work, but one that she hoped he'd be capable of.

The alternative was to climb into the ship while it was on the ground, and be inside it while it took off. Personally, Major Ketta would rather have had a chance to run if things started to go awry.

She led the group out; a couple of shocktroopers behind her, then the three prisoners, and the other four troopers at the rear. As soon as they were all out of the gate, she signalled the pilot.

The fusion drives kicked in with a throaty whine. Power fed through dampers into the grav-lift system, and the landing craft shifted on its bed of debris. Ketta heard masonry sliding back down into the courtyard, slamming into the dropship's armour

She found she was holding her breath.

The craft came up, over the top of the wall. She saw it slide sideways through the air as the port wing scraped down over the rubble pile, then it righted. The grav-lifters were kicking bits of stone and plaster everywhere.

The ship turned in the air and edged out of the courtyard. Ketta almost felt like cheering.

Next to her, one of the shocktroopers made a peculiar sound, as though he had started to say something and then cut it off. She glanced at him, ready to rebuke the man for giving in to emotion, and saw that half his head was missing. He toppled.

A shot whined past her, another clipped her shoulder armour, sending her stumbling. "We're under attack!"

The shots were coming from the monastery. "It's the attendants," one of the troopers snapped. "They have weapons."

"Really! You think?" Ketta hauled out her plasma carbine and began firing back through the gate. She shot an attendant in the head, splashing him apart from the neck up, and blew another's guts three metres past his backbone. "Return fire! You two, cover the prisoners! Stake them if they move!"

Attendants, wild with fear, were scrambling out into the courtyard. From what Ketta could see, only a couple of them had weapons, slender gauss-rifles, but they were making good use of them. Another shot hissed past her head.

What had they been doing with guns in a holy retreat?

The landing craft was above her, blocking out the orange glow of Mandus. She could feel the shivering weight of the grav-field as it came down.

She glanced back. The dropship's landing-spine was down, leaving the upper part of the ship looking eviscerated. Most of its bulk was in the huge box-like ark at the end of the spine – retracted, this was the belly of the dropship.

The ark was down, held horizontal, hatches gaping. The pilot was holding the ship as steady as he could, but the loss of the landing gyros was making things difficult. The vessel was wavering up and down by a metre or more, the ark occasionally bouncing down off the ground. No way she could have had the heretics loaded into that.

"Fall back! In twos, covering fire from burners!"

Two of the troopers stood shoulder to shoulder at the gate and opened up with their incinerators. Twin streams of fire erupted back into the courtyard, washing it with flame. Attendants, caught in the blast, shrieked as the burners cooked the flesh off their bones.

Ketta stood next to the ark. Two troopers went in, jumping aboard and racing to the back, covering the doorway. Godolkin and Harrow were next. "Get in!" Ketta snapped. "Or you'll die where you stand – your choice!"

They each stood with their hands clasped as if in prayer, locked together and to their necks with Iconoclast binders. For a moment it looked like the mutant was going to make a break for it, but Godolkin stilled him with a glare. A heartbeat later, they were on.

Shots were still ringing past the ark. The burners hadn't entirely scoured the monastery. Ketta ordered the remaining Iconoclasts into the dropship and scrambled aboard last. She slapped the emergency linker, set just inside the hatch, with the heel of her hand. "Go!"

The ark rose in a tortured whine of motors, the ship wallowing. Ketta closed the hatch, seeing the foamy surface of

Lavannos falling away. It was one of the nicest things she had ever seen.

There was a series of metallic clatters as the ark locked into position, turning the landing craft into one solid shape again. A hatch slid open, connecting it to the cockpit, and Ketta stuck her head through. "Pilot, get us out of here."

"I am trying, major."

Ketta almost panicked. "Try harder!"

The ship pitched wildly sideways.

The drives were screaming. Ketta rolled out of the hatch and fell uncontrollably across the ark, slamming heavily into the port wall. Her head connected sharply with the metal, and lights danced in her eyes. Towards the back of the ark, shouting erupted.

Godolkin was free of his cuffs.

Ketta groped for her carbine. She saw the heretic slam the head of one of her troopers into the wall, shattering his skull, and in an instant Godolkin had the weapon off his arm. Staking pins slammed out in a chattering stream, catching two more troopers and hammering them across the ark. Two others were already unconscious from the fall. The last one had Godolkin in his sights.

The wing of the dropship hit the ground. The craft slewed wildly around, flinging the trooper off his feet. With the holy weapon covering his right arm and the bulk of his armour hampering his left, there was no way he could stop himself from falling back across the ark. A staking pin found his throat before he hit the far wall.

Godolkin was racing across the pitching, heaving deck towards her.

She tried to pick the carbine up, but he was too fast, slapping it from her hand. He raised the bolter.

It flared. Pain flooded Ketta's entire left side. She screamed, her fingers clawing at the staking pin that had appeared in her shoulder, fixing her solidly to the deck.

He aimed the bolter at her face. "The restraint key."

"Go to hell!"

"I've just left there. Do you wish to return with me?"

"She's dead, Godolkin! Give it up!"

"I still feel her teeth in me, major. She lives. Now, one last time – the key."

Ketta writhed around the pain. "Curse you, heretic! On my belt, crypt-code 'holy fool'."

"Apt." Godolkin took the key and tapped in its code. The broken remains of one cuff fell off his wrist. A few seconds later Judas Harrow ran past him, thermocowl flapping around his knees, stopping to scoop up Ketta's carbine.

The mutant darted to the hatch, poked the carbine inside. "Pilot, I suggest you lower this box."

She heard the pilot call out to her. "Major? Shall I–"

"Yes! Drop the cursed thing. If they want to go, let them go!" Her vision was wavering. Blood was slicking around her injured shoulder. Her altered biochemistry had stopped her bleeding to death, but she was still critically injured.

The ark began to descend. Ketta slumped back, holding the end of the pin. Godolkin and Harrow were at the hatch. As soon as it opened, they jumped free.

"Major?" That was the pilot again, over the internal linker. "Your orders?"

"Raise the ark," she coughed. "Then take us up. And try not to crash this time."

There was a sudden movement at the back of the ark. Ketta twisted herself up to see. The abbot was on his feet, stuffing something into his mouth past the breath-mask. As he saw her, he began to run towards the hatch.

"Not you too," Ketta snarled. She grabbed the end of the staking pin and, with an agonised strength, tore it free of the deck and her own flesh.

The abbot was standing at the hatch rim. The landing craft had bounced up on its faltering drives, and the drop was too much for him. Ketta drew her good arm back, and flipped the staking pin into his back.

It took him in the spine, dead centre, pinning his robe to his flesh. He stumbled back, turned halfway around, and fell on his face. His hands scrabbled weakly at the deck.

"Pilot," she grated. "Immediate dust-off. Get us in the air now!"

The ark began to rise again. The ship tilted forwards and Ketta saw the abbot trying to crawl towards her. He reached out imploringly, but by doing so took one hand from the deck and loosened his grip. He started to slide out of the hatch, leaving a track of blood on the deck as he did so. "Help me," he shrieked.

"Help yourself."

Just before the hatch doors met, he was gone.

Ketta felt the ark lock into place. There was a groan behind her as one of the surviving, but stunned shock-troopers started to come round. "Pilot?"

"Yes, Het Major?"

"It's all gone really wrong. In a minute, one of the troopers will ask you for a medical kit. Please let him know where it is."

"Thy will be done, major. Are you all right?"

"Not really." She flopped back on the deck, quite hard. "I think I'm going to pass out now."

She was right.

16. CEREBROPHAGE

Godolkin still had the holy weapon. It was huge, a flattened egg of metal that enveloped his right arm to the elbow, the forward end a gaping mass of barrels and sensors. It must have been heavy; as far as Harrow knew it would normally link into Iconoclast armour, with power-assist units helping bear the weight. Godolkin was carrying it one-handed as though it was a pistol.

He looked up. The landing craft was wavering away, more steady than it had been, but still unable to gain much height. "Will they make it?"

"They might." Godolkin had aimed the weapon at the craft for a while, but had obviously decided to hold fire. The bolter was a fairly short-range piece anyway. "Even in this low gravity, they will have to make several orbits before leaving the atmosphere."

Harrow understood enough about starship operations to know that the dropship's pilot couldn't engage the main drives while there was any more than a wisp of air in the tubes. He'd blow the engines apart if he tried. "Just as long as they don't try strafing *Hunter* as they go past."

"Something tells me they might have other things on their minds." Godolkin strode past him, moving easily in the light gravity, towards a crumpled mass of robes a short distance away. They had both seen the abbot fall, from what would have been a fatal distance on any normal-sized world. Even on Lavannos, he had built up quite a speed before impact.

Harrow followed the Iconoclast. The abbot, he saw with some surprise, was still alive.

The man was twisted horribly on the cold ground, his shattered legs facing almost completely in the wrong direction. He must have been in little pain from his injuries, though. Harrow could see that a staking pin had parted his spine.

Under his breath-mask the man's mouth was full of blood and greyish fragments. Some kind of dried food, like a fungus. There was more in his fist; Harrow reached down and parted the man's fingers, took a slice of what he had been eating from him, and almost sniffed it before he remembered his own mask.

It was thin, and flat, and oddly wrinkled around one edge. Harrow frowned, holding it up to the light.

And dropped it with a cry of horror. The abbot, it would seem, had not been giving everything he collected to the Mindfeeder.

The abbot chuckled weakly. "It isn't to everyone's taste," he whispered. "Even crumbled in tea, it affects different people in different ways."

Godolkin was grimacing. "You fed me that foul brew?"

"It helped the dreams."

The Iconoclast put the barrel of the holy weapon very close to the abbot's face. "Say your prayers, monster."

"Go ahead, Matteus. Pull your trigger." The man grinned, bubbles of blood soaking up between his teeth. "He'll be awake soon. Hungry. He couldn't live here, not properly, not be awake in our reality, the stars weren't right. But we kept him ticking over, five hundred years of sacrifice."

"Did you think he'd be grateful?"

"Oh yes, Iconoclast, as grateful as a man is to the bacteria in his gut…" He coughed, spattering the inside of the mask with blood and fragments of dried brain. "So go ahead and shoot. And then await his glories!"

Godolkin reached down and picked the abbot up by the front of his robes. The man gave a weak cry of pain. "If you think that I would desecrate a staking pin in your flesh, abbot, you are sadly mistaken."

And with one hand, he hurled the man through the air.

Harrow saw the abbot fly past him, in a high arc, slam back onto the ground and bounce towards a crater. He clawed at the stone for a moment, but it was too smooth. He slid down into the depths without a cry.

Godolkin was already striding away.

Harrow ran to catch up, the thermocowl flapping. "What did he mean? About the stars?"

"Old legends, Harrow. Nothing that you'd be wise to think about." The Iconoclast stopped and turned to Harrow. "We must return to the monastery. The Blasphemy is there, trapped beneath."

"I agree. We'll find her together."

"No, Judas Harrow, we will not." Godolkin glowered at him. "I will locate Durham Red. You will return to the ship and await my signal."

"Why me?"

"Because it's your ship."

"Oh. Of course..." *Hunter* was still slaved to his crypt-key. It would need his bio-signs, or those of Durham Red, to lift off. "It's a long way."

"The dead shocktroopers have integral grav-chutes still attached to their armour. I will adapt one for you."

They set off, towards the broken, burning shape of the Church of the Arch.

17. HELL AND BACK

Red still couldn't believe how big the Mindfeeder was.

She'd been imagining something the size of *Crimson Hunter*; massive, but not unthinkable. She'd encountered some pretty large creatures in her time, and most bio-viable planets had at least a history of megafauna. Antonia had made a mistake, she thought at first; the woman must have been looking at the wrong diagram or brought up an erroneous file. But the more data she'd collected from the ops room's systems, the more certain she had become.

This animal was almost the entire size of the Moon.

No. Animal was the wrong word. She had felt much more than mindless hunger when the thing's scream of awareness had hit her. This Mindfeeder, as the abbot had called it, was an intelligence of unimaginable proportions.

If it ever truly awoke, the universe would be in very serious trouble indeed.

"Toni? You still with me over there?"

"In body, Blasphemy." Antonia had taken her helmet off. Her hair, freed of constraint, was shoulder-length and auburn. Her arm was strapped immobile over her chest, splinted by the armour's internal medical systems, and her leg looked as though it was still giving her a lot of trouble. She was, however, a picture of furious concentration, hunting through the ops room's files for something, anything that would give them an edge.

Red would have liked an edge, but at the moment she would have settled for a clue. She trotted over to Antonia's workstation. "Anything?"

In reply, the Iconoclast brought up another lunar cross-section. "This is a real-time scan. The builders of this complex had the entire Moon wired for study – if nothing else, we can track whatever the creature is doing, at all times." She pointed, tapping the glass. "It's moving."

The perimeter of the mass, a few kilometres below the surface, was in constant motion. It writhed and billowed. "Nasty," said Red. "Makes me feel seasick."

"My sentiments entirely." Antonia turned the chair round to face her. "Durham Red, we both know this entity must not be allowed to awaken. The psionic weaponry it uses might not be constrained by distance."

"Don't tell me you've seen thing kind of thing before!"

"Not entirely. But there have been powerful mutants, psychers, able to kill at enormous distances." She raised an eyebrow. "And none of them were the size of a minor planet."

"Point taken. And believe me, I want to see this thing fry as much as you do. But we don't even have a blaster between us."

Antonia turned back to the workstation. "Elementary military tactics, Blasphemy. When faced with overwhelming odds, fall back and observe. Information is power."

"Yeah? When faced with overwhelming odds I normally go in with all guns blazing and kill them all."

"We don't have any guns."

"True."

It was Red who found the video files.

She had been working on the map table. Most of the controls in the ops room were extremely self-explanatory. Two hundred years of technical progress had, it seemed, finally taught software designers that vast amounts of surface complexity were not the best direction to head in. The active, constantly self-modifying panels were a help too, as they quite often simply moved irrelevant controls away. Red still found quite a lot of dead ends, but she made far more headway than she had been expecting.

Antonia, used to the baroque technologies of the Accord, was having more trouble. "These systems are a nightmare. They do not respond to any sensible protocols."

"Just press things."

Red had found a library of data files. She was scanning through them, awed at how many there were. "You know, I'm starting to get a feel for this place."

"Meaning?"

"Well, look." Red gestured at the screen. "This thing is chock-full of sensory data. I mean, real minutiae. Seismic readouts to ten decimal places, microwave monitors, lidar, graviton detection... Who the hell would need all this stuff? Two hundred and twenty thousand measurements of the distance between two gold plates a metre away from each other." She gave the side of the table a slight kick. "It's a metre, guys! Move on!"

"Blasphemy..."

"Oh, right. What I mean is, this place is just one big laboratory. They didn't just move the Moon, they had sensors and computers and scientists set up to record absolutely everything that happened when they did it."

"A test bed," breathed Antonia.

Red grinned at her. "Bonus points! If you wanted to move something really important, like the *Earth*, say..."

"You would test out the theories on something expendable first."

The Moon. These people had thought the Moon expendable.

The Earth must have been proofed against its loss. Possessing the satellite did far more than simply give the world tides. Red was no geologist, but she knew that simply removing the Moon would have dire consequences for the Earth's crust.

She blinked. The file tree she was scanning through had modified, and she'd been so lost in thought that she had missed it. She scrolled back. "Hello..."

"What have you found?"

"Videos, I think. Hope it's not someone's collection of porn."

Antonia had risen from her workstation and was trotting down the ramp. "Of what?"

"Never mind." Red found a file and brought it up. "Holy crap."

A rectangle of black had appeared on the panel, filled with crisp white text. *Tycho-Alpha Translation Centre – Synchro Test. 11.00AM EST 20-02-2395.*

"Twenty-three ninety-five," Red breathed. "We were right – more than two centuries after I went into the tube…"

The black rectangle vanished, replaced by a camera-view of the ops room. Dozens of graphs and readouts lit up at the edges, jumping and fluctuating in constant motion.

The ops room was full of people. Every workstation was occupied.

A man appeared on the screen, dark-skinned, young. His hair had been dyed vivid silver and he was wearing a slender piece of technology on one side of his face, a combination data-monocle and microphone. "TA synch test one," he intoned. "Initiating primary sensor array Delta-Tango eleven. Modifying for feedback. Recording. Initiating primary–"

"Dullsville." Red hit the fast-forward. The scene blurred.

"A thousand years," Antonia whispered. "That man lived and died a thousand years ago."

"Mmm." Red had to admit she was impressed. The recording must have been stored in a crystal matrix to have lasted so long intact. But then again, if the complex had been designed to test the translation of the entire Moon, and bring back the gigabytes of sensory data needed to make sure the same process was safe for Earth, they would have built it to last.

They would have built it to withstand anything. Even time.

The recording ended. Red cursed and scanned back a few stops, until the man's face reappeared.

"Synch-test in T-minus five," he told the screen. "Four, all baffles holding. Generator online. Datalink confirmed. Two. One. Mark."

Red held her breath. She could hear Antonia doing the same.

The man smiled broadly. "That's a wrap, people! Good job!"

Antonia gaped. "That's it?"

"Good data coming in from all the other centres: Mare Marginis, Robertson, Kulik all giving good returns…"

Red stopped the video. "Other centres?"

Antonia raced back up to her workstation, as fast as she could with a dodgy leg. "So that's what it meant."

"What meant?"

"Mentions of those areas." Her fingers blurred over the panel. Apparently she'd gotten the hang of it. A wire frame globe drew itself onto the big screen above her workstation, studded itself with craters and became a hazy, translucent image of the moon as it had once been. Red looked up at it, and felt a surge of homesickness.

Smaller spheres appeared on the screen, under the Moon's surface. There were four of them, arranged in a rough cross, on a tilted equatorial line. Tycho, Robertson, Mare Marginis, and Kulik.

Four translation drives, each with their own research complex. Tycho-Alpha was only one-quarter of the system.

"Once again," said Antonia quietly, "we have been seeing only one small part of the greater whole."

Red was about to agree, and probably to swear, when the floor under her feet shifted. "Oh sneck, not again…" She grabbed hold of the map table and held on.

It was under the floor, close under, just beneath the mesh. She could see the way the ancient foam bulged very slightly upwards, emitting small puffs of blue dust. Bucket seats swivelled on their bearings. A skeleton sagged slightly, and toppled onto the floor.

Red watched its skull roll past her and come to a halt against a ramp. She was waiting for the scream.

It never came. The feeling of motion went away. She let out a long breath and sagged slightly against the table.

Antonia had her real-time map up again. "Blasphemy," she hissed, as though unwilling to raise her voice. She pointed at the screen.

A loop of unknown material was sliding away from beneath Tycho-Alpha, unravelling as it did so. More loops were showing around the circumference of the mass, odd-looking prominences rolling lazily under the crust.

"It's stretching," said Durham Red. "Not long now."

There was one more video she wanted to see. The last one.

It was a long file, the biggest one in the list. She scanned down to it and brought it up on the map-table screen.

Antonia had joined her again. "I don't know what this will achieve."

"I just need to see it. What happened."

"What does it matter?"

Red snarled. "It matters to me, okay? Now shut up for a minute and let me watch!"

The text on the rectangle read "25-12-2396". They'd moved the Moon on Christmas Day. Red thought that was quite typical, actually. From Boxing Day 2396 onwards, lovers would no longer have anything silvery to meet under.

The ops room, when it reappeared, was less crowded than it had been before. The dark-skinned man was still there, however, with a slightly more attenuated version of the monocle-microphone at the side of his head. They had been updating the whole time.

His hair was golden, now.

There was a lot of preparation and counting down. Red forwarded through most of that. "Come on, come on, cut to the chase."

"Sequence begins. Final translation in T-minus five. Datalink confirmed. Optimus programme is go. Two. One. Mark."

The screen dissolved into static. "Sneck," Red yelled, slamming her fist into it.

"Wait," Antonia told her.

As if in reply, the screen cleared again. The ops room was in a state of controlled panic. "Control, come in," the man was calling, pressing the headset into his ear. "Control?" He leaned back, yelling over his shoulder: "Does anyone know where the hell we are?"

"No returns! Negative telemetry!"

"Sir, surface temperature is rising, fast. One hundred fifteen, one-twenty, one-thirty…"

"Holy shit, have you seen what's out there?"

There was an incredible, awful sound, and the picture tilted wildly. That was when the screams started. The picture returned to static very soon after that and stayed that way for a long time.

The only reason the file was so big was that there had been no one to switch the recording off.

"I've got a ship waiting," Red told Antonia. "On the landing field, about forty kilometres from here. If Harrow's alive, he'll be there. If he isn't, well…"

"We detected no ship," said the Iconoclast.

"You're not supposed to. He'd had some modifications made."

Antonia smiled grimly. "I'll pass the knowledge on. It will prove useful. In the meantime, what's your plan?"

"The key to this is the Optimus programme. I reckon it's the system that links all the drives together, gets them to fire all at once. If we can find that and activate it, the drives should charge, fire, and send this place back where it belongs."

"Which is?"

Red tapped the screen. "You heard those poor bastards. Somewhere hot. Admiral, think about this: the Moon vanished a thousand years ago. Saint Lavann saw it reappear, glowing red, five hundred years ago. So where do you think it was in the meantime?"

"In hell." The Iconoclast nodded to herself. "Five centuries in hell. While this thing grew like a cancer in its bowels."

"I think this orbit was where it was supposed to go – it's too stable to be a coincidence. They must have set the programme up way in advance, to send the Moon somewhere far away, but safe, around a big landmark. A gas-giant. But it didn't go here at first. It stayed in transition, for five hundred years, then finally completed the journey."

"You're guessing."

"Got any better ideas?"

"At present, no."

"Great." Red began adjusting her clothing, ripping away the tattered remains of the bodice, her remaining glove. She took her broken boots off. "Your job is to stay here and get the Optimus programme running. You've worked starship ops all your life. It shouldn't be too much different from a light-drive jump."

"You are insane!" Antonia's eyes had gone wide. "A thousand year old computer programme, on unfamiliar hardware, to trigger four wormhole generators simultaneously? Oh, and with a suitable time delay so you can retire to your vessel! Have I missed any–"

The ops room shuddered. Dust drifted down from the ceiling and three lumes above their heads cracked and went out.

"Yeah," said Durham Red. "Getting it done before this place gets eaten for lunch, and us with it."

Antonia gave her the sour eye. "And where will you be, oh great tactician?"

"In the drive chamber. I've got to make sure those mad monks weren't screwing around with the translation drive while they were feeding their new god."

Antonia watched the Blasphemy disappear through the far door, into the maglev car and away.

She snarled a private curse and turned back to her work-station. There were a thousand things that could go wrong with the vampire's plan. The drives could very well be damaged – if not the one at Tycho-Alpha, then one of the others. The Optimus programme might be unusable, encoded, deleted. It might require a simple access code to operate, which Antonia could never know. The fusion core might not have the power to charge the drives fully, or the other translation centres might not have their cores up and running.

A thousand things. It was insane.

Luckily, Antonia had a few more aces up her armoured sleeve.

The mutant was right about one thing – operating the Tycho-Alpha systems was not light-years away from operating a starship. After all, they were both devices for transporting vast amounts of material from one place to another. Technology could, in certain circumstances, evolve and converge.

Not only that, but when the Blasphemy had switched the power back on, the ops room had returned to the same state it had been in when everything had been turned off. Many of the workstation programmes and applications had been in use when the madman in the fusion core had shut the power down, and had sprung back into life mid-command. Antonia, while pretending to be having a hard time learning how the ops room worked, had actually learned some very intriguing things.

How the communications worked, for example.

She set her station to search for all references to the Optimus programme, then switched seats. The comms system in the base was a distant relative of the ones used in Iconoclast starships. After all, it had been her own people, albeit a thousand years dead, who had moved the Moon in the first place. Further development had been largely halted by the Bloodshed. All things considered, they were far more similar than she could ever let the Blasphemy know.

It wasn't easy to reprogramme the frequency-swapping systems of Tycho-Alpha's comms to hunt down an Icono-clast crypt-key, but she managed it.

The maglev car got Red to the drive chamber in just a few seconds, but there was a hairy moment along the way. The service door she had seen before had been blasted free of its moorings and lay on the conductive track, along with a fair amount of rubble. When the car passed over that, it bucked wildly, and Red had visions of it being slung com-pletely off the track by the electromagnetic imbalance.

It didn't quite come to that. When the base had been new and fully operational there probably would have been some kind of inertial damping system to prevent such a wild ride, even if there was a slab of steel on the track. In these troubled times, it was up to the shape of the car itself, and the way it fitted neatly between its braces, to keep it stable.

It did make Red a little wary of coming back the same way, however. She began wondering if there was a way Antonia could switch off the power on the track and let her run back. Then she returned to her senses. This was an Iconoclast she was thinking about. The two might have been working towards a common goal for the moment, but Red was certain that Antonia would try to double-cross or kill her as soon as the opportunity arose.

It was important that she didn't let herself forget that. She tried to keep an image of Wodan, in flames from core to crust, fixed firmly in her mind.

She wondered what had happened to the service door and then realised that it was from there that the monks had emerged to surprise her in the drive chamber. It must have been their way out of the wheel room. Not only that, but the Iconoclast assault on that very place had been con-ducted through there. When Antonia had ordered the corpse-cavern incinerated, the back-blast had sent the armoured door clear out of its frame.

Over five centuries, the monks of Saint Lavann had woven their structures in and out of this lost base. The whole thing was a temple to the Mindfeeder.

She left the car and trotted down the steps into the locker hall. The hatch was closed, but this time the power was on. The control pad opened it without fuss.

Red wondered what she would see past the doors, but there was no sign of any tendrils yet. She edged forwards.

The chamber was as she remembered it, with the vast black globe of the translation drive suspended above its shaft. Greenish light still spilled up from the gap around it. She went to a comm-panel set into the wall. "Toni? Do you read me?"

"I can hear you, Blasphemy. Are you in the chamber?"

"Yeah." No thanks to you, she thought, blowing doors off willy-nilly. "It all looks good from here. I'll start a detailed check now. How's the geek-work going?"

"I believe I have the Optimus programme online."

"Way to go, Toni! I take back everything I ever said about Iconoclasts being stupid, and that's quite a lot. Is there a delay set in so we can scoot?"

There was a pause. Antonia visiting all kinds of curses on her, no doubt. "It seems that a delay will be part of the process by necessity."

Red was able to walk away from the panel and still converse with Antonia as though the woman was standing next to her. Advanced stuff. "How do you mean?"

"Blasphemy, the drives are very nearly autonomous. Once the Optimus programme is activated the drives charge up, each from their own fusion core. To prevent slight changes in the rate of charge causing an imbalance, each drive-sphere contains its own capacitor array. The power does not need to be connected after the charge is complete – each drive will hold a charge for some minutes, until Optimus considers them balanced, and triggers translation by quantum-inseparability link."

"So we can wind them up and let them go?" She grinned. "Brutal."

The gap between the deck and the sphere bothered her. She kept wondering when the tendrils were going to come swarming out if it. This time, with no monks present, she was able to walk up to the edge and peer down into the shaft. "Sneck," she gasped.

"What is it?"

The shaft was empty of tendrils, but impossibly deep. It stretched down away from her, straight and true, for kilometres, set with panels and cables and the glass tubes that were giving off that sickly green light. "It goes down forever..."

"Beneath the sphere? I believe that is a wave-guide."

Red was thinking about how long the tendrils were.

There was an indicator panel set into one side of the sphere, and one of the braces had been widened into a deck to reach it. Red found herself trotting over a plank of metal no more than a half-metre across, set over an endless drop. "A rail or something would have been nice, fellas."

She reached the panel and began running a series of checks. Her studies on the map table had shown her what to look for. "Capacitors at zero per cent, everything else is looking nominal..."

"How much longer?" Antonia sounded oddly impatient.

"Christ, not much!" Red ran through a second series of checks, this time an internal sensor sweep to look for microfractures. Any imperfections in the shell of the drive, and the translation would be aborted. Red had feared time and the continued eruptions of the Mindfeeder's tentacles might have damaged the casing, but the scan came up within acceptable limits. "Okay, I think that's it."

"You wish me to activate the programme?"

There was something in her voice Red didn't like at all. "Yes, admiral. Run it and let's get out of here. Send the bastard back to hell."

"With pleasure, Durham Red."

There was a distant booming sound. The lights in the chamber dimmed, then returned to full brightness, and when Red looked back at the display panel it showed the drive's capacitors, and those of the other three spheres, climbing up from zero. Five per cent, she saw. Six.

"Okay, time to go." She turned away from the drive.

The entire chamber vibrated. From far, far below her came an awful noise, a squealing, grinding bellow. The bridge quivered under her bare feet, and she had to grab at the sphere to avoid being pitched into the shaft.

There was something moving at the bottom of it. A speck, but growing. "Aw crap... Antonia? I think we woke it up!"

There was no answer. Red got her balance and ran off the bridge, back to the comm panel. It was active. "Antonia!"

"Goodbye, Durham Red."

"What?"

"The task is done. The Mindfeeder will return to the dimension that spawned it, taking you along for the ride. You are not the only one with a ship waiting, Blasphemy."

"Antonia! You treacherous bitch!"

"I believe it says that on my warrant-chip, yes." The admiral sighed audibly. "My soul is already forfeit for working at your side, Blasphemy. So, before you say it, you will very likely see me in hell."

The signal died. Antonia had cut the connection from her end.

Red swore explosively and ran through the hatch. The mag-car was disappearing into the distance. She saw it go past the fallen door in a sheet of sparks.

The walls of the maglev track exploded inwards in a dozen places. Tendrils foamed out, hissing and squealing, sparking and drawing back whenever they touched the conductive floor.

She was trapped. And the drive kept on charging.

18. JUMP

"That's it," Durham Red muttered darkly. "Note to self: never, ever trust an Iconoclast."

The maglev track was a seething, swarming mass of tendrils. They didn't like the floor – hardly surprising with thousands of volts singing through it – but they had erupted through the walls and ceiling of the tunnel in more places than Red could count. Shards of panelling had clattered down from the places where they had broken in and lay sparking on the track. Small fires had started, filling the tunnel with grey smoke.

For an effective vision of hell, it was as good as Red wanted to see right now. Unfortunately, with the translation drive charging busily behind her, she was likely to get a better one very soon.

She ran back to the sphere and peered over the edge of the deck. The moving speck below her was closer now, almost close enough to define.

There was a new noise from the tunnel. A malevolent squealing. Red dodged around the sphere to see what it was.

Some of the tendrils had started to solidify again.

This time, they were not doing so randomly. A column of them a few metres down the track had twisted together, forming a mush of raw protoplasm. From this, spidery limbs began spewing out, shaped like the claw-implement from her dream, but expanded and multiplied to carry a vast, razor-tipped horror of armour and sinew and drooling, swivelling eyes.

There was still no real shape to the thing – it was a tangle of squid-grey flesh and translucent bone – but it had already separated from the mass and was climbing quickly away from the tendrils that had given it birth. Its limbs were hammering into the walls of the maglev tunnel as it dragged itself towards her.

The Mindfeeder was awake, and it had detected a foreign body in its system. It was building antibodies.

Red hit the hatch control. The armoured doors began to grind together, too slowly. Two armoured legs, rife with staring eyes, pawed through before they could close, and began straining against the hatch motors.

Snarling, Red leaped towards them, ducking under a swipe that would have taken her head off had it connected. She still had Antonia's knife, stuffed into the back of her belt. She whipped it out and slapped it into the nearest eye.

It popped messily over her hand and the creature screeched in pain. Red felt that screech in her mind, a smaller version of the Mindfeeder's psychic howls. She ignored it, gritted her teeth, and began stabbing at as many eyes as she could reach.

The legs drew back, suddenly, like a hermit crab snapping back into its shell. The doors slammed closed.

For a moment, Red was left in silence. When she listened carefully, however, she could hear the tearing sound of that nameless monster clawing its way up the wave-guide to get her.

Whatever that thing was, it was huge.

The creature in the tunnel was beating mindlessly at the door. The entire drive-chamber rattled with every blow, and chunks of ceiling hissed down, bouncing and shattering on the deck.

Red scrambled back to the sphere and over the bridge. The panel was still showing the capacitor charge level. Eighty-two per cent on each drive.

She began tapping at the controls, horribly aware of the thing clambering up beneath her feet, trying to find a way of shutting the drive down. "Abort, you bastard. I don't want to go! Abort!"

The screen changed. For a moment Red wondered if she might have succeeded, until she read the text flashing there.

The Optimus programme had lost contact with the Kulik translation drive, and was trying to shut down the jump. There were system errors springing up all over the panel, warnings of data invasion, attack by outside agencies. Unknown material in the wiring conduits.

The Kulik drive was still charging, despite the Optimus programme's shutdown call.

Red stepped back from the panel. Suddenly, she knew what was going on. What had been going on since the beginning.

The Mindfeeder was taking control of the translation drives. That was what it had spent five hundred years trying to do, after the first jump from Earth orbit had deposited the Moon into whatever hellish dimension it called home. The inhabitants of the complexes had gone insane from its presence, killed each other or themselves. One had retained enough sanity to try and thwart the Mindfeeder by shutting down the Tycho fusion core.

It had worked, for a while. Until the creature had built up enough of its own power to make the rest of the jump to Mandus.

And now it was going to do it again. It had tendrils in all the cables, all the ducts, every part of every base. Now it was awake, and it had full control of the drives. The Optimus programme was out of the loop.

The Mindfeeder was going hunting.

There was a deafening scream of tearing metal and shattering ceramic. Red ran back to the deck and saw that the hatch doors had been forced out of their frame at one corner. Armoured legs the size of girders were forcing their way through.

She hefted the knife. "All right then, you ugly snecker. Let's go…"

There was a whooping roar from outside the hatch. Red felt the deck shake, saw jets of flame billow through the gap. The armoured limbs went suddenly limp and toppled into the chamber, severed and burning.

More explosions sounded out in the maglev track. This is it, thought Red. The base is exploding. I'm a dead girl.

She hoped the blast, when the fusion core went up, would hurt the Mindfeeder.

The hatches started to open.

One wasn't going to move at all, wrenched half out of the frame, and the other was sparking and jetting smoke from its motors. It ground shavings of metal from its runners for about two metres, then stopped. Red raised the knife and belted around the deck towards the opening.

Matteus Godolkin was in the tunnel.

He was clad in full Iconoclast shocktrooper armour, heavy goggles covering his eyes, the integral breath-mask obscuring his mouth and nose. But Red couldn't have mistaken him for anyone.

His boots were planted solidly in the middle of the track, sending up fountains of sparks. He had a holy weapon on his right arm, some kind of vast particle cannon in his left. Staking pins and cleansing fire were sizzling down the tunnel, ripping tendrils and armoured spider-legs to shreds. As Red watched, open-mouthed, a protoplasmic mass dropped from the ceiling, vomiting legs and claws. The particle cannon flared out a piercing thread of violet light, and the mass detonated, sending shards of grey bone and gouts of fluid everywhere.

The Iconoclast turned away from the carnage, and ran in through the open hatch. "Do you require assistance, mistress?"

Red shrugged. "If you've not got anything better to do..."

"I have not." He whipped around, amazingly fast in the bulky armour, and stitched a line of staking pins into a tentacle, stapling it to the hatch. "There are more of those nightmares than you can imagine out there, mistress. I suggest we leave immediately."

"Sounds good to me, but how? Through that?"

"No," he replied flatly, and pointed at the roof. "Through *that*. Harrow?"

"I hear you, Godolkin, but I'll need a marker." Harrow's voice sounded over Godolkin's integral comm. He sounded charged up and ready to go. Red grinned. Just like old times – fire, smoke and monsters everywhere, and two men who should have been the universe's worst enemies standing shoulder to shoulder, covering her sexy rump.

Godolkin raised the particle cannon and squeezed the trigger. Red looked up, and saw the violet thread boiling up through the ceiling. She remembered what the abbot had said: This stuff runs like water if you get it hot enough…

A massive metal foot exploded down from the roof.

Godolkin grabbed Red and swung her around, protecting her body with his own armoured bulk. Tonnes of black Lavannos rock were raining down from the ceiling, crashing off the deck, shattering as they hit the sphere and spinning away in knife-sharp shards.

The foot crunched down through the hole it had made and slammed down onto the deck. Landing treads folded out from it, flower-like, and a door opened in the flat forward end.

Crimson Hunter's landing spine.

Red jumped up, onto the steps and through the hatch, Godolkin right behind her. "Take her up," he snapped curtly.

The spine began to rise, the foot coming off the deck. Red felt the temperature start to drop, the icy cold of Lavannos chilling her. "Guys, wait. Harrow, hold your position."

The ship halted, bobbing. Red turned to Godolkin and took the cannon from him. "You mind?"

Fifty metres below her, through a jagged-edged hole in the surface of Lavannos, dozens of armoured limbs bigger than the landing spine were scraping up past the sphere.

Red held the cannon to her shoulder, aimed up on the bridge and tugged the trigger back. The gun shuddered against her shoulder and grew warm.

The bridge sheared through. Steam and sparks spurted out of the severed cables.

"Tough luck, you bastard," she snarled, taking out the opposite brace. "You're not going anywhere."

She only had to cut through one more brace. The sphere was massively heavy. It tilted violently, then ripped its way free.

Spider-limbs, severed by the edge of it, crashed onto the deck. Red saw the sphere drop away, vanishing down the wave-guide. "Okay, let's skedaddle. Something's going to happen and I don't know what."

Below *Crimson Hunter*, the surface of Lavannos was seething with greyish monstrosities of every size and con-figuration. Watching it, even through viewscreens on the bridge, made Red's skin crawl. "Tendrils were all it could manage while it was asleep," she said thickly. "That's what it wanted to be. A snecking hive."

The ship was still rising on its grav-lifters. Harrow was strapped into the control throne, hands white-knuckle tight on the controls. "Sacred rubies," he hissed. "What a night-mare."

"It might get worse," said Godolkin. "If the Mindfeeder gains control of the translation drives and appears in an inhabited system."

"I don't think so," Red replied quietly. "I severed the con-nections between it and the Tycho drive. Control will revert back to the Optimus programme, through a quantum link. So it will either abort the jump, or–"

A star of the purest, perfect white, had appeared on the surface of Lavannos.

"Oh shit!" Red slapped the back of Harrow's throne. "Pedal to the metal! Now!"

"We're not out of the atmosphere–"

"Just bloody do it!"

Crimson Hunter surged forwards, the drives stuttering madly as they superheated wisps of thin Lavannos air still

in the tubes. Below, clear on the screens, the star was growing.

Optimus had jumped first.

A sphere of light was growing from the black surface of
the moon. It was utterly opaque, searing bright. As it grew
it seemed to shed layers of itself, each glaring shell of it
splitting away from the core and expanding out, trailing
lines of brilliance until a great network of blinding circles
and threads of starlight filled the screen.

Just when it seemed the star couldn't get any brighter, it
flared so hard for one split second that *Crimson Hunter*'s
bridge was lit blue-white from the force of it. Then it was
gone.

Along with a quarter of Lavannos.

A vast, perfectly regular sphere of matter had simply vanished. In its wake, streamers of pale flesh, kilometres long,
were boiling away into the vacuum

The whole sickening mass of the Mindfeeder was open to
view, cored, eviscerated.

And screaming.

Red could feel thin howls of despair scratching the back
of her mind, but they were weak, pitiful. "It's dying," she
whispered.

Millions of tonnes of colourless fluid, the noisome
blood of the Mindfeeder, were bleeding out into space.
Red watched it pumping in slow, billowing clouds, and
wondered if the thoughts of its victims were finally dying
too. Immortality, the abbot had called it. As if, once her
brain was swallowed by that thing, she would still somehow exist. A disembodied mind, swarming like a mote in
that titan sac of liquid, along with untold thousands of
others.

Could they rest now?

She hoped so. And suddenly, more than anything else,
she wanted to rest too.

Harrow chuckled. "I've found a friend," he grinned, and
changed the screen view.

A boxy, slab-sided ship was powering away from Lavannos. An Iconoclast landing craft. "Hey, Antonia," Red
smiled. "Long time no see."

"Mistress?" Godolkin was reaching past Harrow, operating a series of controls on the command board. "This vessel
is armed with a brace of flayer missiles. You should have
the honour."

"Nah." She shook her head. "Let 'em go."

"Are you sure? One should never let an enemy live."

"Like I said to Toni, I'm no one's enemy. I just took a
wrong turn." She got up, and headed back towards the
spinal corridor. "There's quite a lot of Mindfeeder left, and
it might get a second wind. The Iconoclasts can frag it better than anyone. I'm going to bed." She yawned mightily.
"Wake me in about twelve hundred years."

"Funny you should say that," said Harrow.

He had picked up the cryo-tube on his way to smash
through the roof of the drive chamber, snatching it from the
ruined courtyard with a cargo grab. Once she had found
out, Red had demanded *Crimson Hunter* make planetfall on
the nearest habitable world.

So she stood, alone, on the surface of Kyriad. It was a
small planet, quite barren, just on the boundaries of the
Accord. A place that could support human or mutant life, if
there had been anything much there to attract them.

It was cold and Red was very tired. She had retrieved her
coat from *Crimson Hunter*'s locker.

The tube looked oddly forlorn, lying there. Red had found
a quiet place for it on high ground, sheltered near some
solid-looking boulders. Safe, she hoped, for another millen-
nia or two.

"This universe," she told it, "is just so crap. I mean really.
I live here now, so I should know."

The tube just blinked its lights at her, mutely. A faint
breeze was blowing up, rattling little stones across the
ground, making scrubby plants dip and bob. A tiny lizard

scurried up onto the tube's dome, blinked at her, and vanished.

"So okay, maybe I'm crazy. After all, I'm out here talking to myself, aren't I?" She glanced back to the *Crimson Hunter*, perched half a kilometre away on its slender, angled leg. "But trust me, you don't want to be here right now."

The breeze was getting colder. Red put her hands in her pockets and bounced on her toes, the flaps of the coat billowing around her. "You'll be okay. No one's here, and your power's good for a thousand years, maybe two. When it finishes, the lid will pop. There's a beacon. You'll be found.

"Or maybe someone will find you earlier, like they found me. I hope not. In a thousand more years, things might be better. I might make them better."

She nodded to herself. "Yeah. I'd like to do that."

And then she turned, without a goodbye, and started walking back to the ship.

EPILOGUE
THE LEVELS OF DOMINANCE

The Osculum Cruentus had still not had their temple-asteroid entirely back under control. Sire Vaide Sorrilier, third Dominus of the Citadel of Cados, had been watching its slow tumble for the past two hours.

The ship had been on a slow approach for that time. Vaide had opted to spend the hours until docking in his private bedchamber, with only a few sylphs for company. The ship was not large, but Vaide liked his comforts. The chamber took up the greater part of the pressure cabin.

The temple rotated slowly on his holoscreen. Vaide, lounging on the edge of his bed, gestured at it. "You see, Lise?" he murmured. "The degree of stupidity I have to put up with?"

Lise was his favourite sylph, and was at that moment kneeling before him, lacing up his left boot. She didn't answer. He would have been very surprised if she had. Sylphs were mindless, their cognitive functions wrecked by subtle, yet powerful drugs administered at puberty. They remained functional in all other respects; their senses acute, their reactions speedy. Features such as loyalty, killer instinct, or sexual voraciousness could be added chemically at any time.

Naturally, sylphs were chosen from only the most attractive stock. Lise was no conversationalist, but she was certainly easy on the eye.

With his boots correctly fastened, Vaide stood up and let two more sylphs help him into his coat. He had decided to dress well for the occasion, affecting loose silk trousers, a shirt of golden fabric-metal and one of his very best coats, the one with the silver trim and the brocade. His long, dark hair was caught back with a gold diadem, and on his left hand, next to the signet ring of his citadel, he wore a platinum band set with a natural ruby as big as his thumbnail.

He was dressed to impress, it was as simple as that. He had ordered his navigator to leave jumpspace two hours from the asteroid for the very same reason – he had wanted to let the Osculum know he was coming, so the ship decelerated from superlight a good distance away. He hadn't called ahead, of course: two hours wasn't enough time for the occupants of the asteroid to put their house in order, but it was enough to make them scurry like rats.

The thought of that amused Vaide. He enjoyed making people scurry.

The ship was within a few hundred metres of docking now, and the holoscreen had filled with nothing more interesting than a dark expanse of rock. The view wasn't even turning any more, as the pilot had matched the planetisimal's spin. Vaide turned the screen off with a wave.

"Lise, my dear, I'd like you to accompany me on this little venture." He reached out to brush her cheek. "I apologise in advance for putting you through such a trial, but it would be nice to show my dear friend Tholen one final vision of beauty."

Lise remained standing loosely at the end of the bed. She would stay there until he gave her a direct order. Some in the citadel thought Vaide odd for speaking to the sylphs as though they were people, but he couldn't have cared less. Let one of them voice such a thought out loud, then he'd make it his business to care.

There was a slight impact, far away, and a soft chime. The ship was docked. Vaide turned to Lise and smiled.

"Shall we?"

The temple smelled very bad. It always had done, to Vaide's knowledge, which was one of the reasons he seldom set foot in the place.

Rather than docking with one of the asteroid's concealed airlocks, Vaide's ship had entered the primary hangar and landed there. It perched next to the Osculum's own ships: two battered phase-clippers, used mainly on harvesting missions. Vaide, strolling down the landing steps from his own gleaming vessel, gazed at the clippers with undisguised contempt. Those ships had cost him very dearly indeed.

As he and Lise reached the deck, a hatch opened on the far side of the hangar, and the Osculum's reception committee filed through. Tholen, one of the high priests, was there, along with a couple of the lower orders and a troop of servitors. Vaide only had Lise with him, but he knew with complete certainty that, should push come to shove, she alone was more than a match for Tholen and his sorry crew.

When the cultists got within a few metres of Vaide's ship they halted. Tholen stepped forwards, bowed slightly, and drew back his cowl. Vaide resisted the urge to cover his mouth, the man's scarred, twisted features were an affront to his sense of decency.

"Sire Vaide," Tholen growled, his voice sounding like gravel shaken in a drum. "We are honoured by your visit."

"I know." Vaide glanced around, feigning interest. "You seem to be having some difficulty with your attitude thrusters, old friend. My pilot had a merry time of things, matching your spin."

Tholen gave a light shrug. "A maintenance problem, sire. We have servitors working on it as we speak." He gestured back to the door. "If you will follow me, I'm sure we can make you and your, ah, companion comfortable."

"My thanks." Vaide let Lise go first, her long silken cloak rippling behind her. She was dressed entirely in midnight blue, the colour of his citadel. "There was also some damage to a service lock?"

Tholen nodded, a touch too vigorously. "Yes, yes, a minor malfunction. The lock was seldom, if ever used. We can easily work around it."

The door slid aside for them. Vaide followed Lise through, into one of the temple's maze of corridors. "I quite understand. Operating in such an ancient place must throw up all kinds of problems. I can imagine how frustrating it must be."

"The great work must continue, sire." Tholen led them around a corner and into a long, vaulted hall. Their footsteps echoed on the stone floor as they made their way between the pillars and arches. "Enlightenment requires certain sacrifices."

"What an apt turn of phrase," Vaide grinned. Then, still smiling broadly, he said: "I'd like to visit your high-priestess, if I may."

Tholen almost tripped over his cowl. "Excuse me?"

"You understand, old friend. Just like to see how my investment is doing."

The priest cleared his throat nervously. "She's bearing up."

"She must be extremely resilient." Vaide stopped suddenly, turning to fix Tholen with an imperious gaze. "None of your other priestesses lasted more than a month. Although..." He put a finger to his lips, as though in thought. "I must say that her last batch of produce wasn't nearly as sweet as the others. Is her health faltering, perhaps?"

Tholen closed his eyes, briefly. "Sire, I must confess..."

"Wouldn't a chapel be more appropriate for that?"

"She is gone. There is a new high-priestess, and she is not of the same... quality."

Vaide's eyebrows went up to his diadem. "Really, Tholen? And how did you manage to mislay my investment so carelessly?"

Tholen backed off a few steps. "Sire, we were attacked. The temple was boarded."

"Go on."

"There were several of them, humans, heavily armed. We fought, but they were too much for us. Father Lassad died trying to protect her."

"Good lord." Vaide turned to Lise. "You hear that, my dear? The temple has been desecrated while I've been away." He smiled back at the priest. "Thank goodness you were here unharmed, Het Tholen. Had we lost you I don't know what I would have done."

"Thank you, sire." Tholen bobbed his head. "They were trying times."

"Hmm. Of course, one thing does trouble me." Vaide affected a troubled frown. "You see, when we took the Osculum Cruentus under our wing, Het Tholen, we took the precaution of seeding this place with surveillance cameras. And what they showed me was that you were boarded by one mutant with a light-drill and a silly little derringer."

Tholen's rheumy eyes widened. He opened his mouth to speak, but Vaide silenced him with a gesture.

"His name was Judas Harrow. He used to be a member of the Tenebrae, but now he is the loyal companion of Saint Scarlet of Durham. He'd been tracking you down ever since Gomorrah, Tholen. Ever since your operatives left there in the exact same crumbling starcraft you have used for the last twenty years!"

Vaide's anger had gotten the better of him. For a second he had almost shown the old priest his true face, but that would never do. He willed himself to calm down. A pinch of Dream, sniffed from a compartment in his signet ring, helped enormously.

He sighed, snapping the compartment closed. "Tholen, my old friend. Did I not implore you to update your fleet? When I gave you Durham Red's location, did I not beg you to use a different ship?" He shook his head sadly. "I believe I even gave you an extra kilogramme of Glow in order to pay for new vessels. I shan't ask what happened to that."

Tholen bowed low. "Sire, forgive me. The responsibility is mine, and mine alone. Whatever you require me to do to make this right again, I shall." He looked up at Vaide from under his heavy brows. "The great work must continue, sire."

"So it shall, Tholen, so it shall." Vaide smiled. "We'll have some people come over to beef up your security, fix those pesky thrusters, yes?" He steepled his fingers, tapping them together rapidly; a slightly nervous habit he was not entirely proud of. "In return, it's been decided at the citadel that your production must increase threefold."

"What?" Tholen gaped. "Sire, the priestess will not survive!"

"I'd suggest getting some more priestesses, old friend." He put his hand on the priest's shoulder. "Perhaps you could keep three on the go at once. They could keep each other company!"

After he had touched the priest, Vaide was careful to keep his hand at his side and slightly crooked, all the way back to his ship. Only when he was safely aboard did he swivel the ruby ring around his finger to face the correct way.

He sat on the bed, and carefully twisted the ruby itself ninety degrees in its mount, watching as the tiny needle slid back into the centre of the jewel. The needle was quite long, but slender: it was unlikely the priest had even felt it go through his skin.

The drug was already in his bloodstream, however. Within two hours he would suffer a violent fever, during the throes of which his psyche would come apart at the seams. He would be a drooling lunatic long before Vaide had returned to Magadan and the Citadel.

Vaide shrugged slightly to himself. Enlightenment, Tholen himself had said, required certain sacrifices.

It was a pity the priest had been such a fool. Durham Red's produce had been so very sweet, Vaide had tasted it himself. He had also gained two levels of advancement just from the sale of it.

And as for its more unexpected qualities, well...

He had to have her back. The saint's retrieval was more important than most in the citadel – in any of the citadels – could possibly understand.